I Laugh to Keep from Crying

Anthony: Thank you brother. It was a pleasure being your neighbor at the Houston Black Expo! May God bless you!
[illegible] Williams
5/16/04

I Laugh to Keep from Crying

T. Wendy Williams

Writers Club Press
San Jose New York Lincoln Shanghai

I Laugh to Keep from Crying

Published by Writers Club Press
an imprint of iUniverse.com, Inc.

For information address:
iUniverse.com, Inc.
5220 S 16th, Ste. 200
Lincoln, NE 68512
www.iuniverse.com

ISBN: 0-595-01115-2

Printed in the United States of America

Dedication

To
Mama,
Ganny,
and
Punkin
Forever north on the compass of my soul

EPIGRAPH

To

Those thousands
of women in abusive relationships:

Love should never have to hurt

Acknowledgements

At last my baby has arrived for all the world to see. Words can't express how elated I am. God has blessed my mind, body and soul with a book, and God has given me the chance to finally stand where I have never stood before-center stage.

I am tremendously blessed to have so many inspirations in my life, beginning, first and foremost, with my mother, Barbara Williams, who taught me at the tender age of two, to use my gift of imagination to take me places far beyond my reach.

I have also been blessed to have my sister, Tawanna Williams, in my life. We are practically joined at the hip and I couldn't have made it this far without her love and support.

I want to thank my Grandmother, Freddie Mae Gordon, who instilled within me the wisdom and courage to take adversity and turn it flat on its back. I also want to thank my father, Terry Williams, whose tough love, will never be forgotten.

I also want to thank the rest of my family and friends; Kathy Garrett, Verdell English, Jan Bennett, Debbie Gordon, Henry Lee Gordon, Terry Gordon, Barry Gordon, Larry Gordon, Sharion Smith, the entire Merchant family, April Houston-McCoy, Joni Hall, Bruce Johnson,

Michael McCain, Cedric Johnson, Robert Bennett, Alonzo Hutchinson, Gary Prevost, Walter McCloud, Leslie Leigh, Shirlyn and Bruce Wilson, Jacklyn Merchant, Shanta Crawford, the St. Luke United Methodist Church family, the Unity of Faith Church family, the Windsor Village United Methodist Church family, the Hall family, the Thornton family, the Stribling family, the Solomon family, the Bradford family, and Earl Turner.

I want to give a very special thanks to my editor, Alicia Lacy-Castille. Alicia's motivation and enthusiasm helped me to soar above and beyond. Last but not least, I want to thank Tony Bibbs for promoting my book and getting it out there to the public. I thank you, thank you, thank you! If I left out anyone, please, charge it to my head and not my heart. I love you all and God bless.

Introduction

There was something about the Georgia air that kept the LaCroix family coming back. Relatives from as far north as Michigan and as far west as California would gather each year in Atlanta to feast and catch up on each other's business. Summer school students from nearby Morehouse, Spelman, and Clark dormitories also seized the opportunity to take advantage of the delicious Soul and Cajun-style cooking.

David Leonard, who just so happened to be a medical student from Morehouse, immediately focused his attention on a line of people standing in front of a twenty foot long buffet-style table. The hickory-smoked aroma of barbecue and the smell of cakes and pies made his taste buds water. It also made him pep up his step. As he stood in line, he feasted his twinkling light-brown eyes on the smorgasbord of barbecue chicken, hot barbecue links, baked beans, potato salad, collard greens, and cornbread.

Just as he was about to pick up a piece of potato pie, he was tapped on the shoulder.

Oh no. I'm caught, he thought. He turned around and discovered his roommate, Jerome.

"Hey David." Jerome whispered. "Can I cut in front of you man?"

"How did you get here?"

"I caught a ride," Jerome said as he watched David pile his plate with links, slices of brisket and ribs.

"With who?"

"With Mike and his girl."

"Who's Mike's girl?"

"I don't know her name."

David made his way to the desserts. "Man look at all those cakes."

"Man, look at all these women," Jerome mumbled underneath his breath as he watched two girls waltz pass him. Meanwhile, David's plate was so full he had to set it aside and get another plate. One of the ladies who was serving asked if she could help carry one of his plates. She was middle-aged and appeared to enjoy flirting with younger men by the way she carried herself.

"No ma'am, I can handle it," David replied as he stared directly into her ocean blue eyes.

"Well, you be careful with that plate baby," she said in a sassy voice. David glanced at Jerome.

"Oookaay," Jerome said. "They do get better with age."

As David walked to his car, he noticed some other guys from Morehouse mingling with the relatives, pretending to be related to them in order to get a plate the size of his. David sat down behind the wheel of his 1963 cobalt blue Impala convertible and commenced to bite down on a juicy barbecue rib. Jerome soon joined him.

"David, man there are some pretty women around here. You know how I feel." He turned up a bottle of coke and took a gulp so large his jaws were swollen. After swallowing he said, "I feel like a mosquito at a nudity camp."

"I hear you," David mumbled with a mouthful of food. Jerome picked up a piece of pound cake and stuffed it in his mouth.

"Damn Jerome man, give yourself time to digest the rest of your food."

"This is really good," Jerome said as he began to lick his fingers.

Across the way from their car were four girls sitting in a circle on a checkerboard blanket underneath a huge pine tree. All four had a paper plate full of the same vegetables, meats, dessert, and an R.C. Cola soda caressing their lips. However, they were all giggling uncontrollably, coughing and nearly choking.

One of the girls mustered, "No he didn't; stop it girl!"

They became so engulfed with laughter, that one of them spit R.C. Cola all over the blanket, showering the others with it.

"Tiny," three of the girls responded, but Tiny was still laughing. The other three looked at each other and started laughing again.

A small distance from them were a group of four guys, sprawled against a yellow Plymouth looking in their direction.

"Hey, Duke, man I think they're talking about you."

Duke shook his head. "Nahn, they can't be talking about me. They don't know a thing about me."

"Then how come they're looking at you? Surely they know *something*."

"Man like I said, they don't know a thing about me."

"Who's the real pretty one?" one guy asked.

"Which one? They're all pretty."

"The one with the long hair."

"I don't know. Beats me."

"That's Mike's girl there."

"Oh yeah?"

"Which one?"

"The short one doing all the talking. They call her Tiny."

"Man she's a killer. She won't be tiny when I'm finished with her."

"Red, I bet you won't say that around Mike."

"I ain't afraid of Mike," he said in protest, before stuffing a hot link sandwich into his mouth.

"Duke, I'll put money on it. I bet you won't go over there and talk to those girls."

Duke looked at his friend and grimaced. "Junior please, those girls ain't nothing. How much are you willing to give up?"

"Two dollars."

"Two?" Duke repeated.

"Two," Junior said once more.

Duke rubbed his hand over his smooth bald head. "No problem," he said as he slowly walked toward the girls' direction. He could hear his friends behind him whispering and chuckling.

"Do yo' thing Duke," Junior shouted and slapped high five with Red.

"Look girls," Tiny whispered. "Look who's coming over."

Dorothy, Claire and Mary were giggling so hard, their faces were bright crimson. Duke approached the girls and stood there staring at each one of them. They returned the stare.

"Well," Tiny said, half giggling, half serious.

"How you ladies doing?"

"Fine," Tiny said speaking for the rest of the girls as well.

Duke didn't waste time asking, in a semi-harsh tone of voice that sounded a bit like a Georgia state trooper and an old cowboy out of a western flick. "Was y'all talking about me?"

The girls looked him over once more.

"And what if we was?" Tiny asked.

Duke paused for a second. The response was a bit too much for him, so he smiled a little, but then he remembered his boys behind his back and he took on a serious look once more.

"If y'all was, you ladies need to cool it. That's not right to be talking about a man and he ain't nowhere around to defend himself."

Tiny shifted her weight to one side and titled her head. At four feet eleven she was a feisty character with Creole roots. She was a witty, outspoken Spelman woman with a mind so candid it expressed everything on its surface. She walked up to Duke and looked him in the face. Behind Duke his friends were still chuckling.

"You must have some nerve coming over here, trying to use that line so you and your boys can get in good with us, huh?"

"Say what?"

"What's your name?" she asked, pretending like she didn't know, but she knew Duke from all the gossip about him on campus.

"I thought you knew," he said.

"No I *don't* know."

"Well, I'm the Duke," He replied in the same manner John Wayne would if one were to ask of his name.

"Well Duke," Her voice was very calm, "for your information we were not talking about just you. We were talking about your friends too, NOW." Tiny put her hands on her curvaceous hips and waited for him to respond. Duke turned around and glanced at his friends. Two were once more chuckling and still slapping "fives" all over the place, while a third one was standing with a smirk on his face, shaking his head.

"I wish y'all could hear what my girl just said!" Duke shouted.

"What did she say?" Junior asked walking towards Duke.

Tiny glanced back at her cousins, Dorothy, Claire and Mary who were in awe, as the rest of the guys began to walk in their direction.

"You didn't have to call your friends over," Tiny said. She was still calm.

"What did she say man?" Red asked.

All four of them were now in the girls' territory. To Dorothy, Red and Junior looked cute far away, but close up was a different story. Mary and Claire were still giggling about the story Tiny told them about the guys' reputations back on campus.

"We didn't say anything bad about y'all," Dorothy said.

"Then tell me what y'all said," Duke inquired.

"All right, I'll tell you, right in front of yo' friends what my friend Thelma said, what Minnie said, and Ruthie said…"

"I don't want to hear it," Duke said. "If all of them had to say it, it ain't true."

"Oh, I know the truth. You use to be a real good friend of my ex-roommate, who graduated just recently."

Duke realized who she was talking about and threw his hands in the air. "Annie Mae? That girl lies too much."

"Hmm Hmm," Tiny said sarcastically. "She lies like a rug doesn't she?"

Duke looked at his boys and sneered. "I have nothing else to discuss with you Shorty."

He blinked his eyes in a mock gesture.

"It's Tiny, short for Christine, if you didn't know."

"I'm gonna tell Mike on you," Duke said as he and his friends began to walk off.

"Tell Mike what?"

Duke said nothing more and his friends just followed behind him, glancing back at the girls.

"The last one is cute," Mary whispered. "What is his name?"

"Oh!" Tiny grabbed Mary's hand. "That's Virgil. Now he's the only one in the group with a light in the attic. Come to think of it, you and him would look real cute together."

Despite the minor confrontation, Tiny still had the nerve to drag Mary to the yellow Plymouth and introduce her to Virgil.

When Tiny returned, Dorothy shook her head in amazement. "Tiny, you have a lot of energy in you girl". Tiny talked a hundred miles per hour and she never stopped moving.

"Girls, I got Mary a man. Just look at her and Virgil over there." She pointed to Mary and Virgil who were standing away from the Plymouth talking.

"I know I'm good," Tiny boasted, then she frowned. "What was Duke's problem coming over here in our faces like that?"

"His ears must've been ringing," Dorothy replied.

"Anyway, where is Mike? He's been gone an awful long time."

Dorothy spotted him talking to David and Jerome beside the '63 Impala Convertible.

"He's over there Tiny," said Dorothy pointing in the guys' direction.

"Where?"

"See, over there beside that Impala Convertible."

"Oh yeah, he's talking to Jerome and David. Girls, I want y'all to meet them. They look so good and they both go to Morehouse Medical School."

Dorothy's eyes widened. "Medical school."

"Uhn huhn," Tiny said. She grabbed Claire and Dorothy by the hand. "Come on I want you both to meet them."

It amazed Dorothy that Tiny knew a lot of people from around campus.

"Mike!" Tiny shouted. She still held Claire and Dorothy's hands.

Mike nudged Jerome's arm. "That's her," he said. Jerome's eyes wandered from Dorothy's head all the way down to her toes. *What a beautiful creature,* he thought as she approached the car. Her long golden brown hair was blowing carelessly in the wind and her perfume had a refreshing soft scent. When Dorothy smiled it seemed the birds noticed, because they began to sing in perfect harmony. Dorothy's radiant cocoa butter complexion and honey-colored hazel eyes were so captivating, they sent a cold chill over Jerome's muscular physique, not to mention David's.

"Jerome and David, these are my cousins Dorothy LaCroix and Claire Jefferson."

Jerome extended his hand. He was so smitten by Dorothy's beauty that he forgot about the barbecue sauce on them.

"Jerome, look at your hands," David said as he extended his. "Hi, I'm David Leonard."

Dorothy checked out David's sky blue Oxford shirt and khaki pants. "Nice to meet you David," she said softly.

Jerome wiped his hands off with a napkin. "I'm sorry about that. Hi, I'm Jerome West and you two look exceptionally pretty if I may say so." He took Dorothy's hand and kissed it. The touch of his lips upon the top of her hand made her insides quiver.

"Dorothy you have such nice hands," Jerome said as he caressed her soft palms.

"Okay Mister," Tiny said. "Stop making eyes at my cousin."

Dorothy eyed the convertible, she had never seen anything as sharp and clean like it. The car was a deep, sensuous blue, just like Jerome, she thought.

"You have a nice car Jerome," she said.

"Thank you," David said while his hand fumbled inside his pocket with what sounded like car keys.

From the car radio, the song *Heat Wave* by Martha and the Vandellas was playing. It couldn't have come at a more appropriate time, because it accurately described the way Dorothy was feeling. She needed cooling down a notch.

"I'm gonna get something to drink," Dorothy said as she felt a bead of perspiration from her forehead. "Anyone else want something?" She asked.

Everyone except Jerome shook his head. Tiny smiled at her cousin. "No, Miss Dot," she said. "You're the only one burning up around here."

"I'm not stuttin' you, Tiny," Dorothy said underneath her giggle.

"Mind if I walk with you Sunshine?" Jerome asked. "I hope that's not asking too much."

"No, not at all."

"Hey, Jerome!"

Jerome turned around. "What David?"

"Bring me a soda pop back!"

"I thought you didn't want one man!"

"Just bring me one; it doesn't matter!"

The summer sun was beaming directly upon Dorothy and Jerome as they made their way through a crowd of Dorothy's relatives.

"I heard a lot about this family reunion," Jerome said. "It was the major talk on campus." Then he paused as if to think of something else.

"Really?" Dorothy responded. "What was everybody saying?"

"How nice the people are, how big it is, and how many pretty girls like yourself would be here."

Dorothy found herself blushing.

"Did they say anything about how good the food was?"

"They said everything about the reunion. They said even if you weren't part of the family you could still come."

"Why did you come Jerome?"

Jerome looked around at the people and shrugged his shoulders. "I came because I was invited."

"I'm just curious. Most people from the A.U. Center come just for the food."

"What are you saying Sunshine?" Jerome playfully pinched her on the side. "You saying I came just for the food?"

"I'm not saying anything." Dorothy opened up a cooler and grabbed an R.C. Cola for Jerome, one for David and one for herself.

"You know Dorothy," Jerome began, "you make me feel kind of guilty."

"Guilty about what?"

"Guilty because I came just to eat, I should take the time out and get to know everyone, especially you pretty lady." He smiled exposing a row of pearly whites.

Dorothy took a sip from her pop. "I have lots and lots of relatives as you can see."

They passed by a table of young, middle-aged and elderly men playing dominoes. One of them shouted, "Big six!" then slapped the table with a loud whack.

"I have a sister around here somewhere."

"Is she pretty as you?" Jerome inquired.

"I think so." Dorothy replied.

"Dorothy LaCroix." Jerome pronounced her name as if she were about to make a grand entrance at a panache venue. "That's Creole isn't it?"

"Yes." Dorothy blushed.

"Are you from Louisiana?"

"Yes, New Orleans."

"Tell me Dorothy, do you practice voodoo?" Jerome's eyes widened when he said voodoo. Dorothy had to laugh.

"Why is it that every time a woman says she's from Louisiana, she has to be involved with voodoo?"

"Did I offend you?"

"No."

"I was told Louisiana women reel in their men-folk with voodoo."

"That is the most silliest thing I have ever heard, and you say you go to medical school?"

"Yes, but what is that suppose to mean?"

"You are beginning to sound pathetic to me. I don't expect a conversation of this type coming from an intelligent man."

"Pardon me, as of right now this man's mouth is closed." He took a sip from his cola. "Except when I drink my cola you understand."

"If you saw the majority of the women in New Orleans, then you would realize that we don't need voodoo to reel in a man. Our looks alone do just fine."

"Lord have mercy," Jerome said as he touched her soft cheek with the back of his hand. "You're right about that. If beauty was worth money, you would be a million dollars."

Dorothy found herself blushing. Jerome didn't hesitate to call her out.

"I see you blushing girl."

"No, I'm not," Dorothy replied with a wide smile.

Jerome took her hand and examined her slender body. "Your shape is so fine; your skin is soft as felt. If God made anything better, I'm glad he kept it to himself."

Dorothy laughed in a giddy, school girl sort of way.

"I got a lot more to say if you want to hear it." Jerome replied.

Around eight that evening the park began to clear. The smell of barbecue had slowly simmered down, as did the pies and beer. The music from the cars ceased and the last of the LaCroix family were loading up chairs and tables onto the trucks and trunks of their cars. Their voices were echoing out their last good-byes, as they embraced one last time until next year when they are to meet at the same place once more. Dorothy and her sister Ophelia gave their cousins Mary and Claire one last hug.

"Are you coming to California to see us?" Claire asked.

"Yes." Dorothy and Ophelia said in unison. They watched as their cousins drove off still waving.

"I'm glad we don't live in California," Ophelia said.

"Thank God," Dorothy replied.

"Dorothy!" She heard her father calling from the car. Papa LaCroix was underneath the hood of the station wagon. When he raised up to wipe his hands on a towel his face was drenched with sweat and his cold black naturally wavy hair was curled tightly like a nest of honeybees. "Look in the back seat there and get me a can of that oil."

"What's wrong Papa?"

"The car is a little low on oil," he said.

HONK! HONK!

Dorothy looked up and saw Tiny and Mike, behind them were Jerome and David.

"Bye." She waved.

"Who is that?" Ophelia asked.

"David and Jerome."

Ophelia's eyes widened. "You know them?" She asked.

"Yes, I know one of them pretty well."

Ophelia looked her sister over. "How well?"

"Well."

"Dorothy!" Papa's voice sounded muffled and agitated from under the hood.

"Okay Papa, I'm getting it! Golleee," she mumbled underneath her breath.

"Watch your mouth, Dot." Dorothy couldn't believe he heard her.

Uncle Billy, Papa LaCroix's brother, approached the car with a brown paper sack in his hand.

"What's wrong? The oil run out?" he asked.

Papa LaCroix retrieved the can of oil from Dorothy. "Yeah, I just filled it up yesterday. What a raggedy piece of junk."

Inside the car, Dorothy and her sister Ophelia sat and talked about the reunion and Dorothy's new friend Jerome.

"Ophelia, I was looking everywhere for you. I wanted you to meet David, Jerome's friend."

"How did he look? Was he fine?"

"Yes, he's very cute. He looks like he has a lot of money by the convertible and by the way he dressed today. He's quiet, very quiet and very observant, unlike Jerome."

Dorothy's eyes wondered into a field of trees. At one point during the day, you could not see those trees for all the people, but now it was empty and there wasn't a soul in sight.

"I want to go see them tonight," she said.

"Papa's not gonna let you go."

"Why not?"

"He's not gonna let you go anywhere in this raggedy piece of shit." Ophelia lowered her voice when she said "shit."

"I'm not going in this car. I'm getting Tiny to pick me up."

Papa LaCroix closed the hood on the car. Billy got in on the passenger's side.

"Hey, Uncle Billy, you have ten dollars?" Ophelia asked. To her surprise, he didn't hesitate to reach into his pocket and pull out his wallet. He gave Ophelia ten and gave another ten to Dorothy.

"Uncle Billy you're so nice," Ophelia said. "I was just playing. I didn't know you was giving me ten dollars for real."

Papa LaCroix got in and shut the door. He was still cursing about the oil to Billy.

"Boy I tell you, if it ain't one thang, it's a million others." He started up the engine, it was so loud and cranky you had to scream to hear the next person talking. The car smoked so much that everyone nicknamed it "Squita" because the soot and carbon dioxide was enough to kill all the mosquitoes in Summerhill.

Chapter 1

I was in desperate need of a ride to the A.U. Center. Ophelia and I were sitting around Papa's house just looking at each other with our faces a mile long. The thought of taking the car came to mind, but then I thought, I'll never hear the end of Papa's punishment. Instead of him sending me back to Louisiana on the bus, he'd be sending me back in a coffin instead. So I went to sleep that night with Jerome on my mind. I wanted so much to see him and be next to him, and have him tell me all the wonderful things he had been telling me at the reunion.

I didn't see or hear from Jerome until four days later when he stopped by Papa's house unexpectedly. I was sitting on the sofa all sweaty and damp when I heard this voice say.

"Hellooo." He scared the life out of me when I saw him standing there wearing a light blue shirt with a dark blue tie and dark blue cuffed trousers. He had the body of a god; it was strong looking, firm and sexy. I sat there on the couch and all I could do was stare at him. I didn't know what to do with my hair; I didn't know what to do with my clothes; I didn't know what to do with myself period, but just sit there and look at this guy watch me through the screen door.

"Hello, Jerome." I got up and walked towards the door. At eighteen years-old, seeing Jerome standing there at the door made me heat up like an incinerator. I mean I was a walking blow torch with a flame five feet, six inches tall. When I got to the screen door he said hello again. I said hello in an unusual tone that didn't sound like me, but like some seductive older woman. We were separated by the screen door, which I didn't realize due to the fact I was so captivated by his rich dark chocolate complexion and the tantalizing smell of his cologne.

"Dorothy, may I come in?" he asked.

I laughed you know to break the tension I felt mounting up inside of me. "I'm sorry Jerome come in," I heard myself say and I opened the door. He took two steps and gave me a kiss on the lips, not a peck, but a real, long kiss. You could've knocked me over with a feather. I was flimsy like a piece of paper and my knees were practically rubber. Jerome sat down on the sofa and motioned for me to come over and sit beside him. I stood there debating. Should I or shouldn't I? If I did what would happen? Could I handle it if it did? What if I were to join him on the sofa and what if literally a push came to a shove? Would things be the same between us? Why am I thinking this way? The guy only asked me to sit by him. He didn't ask me to come over and get fresh with him. Or did he? Forget this. I only met him four days ago, and we were in each other's company for only a couple of hours. I haven't seen nor heard from him since then, he had my number he could've called. I demanded an explanation so I asked him, "Jerome why haven't you called?"

"I lost your number," was Jerome's lame reply.

"Oh," was my response as I sat down in Papa's favorite lounging chair. "How did you know where to find me?"

"I asked Tiny. Was that a problem?"

"Yes. I mean, no, no, no, it was okay." I laughed. Jerome had me feeling goofy all of a sudden. Jerome looked around the room with his eyes, you know how people do when they come to your house for the first time? They look at your pictures hanging on the wall, they check out your furniture and then they say something like, "This is a nice place you have here." I knew Jerome was lying. Papa had absolutely no taste when it came to decorating. The furniture was old as dirt, and the walls were beige and bare. The only pictures Papa had were old pictures of himself when he was in the service back in the '40s and an old picture of his mother, Grandma Pat, beside the *Lord's Last Supper*. Jerome looked at me and smiled. He had such pretty teeth, and nice round lips; not to mention nice, ebony eyes; and when they met mine, they told me more of what Jerome was thinking than words ever could.

"You thirsty?" I asked.

"No." He shook his head. "I just stopped by on my way to lunch and you came to mind." I took that as Jerome's way of getting fresh. I got off the subject and asked him about school. He said he'd been studying for a lab practical.

"Tell me about medical school?"

"What do you want to know?"

"What field of medicine are you studying?"

"Anatomy."

"Anatomy is pretty broad, what type of anatomy?"

"Dorothy's anatomy." He winked at me with those playful eyes. I felt goofy again and I laughed it off.

"I want you to sit here." He patted a spot on the sofa. I sat there in Papa's chair looking at him like he was crazy. Although he didn't come right out and say it, I knew what he was up to. I was apprehensive about it, but I got up anyway and sat down beside him, and before I knew it, Jerome's arms were wrapped around my shoulders just like I had figured. When he brushed his lips against mine I could smell his breath which reminded me of licorice. So I sort of pushed him away slightly.

"What's wrong?" he asked.

"I'm hungry," I said.

He glanced at his watch. "If we hurry we can catch the last of the lunch special at the diner."

"Let's hurry," I insisted.

For the last seven summers that I had been visiting Papa in Atlanta, never in my life had I been on any of the campuses at the A.U. Center. I always wanted to visit, but I never had the chance until I went with Jerome to a small diner which was nestled between Morehouse and Spelman. While I was there, I ordered a chili dog while Jerome ordered a king-size hamburger. He didn't have much to say, and when he finally did, he inquired about my chili dog. I should've told him that my sausage was raw, my chili was warm, and it was the nastiest thing I had ever tasted since Castor Oil, but I didn't. Instead, I gagged it down and drowned it with a bottle of R.C. Cola.

"This is okay. I guess."

"It's either good or nasty, which one is it?"

"If you really want to know Jerome, it's nasty."

"Then why did you get it?" he asked. I couldn't tell if he was serious or not.

"It was the only thing on the menu that looked good."

"Give it here." He took the soggy bun briskly out of my plate and put it in his. I was appalled by his rude attitude. Inside of that beautiful black body of his was a potential nut case, I just knew it. But I didn't let him know he was working my nerves, I just sat quietly drinking my soda while he watched every skirt that passed by on the sly. Then he had the nerve to glance at me quickly to see if I was watching him.

A few moments later, David walked in accompanied by a girl, who I assumed to be his girlfriend, due to the fact he had his arm around her. He was dressed in a suit and tie and she in her Sunday best. They looked like they were on their way to church and it was only Thursday. David pulled out her chair and she sat down, bouncing a couple of times before she settled in.

"Hello Dorothy," he said.

"Hi, David."

"Dorothy, this is Bettye." He pointed to his friend. She was pretty like the typical college girl around here was. I bet she went to Spelman, because all Morehouse men dated Spelman women, or so it seemed to me. I asked her just to be sure and her reply was Atlanta University. I guess that statement didn't always hold true. Then I looked at her closely. She'd be a lot prettier if her glasses weren't so thick. The glasses she wore made her eyes smaller than they were. With those triple-bifocals I wondered whether she could see what was going on in my family room at home in New Orleans. When she read the menu she put it right up to her face. *Poor creature,* I thought. David was eyeing me with those piercing browns of his. I knew, because every time I looked up from sipping on my soda, he was staring at me. Then he'd quickly glance at his girlfriend to see if she was looking at him. She was busy looking elsewhere. David was kind of cute. I liked the color of his skin, it was golden brown and flawless. His hair was trimmed nice and neat with tight curls that gripped the corners of his forehead and the nape of his neck. His body wasn't that bad either. He was about six foot-one, and about two hundred pounds. If he wasn't a medical student, I would've easily mistaken him for a basketball player. He asked me if I had had anything to eat. I said, "yes, a sorry chili dog."

Jerome butted in, "It was not sorry."

"It tasted like rubber."

"You tasted rubber before?" He replied with a chuckle and glanced at David to join him.

"Shut up Jerome," I heard myself say. I felt sweat tingling underneath my arms.

David gave Bettye a dime for the jukebox.

"What do you want to hear?" she asked.

"Put on Sam Cook, or Ray Charles."

She searched until she found Sam Cook's *Bring It On Home to Me.*

"You like that?" she asked David.

"Yes, that's fine, thank you."

Jerome looked at his watch. "Damn I have two minutes to get to my lab?" He jumped up.

"David can you and Bettye take her home for me."

I looked at Jerome and shook my head. He treated me like I was some package of mail you dump on to the floor at the post office. I was so embarrassed; I felt my face reddened. He didn't even say good-bye or see you later, he just took one last bite out of that soggy bun, grabbed his books and dashed out of the place.

"How rude," Bettye said before she sipped her shake.

"Is he always like that?" I asked.

"Like what?" David asked.

"Aggressive, fast moving." I tried to get out all of the decent words synonymous with Jerome. David didn't respond.

"How long are those labs?" I asked.

"Well it depends on what lab he's taking. If it's a gross anatomy lab, he's looking at three hours max."

"So I'm stuck here for three hours." I was fuming when I said that.

"No. Bettye and I are taking you home, don't get upset." He playfully slapped my drumming fingertips. Bettye glanced at David not saying a word. I guess she was upset because he touched my hand. David glanced back at Bettye. "What's wrong?" he asked.

I saw her throat bobbing. "Nothing," she replied. At that moment I felt uncomfortable. I wondered if she noticed the way he kept staring at me.

I didn't want to make eye contact with neither one of them so I glanced at my watch. It was ten after one. David mentioned something to Bettye about a lab practical he had to take around two and then asked me if I lived far? I told him Summerhill was only fifteen minutes away. If he didn't have the time I could walk there.

"That's not a good idea. Me and Bettye'll take you home."

"Thanks, I really appreciate this." I finally glanced at Bettye. She didn't look too happy about the invitation.

I rode home feeling let down by Jerome. My day would've gone just fine had I not thought about him so much, and had he not come over. I wanted to cry. To me he was just like any other loser I had ever been with. The only thing he had going for him was his education, and if it wasn't for that he wouldn't be shit, because good looks don't amount to a hill of beans nowadays.

David turned on the radio and a smooth melodious voice came over the air that said. "Today's high is eighty-nine degrees. Who loves you Atlanta? No one but your own. This is Yours Truly giving you the best of old and contemporary hits. Here's an old tune from Frankie Lymon and the Teenagers. It was a number one hit in 1955." It was *Why Do Fools Fall in Love* .

David and Bettye were in the front seat moving their heads to the beat of the music. I heard Bettye singing then she leaned over and kissed David on the jaw. He glance at her with a look on his face that said, *What did you do that for?* If looks could kill, Bettye would've been dead. I didn't quite understand the private communication among them, but the mood was so intense that I couldn't wait to get out of the car. When David adjusted his rear view mirror, I saw his eyes meet mine, but I thought nothing of it.

David and Bettye dropped me off at 617 Mulberry Street. I got out the car and apologized for any inconvenience. I wished David good luck on his lab practical, and I told him to tell Jerome I was very upset for his storming out on me the way he did and not telling me good-bye or see you later. I wished Bettye good luck as well and stood there in the yard and watched as the car made its way up the street before it turned right and disappeared.

"What's wrong with you?" Papa asked.

"Nothing," was my reply.

"Yes it is. You been walking around here, moping with your mouth hanging down a mile. You didn't eat, and you know it's not like you to turn down my smothered pork chops. What's wrong baby girl?"

I didn't want to tell Papa I was having boy problems, but then I thought he'd be the most qualified person to discuss this matter with. He could probably get to the gist of the matter. After all, he was young once like Jerome. He too had thought the world revolved around a piece of tail. So I asked him, "Papa, when is the best time to fall in love with someone?" I also wanted to ask is it before or after you have sex with them, but I dared not to. Papa's eyes wandered about the room. He had a look of stern concentration and I knew his brain was probably flooding with answers.

"Why? You thinking about having sex?"

"No sir," I said cutting him off. "I just want to know that's all."

"When you know for sure that your heart is right, your mind is made up, and you have no doubt about your feelings. That's when you know you're in love."

"Papa, were you ready when you married Mama?"

"Let me tell you about that situation. Now, I married your mother because I had to. It was out of obligation. Let me tell you this, don't ever marry anyone just out of obligation. You marry him because you truly feel that deep down inside your heart you love him."

Daddy made sense. "I didn't love your mother when I married her. Sure I cared about her, but I felt since I got her pregnant, I owed her and her family something. Hell, what did I know about love at seventeen?" Papa coughed. It sounded like an old car engine rattled in his lungs. He had to put our conversation on hold and cough for about a minute. I got up and rubbed his back. When he coughed his whole body shook and vibrated. He assured me it wasn't nothing that a good dose of Castor Oil couldn't cure, he'd get over it in no time. Papa had been saying that for the past year. He wiped his nose with a white handkerchief and put it in his pocket.

"Now when I was seventeen..." He coughed again for about a minute. "Now, when I was seventeen all I cared about was running the streets and trying to figure out a way to dodge the draft. I didn't care about no love, I didn't care about responsibility, I be damned if anyone told me I had to baby-sit your big sister Katherine, when I was seventeen." Papa leaned forward and retrieved a cigarette from inside the coffee table drawer.

"Papa, now you know better." I said. He knew it aggravated me to see him smoking.

"Papa remember what the doctors said."

He proceeded to smoke like he didn't hear me. "I know what the doctors said and I told them doctors like I'm telling you, smoking ain't the only thing that's bad for you." He thumped his ashes in a nearby ashtray and made the speech I had heard a million times about all the things that were bad for your health. On the television there was a segment mentioning Medgar Evers, who was gunned down a little over a week ago in front of his home. Papa stopped talking and started watching television, I assumed our conversation was over so I got up and walked towards the kitchen.

"Dot, where you going? I'm not finished talking." His eyes were still on the television. I came back and sat on the sofa beside him. "Get your sister, I want to talk to her too."

Ophelia was in the kitchen with her ear glued to the phone. "Ophelia, Papa wants to talk to you."

Ophelia put her index finger over her lips. "Shhh," she whispered and placed her hand over the speaker, "Bobbie Jean's parents are fighting." I rolled my eyes and told her what Papa said. She hung up the phone slowly and walked into the family room where Papa was. "Yes Papa?" She said.

"You and Dot sit down I got something to tell you two about love." Ophelia's face grimaced.

"Love?" she asked.

"Just sit down," he insisted.

Ophelia looked at me. "Are you in love?" she asked. Ophelia should've known I wasn't going to answer that question in front of Papa. Papa puffed on his cigarette. "Ophelia, I was just telling Dorothy that you should never marry someone out of obligation, you marry them because you really love them."

"Why are we talking about marriage?" She looked at me again with the same confused look. "Are you getting married?" I wanted to slap my sister for being so anxious to jump to wild and crazy conclusions.

"No, silly. Me and Papa was talking about his relationship with Mama and when was the right time to fall in love." This time the look on her face got even crazier. I knew what she was thinking, *y'all call me off the phone for this*? Papa began, "I want you girls to not be afraid to talk to me about anything that's bothering you. If you want to talk about boys, I can tell you anything you want to know." Ophelia and I just nodded at Papa. Papa was such a beautiful person, just talking to him lifted a burden off my shoulders. I could talk to Papa better than I could Mama. In fact when I started my period, it was Papa who found out about it and he took me to the store to get the sanitary napkins. I had friends who would swear up and down their fathers were the last people on earth they could talk to. They rarely saw their fathers, let along talk to them.

I often heard some people say that when you return alive from a catastrophic event like a war, that you're a changed person. You've either changed for the better or for the worst. I think the war made Papa change for the better. I think seeing all those people wounded and killed changed his outlook on life. It made him appreciate his family and friends more, because when it came to his family and friends, no one could out-love him. If we were hurting, then he was hurting and he'd try with his might never to see us hurt again. Mama, on the other hand was a different story. I loved her very much, but I despised the way she mistreated Papa. Mama never appreciated what he did for her, it was like his best wasn't good enough. Like the time he and Mama went looking for a house. Papa bought a house he could afford out in the country. Mama complained every day how she hated the long drive into town and she always found something wrong with the house. She never failed to stop complaining until Papa moved her into a house she wanted. But he struggled to keep up because the payments were an arm and a leg. Mama complained that the car they were driving was raggedly and she needed a new one. So Papa worked three jobs and got her a 1948 Plymouth, she got mad and said she wanted a Ford. It seemed like nothing he did pleased her. She was always complaining and finding fault. Papa didn't want to separate from Mama, but he did. When I was eleven it was the saddest thing I had ever seen. It was the first time I had ever seen Papa cry. It wasn't a sorrowful cry, but more like a cry filled with anger. Mama allowed us to see Papa during the summer months. To tell you the truth, those were the best months of the year.

"You know when a young man says he loves you, nine times out of ten he doesn't mean it." Papa looked at me and I nodded, recalling over and over the many times I had heard guys tell me that. Then Papa told me something that I'll never forget, he said. "Dot, let me tell you and your sister something. The only people who truly love you are me and your mama. Always remember that." Ophelia pretended to cry. "Oh Papa that's so sweet."

Papa sat back in his chair and took one last puff of his cigarette. "I'm serious," he said. That night I went to sleep, sleeping a little better than I did previous nights. I only thought about Jerome once, and that was when I went to the bathroom.

Chapter 2

Jerome had his hands underneath my blouse. I pushed them away and soon afterwards he was wiggling his tongue in and out of my ear. It felt cold and slimy at first, but then it began to tickle.

"Jerome."

"What?" he responded, sounding a bit irritated.

"Don't."

"Don't what?"

On the radio, Marvin Gaye's *Stubborn Kind of Fella* was playing.

"Don't touch me right there; that tickles."

Jerome eased away from my ear and stared straight ahead. In the back seat Bettye and David were slurping and kissing loudly. I heard her blouse pop open and David's zipper easing it's way down. Jerome took my face in the palm of his hand and kissed it once more. "Let me make love to you girl," he whispered. "Let me show you what I'm made of." He unzipped his pants, then staring at me with those piercing dark eyes of his, he reached into his pants and pulled out the tip of his penis. *Oh my God*, I thought. I had never seen a man's penis before in my life. My heart was beating so loudly and fast. I imagined David and Bettye could hear it over their loud slurping and kissing. Jerome moved in closer and put his strong black arms around my shoulders and pulled me to him. I closed my eyes and squeezed them shut.

"Dorothy, come on," he whispered.

"Jerome, no. Don't ask me again." He had been trying all day.

"Come on."

"No!"

"Forget this!"

He removed his arm from my shoulder and furiously opened the door. "Of all the beautiful women in Atlanta, I had to end up with a woman like you, A NUN. Won't give me NUN, ain't had NUN, and wouldn't know how to handle it, if she got some." He shut the door and walked towards the forest ranting and raving like a madman. I saw him stop to pick up something. He held it in his hand a while before he threw it out into the darkness. I got out of the car to walk towards him. He picked up a pebble and threw it. It made a small splash in a nearby pond.

"Jerome, is that all you think about?"

Jerome didn't respond. He just picked up a pebble and threw it, making the same splash as the first one he threw. From the car I could hear Bettye moaning. It sounded like David was whipping the living hell out of her. The windows were foggy and the Impala was sort of rocking. I looked at Jerome. This time he had a rock in his hand, and when he threw it the rock made a louder splash.

"Dorothy, why do you make things so difficult?" he asked. I noticed his pants were still unzipped and an array of strange thoughts came to my mind. "Why Dorothy? All I ask is that you give me a chance to love you."

"You don't love me?" I told him while in the back of my mind I recalled the conversation I had with Papa and remembering what he said about guys and love. Papa said don't believe it when a guy says he loves you and don't give him the chance to try and prove it either.

"Dorothy, you don't know what you're missing when you turn down a man that wants to love you." He proceeded to throw another rock into the pond.

"Jerome stop kidding yourself. You don't love me and you know it. Besides, I thought you was smart enough to figure out the different between love and lust."

"Dorothy, you obviously don't know me so don't jump to conclusions."

"My point exactly. I don't know you, which is one of the reasons why I'm not giving in to you."

"You think every time I see you I got sex on my mind don't you?"

"Yes."

He didn't say anything. Meanwhile inside the Impala, I could hear the sound of the springs squeaking, just like the sound a bed spring makes when you're making love in it. Then I heard Bettye scream out, "Oh David!" Then I heard David scream out, "Oh God!"

I was rendered speechless. I didn't know whether to stand there like an idiot and listen to them, or stand there like an idiot and watch Jerome throw every pebble, rock or whatever he could get his hands on into the pond. This was mind boggling. Jerome stopped throwing rocks and turned around with his back against me.

"Jerome what are you doing?"

"Turn your head and leave me the hell alone," he said.

"Don't play with yourself; you know that's not healthy."

"You would know, huh?"

I heard the sound of water drops hitting the grass and saw Jerome's urine glistening from the moonlight. I turned my attention to the Impala. The windows were ice white and the noise had ceased. I assumed they were finished. Just then David got out of the car with his shirt unbuttoned and his pants unzipped.

"Whew!" he shouted. It seemed like the sex had taken all the strength out of him and the sigh was all he needed in order to regain it. He ran towards Jerome and I heard him yell out again, "Whew!" followed by the splatter of urine hitting the grass. I walked to the car. I could imagine what it looked or smelled like inside. I opened the door and sat down on the passenger's side. The car smelled like a combination of sweat and after shave. I glanced over my shoulder at Bettye, who was fastening her blouse, her neatly pinned French roll now scattered on top of her head looked like a destroyed bird's nest.

"I heard you and Jerome arguing. I hope everything is all right."

"Not hardly," I said examining my hair in the rear view mirror.

"Is he acting up again?" she asked looking much different and much younger without her glasses.

"Need I say more?" I replied as I started wiping the mist from my window.

"What are they doing out there?"

"Springin' a leak."

Just then Jerome opened the door. It startled me, so I screamed.

"Hey what's your problem!" he shouted. I guess it startled him too.

"I didn't see you coming Jerome."

"Yeah, now could you get in the back seat?"

David opened the door to the driver's side and got in. "David, do I have to move?" I asked. David only looked at me and smiled.

"Yes you have to. Now move." Jerome reached for my leg.

"Jerome don't you dare."

"Then will you please get up and get in the back seat, that's all I'm asking."

For some strange reason I wanted to make him mad, I was a bit angry about what went on earlier in the day with the unexpected guest.

"Well Jerome, it looks like you're going to have to put me back there yourself," I said.

Jerome's hand was fastened on his hip. "Dorothy, I'm trying my hardest to be a gentleman."

"Really?" I responded. I noticed his temples were jumping.

"Yeah, you'll think I'm crazy if I take you out of this car and throw you on the ground."

I wanted to see if he was going to do it, so I didn't move. "Well I'm waiting Jerome."

At that point, David got out and got in the back seat. "Now Jerome, drive."

Jerome replied, "David, you don't have to get back there. Let Dorothy put her Geechie ass back there." See he didn't have to go there. "Geechie!" I shouted. I almost got out to stomp his behind senseless.

"Dorothy don't make me throw you out."

"dammit man just drive the car!" David shouted from behind me, startling me.

"You stay out of it David," Bettye said calmly.

"Will someone please make up their mind. Shit this is ridiculous!" David shouted.

"Don't yell at me!" Bettye shouted.

"I'm not yelling at you!"

Everyone was shouting and to tell you the truth, that was the most fun I had had this whole wretched day. Once Jerome plunged into the driver's seat, he slammed the car door. "Hey J, take it easy on my door!" David shouted. Jerome started the engine and looked at me, "You are worrisome you know that?" He put the car in reverse. "I'm going to be nice and keep my cool, because you Creole women get rowdy during a full moon."

"You leave Creole women alone." I pointed my index finger at the tip of his nose. He pushed it away, I put it back, he slapped it away again.

"Dorothy you think I'm playing."

"Don't ever call me Geechie again."

The ride going home was a long one. One minute I heard David and Bettye slurping on each other, about ten minutes later they were asleep. I glanced at Jerome. He was concentrating really hard on the road. His eyes blinked constantly and his mouth was pressed shut, though it drooped slightly. Sitting quietly I recalled a review of this whole day. I knew it was going to be messed up. Jerome picked me up and we went to the diner to eat. There, we bumped into his girlfriend. Yes. Jerome had a girlfriend, but no one really liked her. Anyway, she saw us there sitting together. She didn't hesitate to come over and confront Jerome and had the nerve to confront me. She threw her books on the floor and told me to get up and fight her. When I didn't, she reached for my hair. While this was going on, everyone in the diner was crowding around us. Jerome was trying to break us up but the girl had a huge strand of my hair and he had a difficult time trying to pry open her hands. When I finally got untangled from her grip, Jerome pushed her away. "It's not over, Jerome West!" She shouted. I looked around me. I had never seen so many people staring at me; it was as if I was a gigantic movie screen. I was so embarrassed. When we got back to the dorm Jerome admitted that he used to date the girl.

"Use to?" I asked.

"I dated her off and on last semester," he said.

Before I could say anything else, there came a knock on the door and I quickly jumped up, remembering I'm not suppose to be anywhere near the boy's dorm. Jerome whispered for me to go into the bathroom and that's where I remained. I heard a female's voice, which sounded like the same girl, then I saw the door knob move and I heard Jerome's voice over her voice. I stood behind the door and listened as the girl screamed at the top of her lungs at Jerome. "I lose my virginity to you and this is how you repay me! I hate you!" I put my ear against the door and listened closely. It sounded like they were fighting. For a little bit I almost opened the door, but I stood there until I no longer heard them. When I opened the door just a little and looked around the room, Jerome and the girl were gone. I walked out and sat on his bed and waited, and waited, and waited. The room was in mad chaos. There were pieces of glass from a shattered picture frame on the floor, Jerome's waste basket was toppled over and there were specks of blood on the floor. This terrible incident took place around noon, around two I was still waiting. When David walked in, he found me sitting on the floor with my arms circled around my legs; my face was flushed red.

"Hello, Dorothy," he said.

"Hi," I mumbled.

"What's wrong?" he asked.

"Jerome. Have you seen him?" I asked.

"I just saw Jerome at the library," he said.

"Oh yeah, was he with someone?"

At that moment Jerome walked in carrying a book. "Speak of the devil," David said.

Jerome looked at me.

"You owe me an explanation," I said.

"I just went to the library to turn in a book. If you don't believe me ask David," He motioned to David.

"Who was that at the door?" I asked.

Jerome had a puzzled look on his face. "You talking about earlier?" he asked trying to think of a lie.

"Yes, earlier?"

"That was nobody." I gave Jerome a you-must-be-kidding-me look.

He laughed. "Why are you looking at me like that?"

"Because you lie too much Jerome. I heard who you was talking to, it was that girl from the diner."

Jerome didn't respond. "Am I right?" I asked him. He nodded. "I had to get her straight," he said. "I didn't appreciate the way she handled herself at the diner." David pretended to read a book.

"It took you two hours?" I asked.

"Yeah, plus I had to go to the library."

"Save it Jerome."

"If you think I'm lying ask David." He held out his arms to convince the point. I felt I was more like a number than a human being to

Jerome. If I wasn't going to give him something, there was always the next girl in line waiting. There was no love and no friendship as far as I could see. He was cruel in the sense he didn't know how to treat a girl like me. Just because he was twenty-three and I was eighteen didn't mean that I was stupid. I had seen guys like him before. My oldest sister Katherine use to date guys like Jerome. Being the beautiful woman she was and still is, they tried to take advantage of her. Unfortunately more than one of them succeeded, but she was prepared for the next guy. Luckily for her he was marriage material and they tied the knot. I couldn't imagine myself marrying a guy like Jerome West. The fact that he was going to become a doctor, made no difference; he still didn't know how to treat a lady. To me he was a creep, he was an educated creep, a fine creep, but nonetheless a creep.

* * *

I looked outside, and high above the rolling pines was indeed a full moon. I laughed to myself thinking back to what Jerome said. He always had something to say about Creole women. I hope someday God arranges for him to marry a Creole woman, someone not as nice as me, but someone who'll put him in line. Whenever she pulls his chain, he'll come running and barking like a dog. When Jerome stopped the car in front of my house, he shut off the engine.

"Tonight is my last night in Atlanta," I said, finally breaking the twenty-five minutes of silence.

"What time are you leaving?"

"Around one."

"Have a nice trip." He said that in a way as if it didn't matter at all.

The light from the porch came on and Papa's huge silhouette figure appeared in the doorway.

"Who is that, your father?"

"Yes."

"He's a big man."

"Would you like to meet him? He's just dying to meet you."

"You told your father about me?"

"Yes, and he can't wait to meet you."

Jerome drummed his hands nervously on the stirring wheel. I rolled down the window.

"Papa it's me!"

"Is that you Dot?" he asked leaning forward. "Who is that driving?"

Jerome looked at me. That was the first time I actually saw him nervous. He pretended to chew gum, though he didn't have a trace of it anywhere in his mouth.

"Are you going to get out and meet Papa?"

Jerome hesitated before getting out of the car. When he approached Papa I noticed Papa looked him over thoroughly.

"So you the doctor my baby girl's been talking about," Papa said while shaking Jerome's hand. "Vince LaCroix."

"Jerome West," Jerome announced in a formal tone.

"Come inside Doc. No need to stand out here son."

"I wish I could Mr. LaCroix but I have a curfew."

Papa frowned. "Come on now Doc, spare about fifteen minutes. That'll be enough time."

Jerome looked at me as if I were going to say something to convince Papa he had to be back by curfew. Papa put his arm around me and Jerome and walked with us inside. Ophelia was fastening the lock to her suitcase when we all walked in.

"Ophelia you met the Doc?" Papa asked while he ushered Jerome to his seat. Ophelia nodded, said a quick "hi" to Jerome and disappeared into her room.

"That's my baby girl," Papa said to Jerome as he sat down beside me. Jerome just nodded.

"Dot baby, you mean to tell me all this time you've been in Atlanta, you haven't introduced me to the Doc until now?"

I couldn't respond for some reason or another I felt goofy all over again. Jerome glanced at his watch on the sly.

"Doc, tell me what kind of doctor are you studying to be."

"A gynecologist, sir."

"Oh yeah. You like bringing babies into the world?"

I was beginning to enjoy this little conversation Papa was having with Jerome. He could more than likely get a decent conversation out of Jerome, which is more than I can say for myself.

"Have you ever witnessed natural childbirth?" Papa asked.

"Yes sir I have."

"I tell you it ain't a pretty sight to see a woman in that much pain; but man it's beautiful when you hear that baby crying."

Jerome chuckled a little. "It amazes me too."

"Yeah, I witnessed all three of my girls coming into the world," Papa said then he looked at me. "My Dot here scared the hell out of me when she was born." He looked at Jerome. "The midwife had hell trying to pull her out of Cleo." I wanted to hit Papa, while at the same time I wanted to laugh at him. Jerome snickered.

"Then Ophelia, my youngest, she wasn't a problem at all. She took no time getting here."

Jerome glanced at his watch again.

"Doc, you ever witnessed surgery being done on a person?"

"Yes sir. Just last week I witnessed open heart surgery. The patient was suffering from atherosclerosis and that is a disease in which the arteries become engulfed in fat. Fat deposits occur and as a result they block the passageway of blood traveling away from the heart."

Pretty impressive, I thought as I heard him speak.

"You know what?" Papa began. "A man I use to work for had to get heart surgery and you know it took about a week for them to perform it."

"Do you remember his diagnosis?" Jerome asked.

"No, I just remember it was done two years ago and it cost him a lot of money."

"I agree, open heart surgery costs money."

"Why come you didn't study to become an open heart doctor?" Papa asked.

Jerome laughed. "You have to be a genius to be an open heart surgeon."

"You say so, huh? Where did you receive most of your schooling?" Papa asked. He started to cough again. When he coughed, his shoulders shook and his face turned red.

" 'Scuse me," he said between coughing.

"Papa you need some water?" I asked.

He shook his head. "No I'm fine, baby girl." He coughed again.

"Is everything okay Mister LaCroix?" Jerome asked.

Papa couldn't talk. He just pulled out a handkerchief and held it to his mouth. He held up his hand when Jerome stood up to help him.

"Papa that's not healthy;" I said. "You need a check up. Don't you think so, Jerome?" Jerome nodded. "A summer cold is the worst cold to have," he said. "Get your father some cough syrup."

Papa's coughing came to a cease. His eyes were watery and his nose was red.

"Good gracious," he said and laughed. "Did you hear all that rambling and wheezing Doc?"

Jerome nodded. "Yes sir, you need to see a licensed physician about your cough. It sounds like you have bronchitis to me."

"Oh, it ain't nothing, I got a bottle of that Castor Oil in the kitchen there." Papa cleared his throat. "Whenever I start to coughing, I just go in there and take me some."

"Papa you always say that," I said. "Your cough sounds too serious. You need to go to the doctor." Papa shook his head.

"I don't need to go to the doctor, baby girl. Those doctors don't do anything but look at you, take your temperature, and charge you an arm and leg."

I gave up trying to convince him otherwise. Papa looked at Jerome. "I bet when you get established, you'll be charging an arm and a leg too, won't you Doc?" He asked.

Jerome smiled. "Well sir it all boils down to the equipment costs and practice costs. You have so many fees that sometimes you have to charge a lot to compensate for them."

"Even us poor folks," Papa said.

Jerome didn't reply.

"Where you from, Doc?"

"I'm from Houston, sir."

"What part of Houston?" Papa asked.

"Third Ward sir," Jerome said in a boastful tone.

"Oh yeah? I got a cousin Vera who lived over there in Third Ward."

"I went to college in Third Ward at Texas Southern," Jerome said.

"My Cousin Vera went to school there too." Papa nodded his head and thought once more about something. "She's doing all right out there in California. She's a pharmacist."

I eyed Jerome. It nearly killed me how nervous and timid he acted around Papa. While staring at Jerome I thought back to the first time I saw him how different he was then. Right now, he was totally opposite.

Then out of nowhere Papa asked Jerome.

"Do you love my daughter?"

Jerome, whose eyes were glued on the television, looked quickly at me and then Papa. I must admit, Papa's question caught us both off guard. I knew Jerome didn't love me, and I had to defend him so I blurted out, "Papa, Jerome and I don't have that type of relationship."

Papa's eyes were now on the television. He stroked his chin and I could tell something was on his mind because he had that look. His eyes blinked continually and he sucked his teeth. "Umm Hmm." I heard him say. "So you and my daughter are just friends."

"Yessir," I heard Jerome say quickly. He was on the edge of his seat and was glancing at his watch again.

"I say that because I love my daughter. I love all my daughters, and I can't stand for anyone to mistreat them do you understand?" When he said that his voice shifted to a serious gear.

"Yessir," Jerome said. He was sweating so much underneath his neck and around his temples, that he had to reach into his pocket and pull out a handkerchief to wipe his face.

"Son, I didn't mean to make your nervous," Papa said.

Jerome laughed at me. "It's hot sir," he said and continued to wipe the sweat.

"But I mean very well what I said," Papa concluded.

"Papa, it's time for Jerome to leave, remember he has a curfew," I said.

Papa stood up and Jerome stood with him. Jerome extended his hand.

"Pleasure meeting you, Mister LaCroix."

"Pleasure's all mine Doc. I wish I could've met you sooner. We could've went fishing together, do you fish son?"

"It's been a while Mister LaCroix; however, my father went last weekend and caught a twenty-three pound bass." Jerome extended his arms to illustrate.

"Yeah? Well a friend of mine caught one about that size too this weekend. As a matter of fact, they still eating on him right now." Papa and Jerome both laughed. When I walked outside, I realized how much more refreshing it was compared to inside. Papa said good-bye and closed the door behind him. Meanwhile, I walked Jerome to the car and sat inside with him.

"Whew," He sighed. "Your pops is one helluva character."

"I'm glad you met him Jerome."

"Yeah, your pop cares a lot about you."

"I don't know why Papa just came out of the blue and asked you that question," I said. Jerome stared straight ahead quietly. "He's just concerned that's all. I know if I had a daughter that looked as good as you, I'd be concerned too."

"Yeah, but you don't have a daughter," I said.

"If you stick around, I will one day," Jerome replied reaching out to touch my chest.

"Shut up, Jerome," I said intercepting his hand. I noticed he was still sweating a little. Behind us, the two love birds were still asleep. David was stretching and grunting. He sounded so much like an old man that Jerome and I laughed quietly to ourselves. Afterwards it became quiet and all I could hear were the crickets chirping.

"Dorothy, I had a good time talking to your father," Jerome said as he started up the engine. I sat quietly. This was the last time I was going to see him for a while.

"When are you coming to New Orleans?" I asked.

"Most likely it'll be around Christmas. I usually pass through on my way to Houston."

"Christmas? That's too long away."

"It's only four months."

"But still," I said.

"But still what?" he asked glancing at his watch.

"I would like to see you before then."

"I got a question for you," he said. "When are you coming back to Atlanta?"

"I don't know, maybe next summer."

"I hope to see you around then, maybe we can get better acquainted, if you know what I mean," he said with a wicked smile.

"You just don't quit," I said. He smiled and those were the last words we said to each other before I got on the bus the next day and rode over 500 miles back to New Orleans.

When Ophelia and I arrived home, Mama was sitting on the couch with a swollen belly between her legs. She was fanning and cursing about how hot it was and how her thighs rubbed a rash between her legs. Mama was eight months pregnant.

"Hello my pretty babies," She said while smiling and rubbing her stomach. Although Katherine was twenty-two, Ophelia was sixteen, and I was eighteen, she still called us babies.

"How was the trip?" She asked. Mama looked like a white queen with her long hair pinned on top of her head, sitting on a red Victorian settee with deep purple curtains behind her.

"It was fun Mama as usual," Ophelia said as she sat down next to Mama and rubbed her stomach.

"Has it been kicking a lot?" she asked.

Mama sighed. "Oh yes. I believe it's a boy, because a girl just doesn't kick this much."

I took my suitcase and walked towards my room. Seeing Mama pregnant just didn't fit well with me. Why in the world did she have to come up pregnant by Louis Dix in the first place? Everyone knew that Louis Dix was a notorious womanizer. There wasn't a woman in New Orleans or Louisiana who hadn't had Louis Dix at one time or another. He had been married two times before and out of those two marriages, he had seven children, who I knew of. Mama's little headache was eighth on the list. When I walked into the living room she and Ophelia were still engaged in a conversation about the summer in Atlanta.

"Dot, I didn't hear you say anything about the trip, did you enjoy it?" Mama asked.

"Yes," was my reply.

"Did your Papa fool around and find him another woman?"

I wanted to tell her for her information Papa was beyond the fooling around stage. He was thirty-nine years old and didn't have any more small babies to take care of, unlike her. It irritated me that every summer when I came back, she always asked me if Papa had found himself a woman. Why would it matter to her if he found another woman? For fifteen years she had had her chance to prove to him she was his only woman.

"No Mama." I said.

"Hmmphf," she said. "I'm surprised he hasn't found a piece," she bellowed out. "He must be worn out." And she commenced to laughing. Her stomach shook like gelatin when she laughed. Sometimes I found my mother in poor taste. She was hard to live with; that's why I always ran away to my Aunt Ruby Jewel and Uncle Herbie's house. My Aunt's house was peaceful and I got along with her and Uncle Herbie so much better. Sometimes I wished Papa had married Aunt Ruby Jewel instead. She appreciated everything in life and she wasn't a gold digger and selfish. Aunt Ruby Jewel was Mama's older sister, but she looked so much younger and was in excellent shape. She couldn't have children because she had an inflamed cervix and her uterus was too small. She said if she were to have a child, it would kill her. But she always said God blessed her to have beautiful nieces to love like her own children. Uncle Herbie felt the same way and they spoiled me considerably. Meanwhile Mama kept asking questions about the trip.

"You know your Uncle Herbie and Ruby Jewel moving to Beaumont."

"Why?" I asked. It was a bit of a surprise.

"Herbie got a job working on ships."

"How did he come across a job like that?"

"His brother, I reckon," Mama said and leaned forward to place a pillow behind her. "I be glad when I have this baby, you know Mama's a little too old to be worried about this shit again."

"Where's Louis?"

Mama sighed and wiggled herself against the pillow. I wasn't surprise she didn't know where he was. Before I could speak, Louis stumbled in the doorway, dressed from head to toe in white.

"Hello, hello, hello." He took off his hat. It reminded me of Barnum and Bailey when the circus announcer gets in the center of the ring and says, "Ladies and Gentlemen, Children of all ages! It's the grrreatest show on Earth!" Louis looked like the little man and acted like him too when he held out his arms and walked into the living room. His hair was still the shape of the inside of his hat, and he smelled like talc powder and spearmint.

"You girls glad to be back home?" he asked walking toward the couch and sitting beside Mama. When he crossed his legs the silver tip of his shoes caught my eyes, not to mention the rings he had on all eight fingers. I noticed one of Louis' eyes wondering, while the other one stared straight ahead at you. It looked awfully strange. It's funny that after all these years, I hadn't noticed his "lazy eye." Louis reminded me of Sidney Portier, except Louis had a mustache and a beard streaked with gray, not to mention a "lazy eye." He had a rich Creole accent, which I thought was more rich than Mama's.

Seeing Mama and Louis sitting there together made me sick. They didn't look right together. They didn't look like they were in love like Uncle Herbie and Aunt Ruby Jewel did. Uncle Herbie was affectionate towards Aunt Ruby Jewel. He always had something kind to say, and he never went a day without telling her he loved her. I would always find them sitting outside on the porch swing, acting like teenagers kissing and teasing each other. Louis and Mama never did that. The only time they touched was probably when he got Mama pregnant. They never said affectionate words to each other. They never touched affectionately, unless you call Louis smacking Mama on the behind, showing affection.

"Louis," Mama said rubbing her stomach, "any day now you got to curse and scream with me when I give birth. I ain't doing this by myself."

Louis rubbed his palm on top of her stomach, his rings were glistening. "I seen my first baby, and that was all I had to see," He said. Mama rolled her eyes toward the ceiling.

"Oh hush up!" she said removing his hand and shifting her weight away from him. Ophelia and I laughed and I turned my attention outside the window to the busy street that ran in front of the house. My mind was on Jerome for some strange reason as I watched a couple holding hands and strolling outside on the sidewalk. Jerome and I never held hands when we were together; neither did Mama and Louis.

Chapter 3

Katherine sent word that Papa was seriously ill and had been for two months. He never told anyone how serious it was until Katherine paid him a visit and he started coughing. Katherine said Papa coughed so much that he began to vomit. She finally convinced Papa to go to the doctor. He did and found out he had lung cancer. When I heard the news, my heart fluttered and for a moment I pictured Papa lying in a pearly white casket. I was praying to God to make Papa better. I wouldn't know how to cope if Papa died on me.

Mama had the baby, a little five pound girl name Jacqueline. I wasn't around when Mama gave birth but Ophelia was. She told me Reverend Montague and the Devereaux sisters came by. Reverend Montague, who was a Catholic priest, decided to read a scripture from the Bible before the sisters, who were also mid-wives, proceeded with the delivery. Ophelia told me through laughter that Mama was cursing and screaming right there in front of them. The sisters started to pray louder. She said after awhile she heard Mama singing, "Swing Low Sweet Chariot, come and take my big ass home." Then she heard a baby crying. I asked Ophelia where was Louis. She said he was in the living room puffing on a cigarette acting like he wasn't concerned. Some man he was. At least Papa was there for Mama when she delivered the three of us. I told my Aunt Ruby Jewel, who was packing for her move to Texas, about Louis, Mama, and the new baby.

"You know baby, until this day, you thought she did mighty right when she got involved with that man." I folded an apron of hers and laid it in the suitcase with the rest of her clothes.

"You couldn't tell Cleo a thing about that man." She paused and frowned at an object I couldn't recognize with my own eyes.

"What are you looking at?" I asked.

"Oh nothing, I was just thinking." Her eyes were still on the object. "You know what?" she said in a falsetto tone of voice. "I thought I put Herb's clothes in the trunk with the rest of the things."

I thought Aunt Ruby Jewel was going to finish her conversation about Mama and Louis, but she excused herself outside instead. I sat staring at the bare walls that were once covered with pictures. There were pictures of people I knew and some who died before I was even born. I had a lot of good memories in this house. I use to sit by the window and stare at a bed full of carnations leading a pathway into a thick forest. I use to play hide-and-seek with Katherine and my other cousins and we'd get lost among the thickets. In the spring when the weeds and flowers reached their tremendous heights, Uncle Herbie cut them down and burned them to a black crisp. We'd pout because we didn't want him to level our emerald fortress. Aunt Ruby Jewel also had magnolias and azaleas which were plentiful and just smelling them reminded me of clean, fresh, Louisiana air. I was going to miss this place.

When Aunt Ruby Jewel came back inside she sat down to join me. "Now." She said. "Where was I?"

* * *

I got a letter from Jerome in the mail. It was about time; after all, I had written him three times. He didn't have a lot to say, just that medical school was putting him through a test and he was walking a thin line between moving forward or just quitting and getting a teacher's certificate to teach. He mentioned something about David and Bettye breaking up. He also mentioned that David asked about me a lot and wanted to know when was I coming back. Then he said how much he missed me, which I knew was a lie, and finally he ended the letter with a p.s., "Hope we can get better acquainted which each other next summer." I laughed. That part of the letter was so funny.

* * *

I was enjoying my life at Southern. I couldn't believe I was actually in college. The people there were friendly and down to earth. I met a girl who reminded me so much of Tiny; her name was Joan St. Julian. We were in the same government and history classes. Joan was a pretty girl who, like Tiny, spoke her mind and never hesitated to tell you how she felt. We were in government talking about the march on Washington and how Martin Luther King's *I have a Dream* speech made us feel.

"I'm from D.C. and I went to the march and I saw all those people and I thought." She gestured with her hands. "It's a shame that after 100 years, Negroes are still talking about dreaming in America." She shook her head. "Why is that Negroes are the only people in this country still having to dream? Immigrants can come over here with nothing and build multi-million dollar corporations. We've been over here 400 years, so called emancipated for a 100 and can't even build decent schools for our children." Everyone just stared speechless at this petite person in front of the room. "When are we as Negroes going to stop relying on the other man and start relying on the brother man?"

Professor Thornton nodded. "Good question," he responded in a northern baritone voice. I looked at Joan whose face had reddened. I guess her blood had warmed over from her frustration. Looking at her I thought, she would make a good lawyer.

There was a gathering at the student union, Southern's chapter of the Student Nonviolent Coordinating Committee was having an interest meeting. Joan was telling me what it was all about and that she was joining it. I didn't want to be a part of anything at all. My intentions were to just rush through Southern and get my degree; however, it wasn't long before I found myself pledging a sorority. Joan and I were on the same line and we both ended up going over. I wrote Tiny to tell her about the news. She wrote back to congratulate me. She told about the time she pledged and how she felt when she finally went over. She ended the letter saying she was going to love being my soror. Then she told me David inquired about me a lot, and that he and Bettye were no longer together. She said David and I would make a good couple a lot better than Jerome and I. She told me Jerome was dating another soror from Clark and she saw them studying occasionally.

"Jerome sounds like a major stud to me," Joan said after I let her read the letter he wrote and told her about him. "I wouldn't let him get under my skin girl, it's obvious where his head is." Joan went on to tell me about her friend from D.C.

"He thought he was slick," she said. "He thought he could run around the country and jump every girl he could get his hands on. The part that's so disgusting was this guy was a minister, he was suppose to be a man of God."

"How old was he Joan?"

She closed one eye and tried to think with the other one. "About twenty-four or twenty-five. He looked much older though, but he was something else. We almost went down the aisle, until I found out he had an illegitimate child by one of the sisters in the church."

"No."

"Not just any sister, this girl was special."

"Special meaning?"

"Meaning she was on the slow side."

"No."

"He was very disgusting, I swear," was all Joan could say.

"Sounds like Jerome, a low down, sleazy, lying…" I was stuttering as I tried to get the rest of the words out.

Joan shook her head. "I know what you mean."

I sat staring at the poster she had of a colored man with a goatee and horn-rimmed glasses on her wall. Underneath were the words, *By Any Means Necessary. Oh really*, I thought.

* * *

Katherine and her husband came by Aunt Bridgette's, Mama's youngest sister's house. Katherine didn't have any make-up on which I thought was really strange. She looked at me and shook her head slowly.

"Papa's not doing too good." Her voice sounded tired and cracked.

"What do you mean?" I asked. I felt my heart thumping. She sighed and said, "Papa's giving up on us. He's not taking his medicine, he's not eating."

Ricky cleared his throat. "We've tried everything."

"Don't say that," I heard myself say to Ricky. It sounded like Papa was already dead, and I wasn't going to accept it.

"Who's taking care of him now?" Aunt Bridgette asked.

"Aunt Naomi and Aunt Theresa," Katherine responded. She looked exhausted from the long drive, plus she felt the same way I did about Papa. His illness was having a drastic effect on the both of us. There were dark circles around her eyes, shaped like coals, and her hair was pulled back into a frizzy ponytail. Ricky didn't look any better. His face needed a good shaving not to mention a hair cut.

"Thank God you two managed to make it here safe." Aunt Bridgette put their suitcases in the guest room. Katherine closed her eyes and laid her head in Ricky's arm.

"We're leaving tomorrow afternoon," she said.

"Why tomorrow? Why not leave the day after tomorrow?" Aunt Bridgette asked when she entered the living room.

"We have jobs," Ricky responded. I heard another sigh from Katherine. It was long and exasperated.

"Really Katherine?"

Katherine just nodded and leaned her head against Ricky's arm.

"Well," Aunt Bridgette responded and sat in her chair and proceeded to sit in silence and watch the two of them.

Katherine smiled. "How's the baby?" she asked. Her eyes were pressed shut and her head was still in Ricky's arm.

"The baby was fine the last time I saw her. She's pretty and fat," I began. "You wouldn't think half of her was Louis."

Katherine and Ricky both chuckled. Aunt Bridgette playfully slapped my arm. "Girl hush," she said laughing.

Later that afternoon, after the rain cleared, Katherine and I went to Mama's. Mama was happy to see Katherine.

"Hello there, I forgot you existed," Mama said as she embraced Katherine. Seeing them embrace each other was like watching someone embrace her reflection in a mirror.

"Mama, where's the baby?"

Mama smiled. "Sleep," she said and plopped down on the sofa. She sighed the exact same way as Katherine. It was amazing how at times Katherine acted like Mama, and sometimes I would catch Mama doing things I remember seeing Katherine do.

"How's your Pappy doing?" Mama blurted out.

Katherine replied. "Papa's fine I guess." She looked at me; I rolled my eyes. Mama had a way with words which we both thought was tasteless.

"You guess?" She leaned forward and grabbed a coin purse from a nearby coffee table. Reaching inside it, she pulled out a cigarette. "Huh?"

"Mama, Papa's been ill for a while now. He has a wheezing cough."

Mama placed the thin white stick between her ruby red lips and puffed twice before she exhaled a cloud of smoke into the air. I watched as it swirled about the room and I thought, why on earth would anyone inhale all of that smoke? I imagined it swirling in her lungs and I thought about Papa. It swirled about a million times in his lungs too. That was before it built a crusty ugly black monster that suffocated him. It had him breathing and panting like a dog and he coughed until his lungs nearly collapsed. I looked at Mama taking another puff and watched as the smoke swirled from her nostrils. She had that smoking a cigarette look. You know the one when the smoke gets in your eyes and you frown with your lips half parted.

Katherine reached into her purse and pulled out her cigarette. "Katherine, now I know you're not smoking," I said in my disgusted-with-you voice. She struck a match on the coffee table and cupped her hands to keep the flame from flickering out. "Yes," She said while putting out the match and holding the cigarette between her small fingers. "Don't look at me like that, Dot," she said.

"Katherine, that's why Papa's in the fix he's in."

Katherine thought about what I said, blew out a cloud of smoke, and smashed her cigarette in the ashtray.

"Well I be," Mama began. "Katherine, I know you not gonna sit there and take shit from her. You're a grown ass woman, shit. Smoke your damn cigarette." Mama opened up her coin purse and handed Katherine another one. "Here don't let this child tell you what to do."

"Mama," I said.

Mama thumped her ashes. "Go to hell Dot. Leave your big sister alone. Let her smoke her own cigarette if she wants to. Ain't nobody gonna end up like yo' Papa. Shit, that man could chain smoke from here to damn near New Yawk."

I didn't argue with Mama, because arguing got us nowhere. I especially didn't want to argue with her about Papa, because she went on for hours talking about him. Meanwhile, Katherine just held the unlit cigarette between her fingers.

"I know I shouldn't smoke, but lately I've been having a lot on my mind."

Mama studied Katherine. "I see. Baby your eyes have bags under them. Where's your make-up? Have you been getting enough sleep?"

Katherine untied her pony tail and ran her hands through her shoulder length black tresses.

"I can't sleep. I worry a lot about Papa."

"Katherine, you let Vince's relatives take care of him. You needn't worry yourself with him."

"What do you mean I needn't worry myself? Need I remind you that's my father." Katherine's voice began to soften.

"You don't have to remind me." Mama stood up and walked lazily into the kitchen. "But getting back to what I said earlier. Don't worry yourself to the point where you go out in public looking the way you do. Child have you looked at yourself in the mirror lately? Baby at the rate you're going you're headed for a nervous breakdown."

Katherine placed the unlit cigarette on the table beside an old picture of Mama, Papa and us in the early fifties.

"Mama doesn't understand." Katherine said.

I heard Mama's voice from the kitchen yell out, "all right! Don't come running here if you go off the deep end worryin' 'bout you papa!"

"Mama would you at least show some compassion for him. My papa needs attention!" Katherine yelled back.

"your papa don't need a damn thing but a peace of mind!"

Katherine shouted, "what are you talking about?"

Mama appeared in the kitchen doorway. "Your father is getting payback for his wrongdoing."

"Mama what payback? We don't even want to get started on you and Papa's marriage." Katherine's voice had transformed into a hard sounding robot. Mama leaned against the kitchen door frame and blew out another cloud of smoke.

"Mama I wish you could put your differences with Papa in the past," Katherine said as she rested her arm on the settee and toyed with her hair. I heard a cough followed by a sharp cry. It was the baby crying in the other room. Mama put out her cigarette and ran into the room. Katherine sighed again and closed her eyes. "God forgive me for saying this, but our mother is ignorant," Katherine whispered.

"I know," I whispered back.

A few minutes later, Mama appeared in the doorway holding the baby in her arms.

"Katherine, look who just woke up?"

Mama smiled and held the baby so Katherine could see her oval shaped face. Katherine's mouth fell open with awe and she slowly eased up to hold the baby.

"Oh Mama she's so pretty! Hello, precious." Katherine kissed the baby's rosy red cheeks. Mama's eyes were glued on the baby. I noticed how they sparkled when Katherine cooed with Jacqueline.

"She's a doll."

Mama bounced the baby in her arms. "Say I know, Big Sister Katherine." Mama pretended to speak for the baby who stared blankly past Katherine's head to the ceiling fan buzzing above her. Mama took the baby's tiny fist and kissed it. "It's feeding time." She spoke baby talk and that annoyed me. Mama sounded like Tweety Bird from the Looney Tunes when she talked like that. Katherine held the baby until she started crying. "Oh I see how you are; you are spoiled rotten already."

After Mama left the room Katherine looked at me and shook her head. "Now Mama know she's too old to have a newborn baby," she whispered as she picked up the unlit cigarette. I guessed she remembered what I said and dropped it back on the table where she found it.

* * *

A day later Katherine and Ricky left for Atlanta. I sat staring out my bedroom window at their car until I could no longer see it. I prayed they would make it home safe and that Papa would be much better. Lord knows I want to see him, but not the way he is.

Outside my window the streets were busy with pedestrians and traffic. Sometimes living on a busy street has its advantages. I liked checking out the latest rides and eavesdropping on the neighbor's fighting and oh yes, the block parties. Our home wasn't grand, but it was big enough for the four of us. Modest would be the best way to describe it. When you opened the gate you stepped onto a pebbly terrace and right in the center was a headless, armless, sculpture of a woman with ivy scurrying around her stone body. Inside, the walls were adorned with pictures of the whole Montague and LaCroix clan. A sign with the words "Bless this Mess" was nailed atop the door frame leading into the dining room with its antique Victorian-style dinning room table, one of the few luxuries Mama acquired from her marriage to Papa.

Looking out the window, I saw an old man and a boy passing by. The man's eyes were hidden behind dark glasses, I assumed he was blind because he held on to the boy's hand. Going in the opposite direction was a man, swinging his arms to and fro' with each short and swift step. Coming across the street in the direction of our house was a man carrying a little girl in his arms. He laughed along with the child as he put her down on the pavement to walk. They stood there for a moment staring at the houses and pointing at the maple, oak, and cypress trees that lined the streets. They turned and looked at our house. I noticed them staring at me looking back at them from my window. Seeing them reminded me of myself and Papa. Papa use to hold my hand the same way. My heart fluttered and at that moment. Something hit my body like a bolt of lightening and I became suddenly nauseous. I closed my eyes for a period of time and wished for this sudden outburst of pain to go away. When I opened my eyes to look outside, the man and little girl had disappeared down the street. From behind me, I heard the baby crying and Mama talking gibberish to her. Outside the window there was a loud squeal from the breaks of a car, followed by a loud horn. I felt my shoulders tighten and my brain throb. I felt that if I couldn't talk to anyone I would explode into pieces. I opened my chest-of-drawers and searched furiously through my under garments hoping to find something to give me peace of mind. I stumbled across the address to Jerome's apartment, then I thought, I definitely didn't want to write him because he was one of the reasons why I was feeling depressed. I didn't want to write Tiny because all she talked about was how childish and inconsiderate Mike was and how I should consider talking to David. Wait a minute; a light came on. Talk to David. He's probably feeling the same as me, depressed about he and Bettye's relationship, depressed about school, or depressed for no reason. I got out a pen and a sheet of paper.

> Dear David,
>
> How are you? I hope you're doing fine, and I hope you're not fretting medical school like other people I know. I'm sorry to hear about you and Bettye. I always thought you two were the ideal couple; full of love and understanding towards each other. I thought Jerome and I could work things out, but some people have what you call a mean streak running through their veins.

I realized that I wasn't making sense. I wanted to write David and talk to him about other things, not just Jerome. So I crumbled up the paper and started over. Then I thought, why am I pouring my heart out to David? It probably wouldn't matter to him how I felt. I had no emotional ties to him; I hardly knew him. Then something told me, Dorothy just write to whom it may concern. So I began writing and thinking. I thought about Mama and my relationship with her. It's not the best relationship in the world and it's not like I hate Mama, but I just can't express myself openly with her. Mama wasn't an easy person to talk to and she wasn't the type of person you expressed your feelings with. If you did, she drew an awful lot of conclusions and she thought that being emotional was so unnatural for a black person. Mama always kept her feelings rolled up inside of her, and Ophelia was the same way. Only Katherine and I were the "soft-hearted" ones, the ones who were easy to figure out because we wore our feelings on our sleeves. We were sensitive too. But as for Mama, it seemed as though there was a brick wall between us and neither one of us would tear it down to see the other side. With Aunt Ruby Jewel and Papa it's a different story. I could tell them more things and I would receive the compassion and pampered treatment that I looked for that only a mother is supposed to give. I could also talk to Aunt Bridgette with her hilarious self; she always kept me laughing. Though it was hard to take her seriously at times. I could talk to my sorors, but some of them had problems too. I put my thoughts into words and addressed the letter to David.

About two weeks later I received a letter from David. I sat on my dorm room floor and proceeded to read it.

Dear Dorothy,

First of all I'd like to take time out to thank you for writing me, I was stressed out, but your letter made everything all right for me and thanks once again. I don't like writing letters but when I received yours I had to make an exception. I know by looking at this letter I don't have the best penmanship in the world, but how many doctors you know do for that matter? So all I can say is make out what you can of my writing.

Dorothy guess what? Jerome saw the letter you wrote. He acted strange when he saw it was addressed to me instead of him. He kept asking me what was up? I said nothing, as far as I am concerned. Everything between me and Dorothy is strictly platonic. He didn't believe me and I finally broke it down to him like this Dorothy. I said, "Look Jerome, Dorothy is a beautiful woman and she doesn't deserve to be treated like she's worthless." I told him, I hate to see a brother not taking care of his business. I said if Dorothy was my woman, I wouldn't mistreat her at all because you must understand that a woman's feelings shouldn't be neglected. I told him that you got to show her there's much more to you than your drawers. Jerome said nothing more to me, but "Yeah, I knew something was going to happen between you and her sooner or later." About an hour later that same evening he hid a girl in the room and she spent the night. I thought, see there, that's why black women are so hard on their men. They can't trust them. They got to keep a leash on them, just like dogs. When he brought that girl over I said, "Dorothy doesn't deserve to be deceived." Jerome told me I was sounding like a female, but I was right.

Well enough of Jerome. He's yesterday's news. In your letter I read you were depressed because of your father's illness. I'm sorry to hear about that. All I can say is take care of him. Make sure you are there for him and don't forget a little TLC. I wish there was something I could do to make the situation easier for you to deal with. I know words can only go so far, and in situations like yours good family support definitely helps. Tiny told me that you and she are very close. I like Tiny. She's a very nice person and she thinks the world of you. She also told me you pledged and were part of the family now. Congratulations. Welcome! I am going to love having you as my soror. You know the sorority and fraternity have a tradition of maintaining strong beautiful Negro women and successful young Negro men.

As you know, Bettye and I aren't together. It's funny. When I broke up with Bettye, it was Tiny who pulled me aside and told me there were a lot of fish in the sea. I wasn't willing to accept it, because for five years I thought the sun rose and set around Bettye. It took me some time to accept it was over, because I had known Bettye since our undergraduate years at Texas Southern. Well, I thought I knew Bettye, but I realized that after all these years the person I grew to love was still a stranger. You asked me if I still loved Bettye and will we ever get back together. I do care about her still, and I hold no ill feelings against her. It's just when the magic wears off, it's gone permanently and that was the case with Bettye. I don't think I will ever get back with Bettye this time. We've separated on many occasions and reconciled, but this time it's over for good. Did Bettye try to hurt herself? Yes, she did and that's something I am very bitter about. When we broke up we both agreed we were not going to be childish and there were no hard feelings. So we left it at that. About a day later I get a call from Bettye's parents. Her father is cursing at me and telling me it was all my fault that Bettye tried to hurt herself, and she tried to act as if everything was my fault. So I drive to the hospital to see Bettye, but her parents are giving me a difficult time. So I told them I didn't provoke Bettye to do a thing. They didn't believe me. That's when I lost it with her parents, after all these years they obviously didn't know me either. So I drew the line with Bettye and her family. I had told

Bettye how I felt, she told me how she felt. She appeared to take our break up well. Apparently, she didn't.

Dorothy, I'm glad you decided to write me, I just wish I could see you. So when are you coming to Atlanta again? When you decide to come, don't forget to look me up.

Sincerely,
David.

I sat on my floor flabbergasted. David had a lot on his mind and like myself he needed someone to talk to. I thought I would bubble over like a pot of boiling hot water if I didn't find a network for my feelings. I guess I found a network in David, because for the next three weeks we wrote each other back and forth. He was a great advisor and very wise and intelligent to be so young. I was looking for someone like that.

I let Joan read the letter and she was impressed. She gave me the okay sign and said I should consider dating David instead of Jerome. She even suggested we go shopping to pick out an outfit for the first date. I thought that was taking it a little too fast besides it was sleazy and distasteful to date a guy and end up dating his best friend later. She said guys did it all the time and showed no remorse. I don't know, I just couldn't picture myself in that situation. It would be awkward for me. How would Jerome react to seeing me on David's arm as opposed to his? Knowing Jerome, it probably wouldn't phase him, he'd find himself some other girl to mess around with.

* * *

Everyone was talking about Kennedy's assassination. It was on every channel and graced the front cover of every piece of tabloid out there. Not one time did I see anything on Papa's death, not even in the daily newspaper's obituary. Papa died on the 23rd of November around nine in the morning. Katherine called and told us. She said when she went into Papa's room to feed him breakfast, she noticed his eyes were pressed shut and his face was still and solemn. When she called out his name he didn't answer, so she called out his name once more, but still no answer. As she told me, I could see a picture of sun rays beaming down on Papa's bed, and I could see his spirit rising from his body and he vanishing into the rays. After calling his name for the third time, Katherine said she dropped his breakfast on the floor and ran screaming out of the house. Aunt Theresa checked on his pulse and felt nothing. Katherine said the look on Aunt Theresa's face was motionless, like she too had died. Katherine said she held on to Papa's corpse and cried.

When I first heard the news of Papa's death, I was sitting in my government class listening to Professor Thornton talk about the assassination. The discussion was heated and as usual, Joan put her two bits in. When the door opened and a student aid came in, I thought nothing of it. It seemed on numerous occasions when I saw someone entering the classroom with a note, my heart would thump louder than a thoroughbred's and a lump about the size of Alaska would form in my throat. I would always say, I hope it's not a terrible message, and those times it wasn't. It just so happened when I least expected it. When I read the letter, I felt like rubber. It wasn't so. I had my bags at home and my round trip bus ticket just waiting to go see him and nurse him back to health. I felt drunk, nauseated and I wanted to throw up everywhere. It had to take some time to set in, but when it did, I exploded. Papa? Dead? It was unbearable to mention it in the same breath. The hardest thing for me to do was go home and face Ophelia and Mama. When I arrived at home Mama was sitting in the living room listening to Mahalia Jackson, of all people. She didn't even look at me when I walked in. The room smelled like bourbon and I noticed beside Mama's right foot was a glass decanter halfway full with the remains of the bubbling golden brown liquid in it. Ophelia was sitting across from Mama absorbing Mahalia's voice. Mahalia was singing the song she sang at the woman's funeral on *Imitation of Life*. Listening to her sing was haunting, her voice sounded like she too was mourning over Papa's death. When Ophelia saw me, she stood up and I saw the tears glistening in her eyes. She sobbed as she walked towards me. I embraced her and we both sobbed and cried on each other's shoulders. Listening to Mahalia's voice didn't make the situation better, she was only adding to the sorrow.

"Dot, Mama's not talking," Ophelia said between each sob. "Since she found out about Papa's death all she's been doing is drinking." I looked at Mama who was sitting with her back to us, staring out the window. Her silky black hair was down and her shoulders were slumped over. I couldn't tell whether or not she was crying, but from the way she swayed from left to right, I could tell she was hurting. I always knew deep down she still had a place in her heart for Papa and her conscious was reminding her; *Cleo you shouldn't have treated him the way you did. You could've still been with him had you not messed around. Vince loved you, you two had a beautiful family and you never appreciated it.* I knew for sure Mama was hurting because she only played Mahalia whenever someone dear to her died, like Grandma Reba. I walked towards Mama, but something told me to leave her alone with her thoughts, so I did.

* * *

On the morning of the funeral, the family started arriving around eight in the morning. There were so many cars lined up in front of our house that it reminded me of Mardi Gras. Katherine arrived from Atlanta in her black chiffon dress with Ricky. I hadn't seen my sister since her last visit, so we embraced. I tried to hold back the tears, by trying to smile a little, but I couldn't. All around I could hear muffled voices and Katherine's voice trying to soothe me.

"Where's Mama?" She asked, her eyes were moist.

"Mama's in her room getting dressed."

She touched my crimson cheeks. "It's gonna be all right, Papa's gone to a better place." I touched her hand and held it to my face, crying. Katherine was fighting back her tears while biting her bottom lip. "Excuse me," she whispered. I watched as she walked through a crowd of Papa's relatives, everyone was trying to hug and console her and she would stop to talk but her mind was on Mama. Meanwhile Louis was near the bar set entertaining distant male relatives of Papa's with his conversation. I saw Uncle Billy. This was the first time I had seen him sober. His eyes were sulked and black from crying, and he stared pitiful-eyed at the wet bar full of cordials. As I stared at him, I didn't see him ask Louis for a drink nor did he bother to bring it up in a conversation, he only walked away and disappeared into the den.

My cousins from California, Mary and Claire, entered the room, both of them decked in black. I knew as soon as we embraced, I would burst out crying again. Their mother Vera, who was Papa's second cousin, embraced me. Afterwards, she cupped my face in her hands. "Be strong," She said. Cousin Vera didn't have to tell me.

"Where's your Mama?" she asked.

"She's in her room."

"Where's Ophelia, Katherine, and the baby?"

Despite the circumstances with the funeral, I thought about being foolish and looking inside my pockets for them, but I noticed I didn't have any.

"They should be with Mama," I said.

She tapped me slightly and walked into that direction. I noticed Joan and some of my sorors had arrived. All three had on their dark green cashmere dresses. Joan was holding a vase with a half dozen pink roses in it. I knew I couldn't be strong; I was going to break down all over again.

At the funeral, I sat with my mind wandering. I saw the minister's lips moving but I didn't hear anything. He couldn't tell me a thing about Papa that I didn't already know. I knew Papa was a good man and a devoted husband who bragged to the world about his girls. I knew Papa had served his country with honor in World War II. I knew about Papa being a devoted church member of St. Mary's Catholic Church up until the day he moved to Atlanta. The minister didn't have to tell me a thing.

I looked at Mama sitting on the corner holding two month old Jacqueline who was sound asleep. I couldn't see Mama's eyes because she wore a black veil over her face. I know when we left home she was wailing about how hard it was for her to make it here to the cemetery. She was saying she never stopped loving Vince LaCroix, and kept fainting everywhere. Louis had to pick her up and carry her to the car. I could hear the people around me humming Papa's favorite song, *Amazing Grace* . I remember when I was younger Papa use to take us to a little diner on the corner of Bourbon to hear his favorite band play. They played *Amazing Grace* , but it had a secular feel to it and people were grooving to it like a blues tune. I'll never forget how the people were dancing and how Papa got everyone's attention with his crazy dance moves. I found myself smiling. I glanced at Papa's casket and pictured him dancing around heaven, making the people up there laugh the way he made me and Katherine laugh and all those people laugh.

At the end of the service, I couldn't stop crying. My mind was saying this is it, this is the last time. My sisters couldn't calm me down; my sorors couldn't calm me down. I flinched every time someone touched to comfort me.

Then out of nowhere I felt a great abundance of warmth. I turned and to my surprise I saw David, and beside him were Tiny and Mike. Tiny had tears in her eyes as we embraced. I felt some consolation. Then Mike embraced me. Then David embraced me. I nearly collapsed in his arms, he felt so warm and tender. I felt his big hands rubbing against my back and for a second I was lost in David's arms. When David and I released ourselves from each other I saw something in David's eyes that I had seen in no other man's eyes. I saw a look of pure assurance, a look that said to me, "Dorothy you don't have to worry anymore; I'm here for you." David took the back of his hand and gently rubbed a tear that was streaming down my cheek. He didn't have to say anything to make it all better for me, David Leonard's touch was enough.

* * *

Dear David,

Thanks for everything. I wasn't expecting you to come down with Tiny. It was an overwhelming surprise and I can't stop thinking about it. I thought Jerome would be the one to come down since he is supposedly my so-called steady. I can't believe he would make up an excuse claiming he was ill. That's the oldest excuse in the book. Sometimes I question Jerome's conscious. I guess medical school can teach you everything you need to know about a woman's body except for her mind. Jerome needs a lesson on sensitivity and compassion, which are virtues that he lacks. I swear the more I think about Jerome, the more I feel sick. I thought he would at least show up and pay his respects. For Christ's sake, he knew more about my Papa than you. Anyway, I don't want to discuss him any further. David I really don't have much to say, I'm sitting in my English class, I'm suppose to be reading, but my mind is on you constantly, I wish we could've spent the weekend together around better circumstances, but we will sooner or later. But as for right now, I would like to thank you again, and I wished you could've known my Papa. He would have loved you David.

Yours truly,
Dorothy

CHAPTER 4

The fall session was over and everyone was gone home for the holidays. I was going to spend my holiday in Atlanta with Katherine and Tiny, and help Katherine remodel and restore Papa's house. All the universities except for the Medical School were closed. David told me they wouldn't go home until the 20th and I thought that was pretty rough. It only gave them five days before Christmas, and those who lived in Detroit and Chicago were the unfortunate ones, if they were traveling by bus. Could you imagine, spending Christmas on a bus? Tiny and I were sitting on the living room floor polishing our toes and talking about it. We polished our toes with intense concentration, and while I polished my mind was going crazy.

"I wonder what Jerome is up to?" I asked. Tiny looked at me and frowned.

"Why are you concerned with Jerome, it's David, read my lips David Leonard."

"But David is Jerome's best friend. I can't see myself going with him. And another thing, I don't think he's over Bettye."

"As much as he talks about you Dorothy, you would question whether he and Bettye ever had anything going in the first place."

I hesitated, "I don't know Tiny, it seems so funny to me."

"Let me tell you something Dot, David cares a lot more about you than Jerome ever will." When Tiny said that she stopped polishing her nails and looked me straight in the eye. "David told me that himself."

I felt myself blushing all of a sudden.

"David told me he has never felt so close to any woman before. On the way back from New Orleans, you were all he talked about Dorothy."

I smiled, "Really!" I said in my high falsetto voice.

"Dorothy, the man talked about you so much that he put me and Mike to sleep."

"I still don't know. He and Jerome are best friends they think alike."

"No they don't," Tiny responded quickly. "David knows how to treat a woman and you don't have to worry about him messing around on you at all. I know he's a man, and some of them have a tendency to think alike when it comes down to treating a woman, but he's different. David is a twenty-three year old man, a very wise one who knows exactly what he wants." Tiny was so sure of herself, I guessed David had told her all this.

"How do you know Tiny?"

Tiny wiggled her toes. "I do my homework."

I didn't respond.

"I think you should call him up tonight Dorothy."

"Tiny I'm scared."

"Scared of what? Who are you scared of? Jerome?"

"No."

"Then why are you scared Dorothy?"

My mind flashed back to the dates I had with Jerome. All four of them were disasters, and I didn't want to go through another disaster date again.

"I'm scared that David might end up treating me like Jerome." A look of disgust was on Tiny's face.

"What?" was all she said. It was like she couldn't believe I thought that way about David. So she laughed. "Oh girl, you been dealing with the wrong one for too long. Not every man is like Jerome West." She wiggled her toes again. "I should kick Jerome's behind for brainwashing you into thinking like that."

"It's not just Jerome Tiny. It's every guy I've been involved with since my sophomore year in high school."

Tiny pointed her index finger at me. "Key word, 'high school. ' Dorothy, you can't expect much from them, and you can't expect much from a man with a high school boy mentality either. You need a man like David Leonard, I'm telling you."

Later that night me and Tiny along with David and Mike rode around town gawking at Christmas lights and listening to Nat King Cole Christmas songs. David looked so handsome in his black, Botany 500 jacket and tie. He dressed like the preppie white boys I saw in the JC Penny's catalogues, and his cologne intertwined with after shave smelled like he had been in the shower for hours. I was nervous too that night. I hadn't seen David since Papa's funeral and I was anxious for a conversation, anything to break the silence and small talk. So I made a comment about his dress attire.

"David, every time I see you, you're dressed so nice. I bet your wardrobe is expensive."

He smiled. I noticed he had a small dimple on the corner of his mouth. "Only the best," he said as he kept his eyes on the road. I looked outside my window at the rows of homes and Christmas lights. Each home had a different theme of its own.

"Dorothy, you look beautiful tonight," he said. "Of course, you're beautiful all the time."

"Wheeww!" I heard Tiny squeal from the back seat. She and Mike started laughing.

"I hear you; say it with feeling," Mike said before he tapped David on the shoulder. David smiled, only a little. I noticed he had a habit of licking his lips to keep from laughing.

"I meant every word of it," He said staring at me. I saw David's eyes sparkling from the incoming traffic lights. My heart started pounding and for some reason I began to perspire underneath my arms.

"David, there's a nice coffee shop on Peachtree that's open until two; we can go there," Tiny said.

When we entered the place, it was jumping and packed from wall to wall with people. Chubby Checker's voice was telling everyone to do 'The Twist' and they didn't hesitate. I saw a lot of arms swinging, skirts twisting, and feet shuffling. I heard a lot of people laughing and singing with the music. Girls were squealing and guys were basking in the glory of their skirts. David took my hand and we managed to find a spot at the counter where David ordered two chocolate shakes.

"This place is jumping tonight," David said. "Can you dance?" He asked.

"Yes I can dance," I said boldly. He glanced at me as to say, *I'm scared of you Dorothy LaCroix.*

"Can you dance?" I asked.

"Yes I can dance."

"I'm gonna give you the opportunity to prove it," I said.

Staring at me with those handsome brown eyes of his he nodded. "Dorothy I will turn this place out," he said just before he retrieved the shakes from the clerk. On the floor Mike and Tiny were all into the music; they moved all the way down to the floor doing the twist. Tiny looked so cute in her blue cashmere sweater, twisting all over Mike. She had this expression on her face that said, *You can't mess with me when I do the twist. Honey I made this gig.* I looked around the room and noticed a lot of girls wearing cashmere sweaters and the guys decked in slacks and shirts with ties. Everyone was so lively. Stumbling through the crowd, Jerome was looking around and about. His eyes were sulked and his mouth was hanging a mile. I saw two girls pass by him and he watched the back of their wiggling hips.

"David, guess who walked in," I said over the music.

"Who?"

"Jerome."

He looked around the room until he spotted Jerome standing in the center of the floor laughing out loud and hugging on Mike. I noticed Mike grimacing.

"I'll be back," He said.

Just as David got up, another guy sat in his place.

"Hello," he said. I noticed it was Duke, the guy from the family reunion. Who could forget a man with a face and a bald head like his. "I noticed you when you walked in baby." He said. "I told myself, I got to talk to this lady. I wouldn't have it no other way."

"Hi Duke," I said and continued to slurp on my shake. He frowned and begin to scratch his bald head. "How do you know me?" he asked.

"You and some friends of yours came to the reunion last summer."

He sat there thinking. "Reunion." He kept saying it over and over. Finally a light came on. "Yeah I remember you. You were with Tiny Jefferson."

"Yeah."

He moved his stool closer to mine. "Anyway, think about what I'm saying."

I thought I could move my stool, but it was too heavy for me to handle, so I leaned away from him.

"What's wrong? I'm not going to bite you," he said. "Where your man at?"

"He's here and if I were you, I would move before he gets back."

Duke moved even closer to me. "Your man being here don't put fear in my heart girl. I love living on the edge, especially when it comes to getting something I want."

"Yeah, people in hell want cold water," I said before I got up and made my way into the crowd. I heard him shouting something behind me, but I paid no attention to what he was saying.

"Dorothy!" I heard an old familiar voice calling out my name. It was so crowded, that I didn't notice I had walked passed Jerome and David.

"Jerome!" I shouted back.

Jerome grabbed me and held me in his arms. I felt his lips touch the side of my neck and when I tried to pull away, he pulled me back to kiss his lips. I got a whiff of his breath and I turned my head because it reeked with alcohol. "C'mon now Dorothy, give me one right'chere." He puckered his lips. I glanced quickly at David who was giving Jerome the evil eye.

"Dorothy, I haven't seen you in so long, girl. Let's go somewhere and talk for old times sake." He put his arm around me and stumbled against me. "You look so pretty tonight! Doesn't she, David!" David just stared at him. Judging his expression, he was extremely upset.

"Jerome man, you are in rare form tonight."

Jerome released me from his hold and just stood there. "Nahn I ain't, Nahn I ain't!" he shouted. "Look man, I can dance, let me show you." He pushed other dancers aside and made room for himself. In a minute Jerome was going to make a complete fool of himself. I felt embarrassed for him. Jerome started shuffling his feet and fell right in the middle of the floor. I felt my face reddened. David grabbed him by the arm, Mike came over, and they escorted him outside. Jerome was still trying to dance. I followed them outside. Now he was cursing and trying to release himself from them. "Let go of my arm; it ain't a damn thing wrong with me." Tiny followed behind me. "Brrr, it's cold out here!" she shouted.

"Dorothy would you open the door for us?" David asked.

"Stop it aiight, I aiin't drunk!" Jerome shouted in David's ear. I could see the precipitation coming from his lips. David and Mike threw him in the car. Jerome just laid there with his head buried in the seat. David slammed the door. "We're taking him home," He said to me and Tiny.

"We'll be back." He and Mike got into the car and started up the engine. Tiny signaled for Mike to roll down the window. He did.

"You alcoholic. What are you trying to do, ruin the night for all of us?" Tiny shouted at Jerome. She and I stood and watched as David drove off into the cold windy night.

"You see," Tiny began. "You see, that's the kind of stuff I'm talking about. Jerome is so low down; he is always trying to scheme and mess up things for everyone else."

The wind picked up a notch. "Come on let's go back inside," she said. My teeth were chattering, and I couldn't wait to do so. I kept thinking of what Tiny said about Jerome's scheming. It did seem awfully strange that Jerome would get drunk tonight. Jerome wasn't a drinker, and admitted on occasions that he wasn't. But I found out, theoretically, Jerome would say and do anything.

Tiny and I walked around the diner until we found a seat. "Tiny, you will never guess who I saw tonight," I began.

"Who did you see tonight?" she asked.

"Duke, our friend from the reunion."

She made a face. "Oh, you ain't seen nobody special."

"Tiny, he tried to talk to me."

Tiny rested her chin in her hand and said nonchalantly, "Girl he'll try to talk to the Virgin Mary if she was here."

I rested my chin in my hand and watched as two couples slow danced in front of us, they were kissing like it was going out of style. I tapped Tiny on the arm. "Look."

Tiny shook her head, "That's a shame. They might as well go home and get in the bed."

I laughed, knowing far too well Tiny was telling the truth.

"So Dorothy," Tiny began, "What do you think about David?"

"He's such a gentleman, Tiny."

"See, I told you he's a gentleman. Watch in two years, mark my words, you and David will be walking down the aisle."

I felt myself blush as I pictured that moment.

"Two Tiny, don't you think that's too soon?"

"I don't know, I'm getting some good vibes."

"We'll see," I said. "I'm going to the powder room. Hold my seat until I get back."

"Don't stay too long, they're playing my song and I want to dance."

I moved in slow motion through the crowd of dancers until I was inside. There were a couple of girls standing in front of the mirror, primping and applying lip rouge. I waited until there was a free mirror and seized the opportunity to check my lip rouge before David returned. Just as I was about to look into my purse, a finger tapped me on the shoulder. I turned around to see Bettye, David's ex-girlfriend.

"I thought that was you," she said.

"Hi Bettye," I said, and for the strangest reason I felt nervous.

"I saw you and David earlier."

I didn't know what to say. So I reached into my purse and pulled out my stick of lip rouge. I didn't know exactly what state of mind Bettye was in, but I was prepared to fight if push came to shove.

"You two look like a happy pair."

I was still speechless.

"Well aren't you going to say anything?" she asked.

"Bettye, if you think I had anything to do with you and David breaking up, I swear to you I didn't."

"Not directly, but ever since that day at the diner, things between us were not the same."

"I'm sorry Bettye."

I saw a tear glistening in the corner of her left eye. "Just a word of advice to you Dorothy."

"Yes?"

"Beware. Things aren't always what they appear, and that's all I have to say to you."

The tear began to fall down her cheek. By that time I wanted to cry. It was obvious, Bettye was still hurting from their break-up and for a moment I was having second thoughts about David.

"I wish you the best of luck. Make him change; God knows I couldn't."

She grabbed a tissue nearby and removed her glasses from her face. I watched silently as she wiped the tears from her eyes and walked solemnly out the door. I wanted to grab her and say, *Stop, please come back and tell me more*, but I couldn't. I was numb and trembling and it felt as if I was in the twilight zone and everything, including myself, was moving in slow motion. I gathered my things and walked back out into the crowd. My eyes searched high and low for Bettye, but I didn't see her. I found Tiny sitting at our same spot, dancing and having herself a good time.

"Hey Dot, remember this song?" she asked, while popping her fingers and moving up and down like she was on a see-saw.

"Yes girl," I said, pretending to sound upbeat and in high spirits.

Twenty minutes later, I saw David and Mike coming inside. David was looking around the room for us.

"Tiny, I just spotted David and Mike by the door. I'll be right back."

I got up and walked to their direction. It was hot and damp as I walked deeper into the crowd.

David spotted me and we hugged like we had never seen each other before.

"How is Jerome?" I asked.

"No different than he was before. We left him with another frat brother of ours."

I took David's hand and lead him to our table. He and Mike pulled up a couple of chairs.

"I hope y'all took Jerome's stupid behind back to the dorm," Tiny said.

Mike just stared at her. I glanced at David who was eyeballing the couple on the dance floor. His mind looked as if it were engulfed in a million thoughts. I wondered if he had run into Bettye. I just couldn't get her words out of my mind, and what really shocked me was how she managed to stay calm. Most girls would've fought tooth and nail over their man, but she didn't. Maybe she was just trying to scare me. I don't know.

"Come on Dorothy, let's dance," I heard David say to me. I took his hand and followed him to the edge of the dance floor where it wasn't so crowded.

"I like this song." David said. It was Ray Charles' *Georgia on My Mind* I waited until David lead the first step before I followed. He was a great dancer, and I just loved the way he held me. Now and then I would look up to see his eyes. He would smile and continue leading me along with him. I definitely didn't want this dance to end.

That night after we left the coffee shop, we rode back to Tiny's, the four of us, sitting in David's car, listening to Nat King Cole, and joking about everything. "Mike is it true?" Tiny asked out of the blue. Everyone stared at her like she was crazy.

"True about what?" Mike asked with a puzzled look in his honey-colored eyes.

"Do you remember Eunice Taylor?" Tiny asked, while at the same time staring Mike straight in the eye.

Mike shook his head. "No."

"Stop telling a tale."

Mike started chuckling, "Honest Tiny I don't."

"Anyway, is it true that you and her got caught in your dorm room on campus and she was on her knees?" Tiny was anticipating a quick answer.

I covered my mouth in shock. David started to laugh, and Mike hesitated. "No, heck no, that was Mike Thomas not me." Though it was dark I could still see Mike's light brown complexion reddening. David was so tickled, he slumped over the stirring wheel, his shoulders shaking. It tickled me to see him laughing, because I was so accustomed to seeing him act serious. He laughed so hard he nearly choked.

"What's so funny David?" Tiny eyed him suspiciously. "You know something I don't?" He was still laughing. Mike started to snicker himself. Tiny slapped him on the arm. "Stop laughing Mike, you working my nerve." Mike stopped and fought his laughter with a phony smile.

"I still say you're telling me a tale."

"Okay, Ms. Tiny Jefferson, answer this. Did you key my car and put my tires on flat?" Tiny sat there silent for a second. "What?" Her eyes studied Mike intensely.

"Don't what me."

"I-I-I."

"I-I-I my foot, you did it and I know you did it."

"Prove it."

"I don't have to prove anything; I know you."

"No you don't. I let you know what I want you to know."

Mike waved his hand. "I don't want to hear it, besides I'm tired of you anyway."

"I'm tired of you too, now." Tiny said before licking out her tongue like a young, immature school girl. She glanced at me. "So Dorothy, have you and David had sex yet?"

I began to blush. Sometimes Tiny can be far outlandish for her own good. "For heaven's sake," I responded quickly.

"Come on girl stop pretending and tell the truth."

"Hey Tiny, don't you think you're getting a bit carried away?" David asked.

"Well?" Tiny asked.

"Tiny you know I would never do anything like that."

"Not yet anyway right?" she said smiling with her chin resting on top of the seat.

"Tiny Jefferson, you are a pervert," I said.

"There's nothing wrong with it; you and David ought to try it sometimes."

Then she bounced up and down like a kid. "I bet you two haven't even kissed yet."

I glanced at David who glanced over his shoulder at Tiny. "That's none of your business."

"I dare you to," Tiny challenged us.

"No," I said quickly.

"That's because y'all scared," Tiny concluded.

I heard Mike tap her on the arm. "Stop instigating."

Tiny began to bounce up and down like a kid again. "Lay it on him Dorothy."

I rolled my eyes and glanced at David. David smiled and licked his lips. "You sure you want me to do this?" he asked.

Tiny was still bouncing in the seat. "Kiss him, girl."

David turned towards me, his right arm hung lazily on top of the car seat while the left arm rested on the stirring wheel. I was anticipating a long French kiss, but David just gave me a peck on the jaw.

"Is that it?" Mike and Tiny said in unison.

"You thought I was going to French kiss her or something?"

"Yes," they responded in unison.

Tiny started bouncing again. "Do the kiss over again, and do it right," she said.

"We did it right," I told her, and glanced at David who winked his eye.

"Ummm hmmm. Well, it's getting late; my cousin and I need our beauty rest." Tiny opened the door so she and Mike could get out. "Dorothy are you coming?"

"I will, just give me ten minutes."

Tiny rolled her eyes until the whites showed. "Good night David, and don't do anything with my cousin."

"Don't worry about us, you just keep an eye on Mike."

I turned to David, I was still mesmerized by his small kiss, it was soft and tender just like he was.

"Good night David, I had a good time with you."

"Well, you know anytime you want to go out, just give me a call."

"Sure David."

He took my hand and held it. "You know," he began. "I have so much to tell you."

I blushed; his voice was mellifluous and sensuous. He pulled me closer to him. "Dorothy I really like having you around, you're beautiful, you're smart, you're all the things a man looks for in a woman. I remembered the first time I saw you at the reunion."

I laughed, it was the second time tonight, that the reunion was mentioned.

"You looked so beautiful, and I thought, how could I get the chance to be with a woman like that. You seemed so untouchable."

My mind rewound to my meeting with Bettye. "Is that what you thought?"

"Yes." His expression was so intense it burned right through me.

"You can have me, if you so desire." I heard myself say.

He moved me even closer and touched the tip of my chin with his finger; lifting my head, he stared into my eyes. "You don't know how it makes me feel to hear you say that."

I buried my head in his chest and lost myself in his warm embrace.

"Dorothy," he whispered against my forehead, "I need a woman like you in my life."

I lifted my head so I could see his eyes again; they were closed. I never felt so secure and so needed in my young life.

"Dorothy, if I told you I loved you, would you think I was rushing our friendship?"

"I can't stop you David if that's how you really feel."

"How do you feel, Dorothy?"

I fought back those feelings of doubt I had earlier and took a deep breath. "To tell you the truth, I feel for the first time in my life I found a guy who truly cares about me."

"I do. I want you to be my girl. Would you be my girl?"

I nodded. On the radio was Nat King Cole singing, *Unforgettable, Oooh yes, that was my song*, I said over and over inside my head as David and I embraced. At last, I was in love.

Chapter 5

After a blissful year and a half courtship with David Leonard, I finally had my ultimate pleasure fulfilled. I took a pilgrimage to the Kingdom of David, and when I returned I was satisfied to the fullest. It was a once in a lifetime experience. At twenty years old I was no longer a virgin. I was "ripened," and frankly I couldn't have asked for a better birthday present. The day started with David's graduation from medical school. I was prim and proud that day, sitting beside his parents. My first impression of the Leonards? They were kind and caring, somewhat too caring that at times it seemed phony. I often heard horror stories of in-laws from hell, but it wasn't that way with the Leonards. When I first met David's parents a year ago, they welcomed me with open arms. Mrs. Leonard fell in love with me the moment before David introduced us. She hugged and told me, "Welcome to the family." Mrs. Leonard was beautiful. She had a soft café au lé complexion like Dorothy Dandridge, and she moved with grace and spunk like Eartha Kitt. She had a niche for lavishing her body in expensive clothing, because she wore the sharpest double-breasted suit I had ever seen on anyone. It was off white with a long fish tail gathered around the ankles. Now I knew where David got his character and exquisite taste in clothing from. David's father was a stocky, medium height, brawny man with a loud voice and a loud laugh. Doc Sr. in my opinion, had the characteristics of a prestigious doctor; he had a clean, bald head, moustache-free look, which made him look a lot younger. He was very affectionate towards me, which made me feel uncomfortable at first, but then I realized that was part of his personality. I also noticed he was affectionate with a lot of women. Anyway, David's parents were jumping the gun and claiming me into the family. They already had us married and living in a posh neighborhood in Southwest Houston. I didn't like Houston because it was too big and it took you forever to get where you want to go, but since I was David Leonard's woman, his home was my home.

When David graduated, I felt on top of the world. That was my man, I said to myself when he glanced at me and his parents. Mrs. Leonard was dabbing her eyes and whispering, "That's my baby, my handsome doctor." She said it with dignity and pride; she shared my spot on top of the world too. I glanced at David's father. He had that nod of approval. Underneath his glasses his eyes were pressed shut; it was as though he was praying, *thank you Jesus, the tradition lives on*. A tradition, I discovered, which dates to the turn of the century with David's grandfather, Dr. Alfred C. Leonard. Alfred was the son of a free Negro domestic and her wealthy white employer, who went on to become the president and founder of the Texas Board of Negro Physicians. His two sons, Alfred C. Leonard, II and David Claude Leonard, followed in his footsteps and went on to become doctors as well. David Sr. then passed the tradition on to his oldest son, David C. Leonard II, now a recent graduate of Morehouse Medical School.

After the ceremonies there was a gala in the Alumni Center for the graduates and their families. David was so happy, he was bouncing off the walls and posing for pictures. We must've taken about three rolls of film. I think one roll was on just David alone. There were pictures taken of his parents, me and Mrs. Leonard, me and Doc Sr., me and the buffet table. After three hours of smiling I was plum exhausted, but it wasn't over. Tiny was giving Mike a party at his home around 10:00 that evening.

"Tell Mike we can't make it to the party," I kept telling David.

"Try telling that to Tiny; I bet you wouldn't hear the end of it."

I yawned and fell face first on top of the bed. David and I were staying at one of the finest colored-owned hotels in Atlanta. David was in the shower, singing and "whewing" like he normally did when he was feeling good.

"Dorothy! You ought to come in here and join me!" he shouted over the gushing water.

"I will as soon as I take a nap!" I shouted back.

I laid there for about three minutes, until I felt something wet and slippery, slithering against my legs. I turned around. "David stop!" I screamed. He was dripping wet.

"Stop! Now, you're getting my dress all wet sugar."

"So, I can afford to buy a new one."

He got on top of me and began to unfasten the buttons on my dress one by one. His eyes studied each button carefully as though he were examining a patient in the hospital. Oh God, I thought this is going to be the best birthday present ever. I was actually getting the opportunity to play the childhood game of doctor with a real doctor. After David unbuttoned my dress, he took me in his arms and removed the rest of my clothing. I felt the tickling effect of the water dripping from his flesh onto mine. My backbone arched, and my spine tingled whenever he touched me. He then picked me up and carried me all the way to the shower. Once inside, we kissed and washed each other's bodies. The warm water felt so good beating against my skin that I didn't want to get out. After we showered and dried each other's bodies, we stood in the doorway of the bathroom kissing and occasionally glancing at the reflection of our naked bodies in a full length mirror. David whispered he didn't want to go to Mike's anyway, besides he was having so much fun with me. So we kissed all the way to the bed and collapsed on top of the covers, which felt so cold against my naked body.

He took my hands and kissed them. "Oooh these hands, these hands, these soft and delicate, beautiful, gentle hands."

"What about my hands?" I asked.

"I want these hands to hold me." He kissed each one of my fingers. "Now and years from now. I want them to warm me when I'm cold, and feed me when I'm hungry. I want these same beautiful soft hands to chastise my children when they fall out of line." I was speechless.

"What are you talking about?" I asked.

"I'm talking about a commitment."

When he mentioned commitment, I thought I was going to melt all over. My heart pounded against the walls of my chest.

"Dorothy, I can't see my future without you. Would you be my wife?"

I swallowed so hard, I nearly strangled on my own saliva. David was proposing to me.

"Dorothy, will you marry me?" he asked, and before I responded he slipped a shiny diamond ring around my slender finger. I was at a loss for words.

"Duh—Duh," Was all I could muster of David's name. He held me. "I am more than willing to give you all the love you need and deserve," he whispered against my lips. "I want to shower you with a love that is almost like a daddy's type of love. Dorothy I know how much you loved your father and I know he loved you." He held me tightly in his arms. I listened to what he said and it brought tears to my eyes. He was right. I wanted that daddy's type of love and I knew he was more than qualified to give it to me. In the year-in-a-half we'd been together, he had yet to disappoint me. How could I resist; I said yes. I closed my eyes and received his kisses as they overwhelmed my throbbing body. For the first time in my life I discovered the nature of an orgasm and the feeling of euphoria it brought to me.

David's parents, well his mother, suggested David and I go see a minister for counseling, before walking down the aisle. We went to First United Methodist Church and sat there in the parsonage for two hours listening to Reverend Long pray, lecture, and ask questions. One of which was. "How well do you know the person you're going to marry?" David thought about it quickly. "Well Reverend Long," he began in his authoritative tone of voice, "I know Dorothy well enough that when there's something bothering her I can sense it, and how I sense it, I see it in my woman's eyes." When David said my woman, you could've knocked me over with a feather, I had never had a man, other than my father, tell me how much I meant to him. David held my hand and poured his heart out to Reverend Long. Reverend Long sat there with his fingers crossed on top of his desk listening and nodding. "I know Dorothy will provide for me," David said, "because she has already. I know Dorothy LaCroix is someone who I can talk to, and I don't have to question whether or not she will be there. I know for a fact Dorothy will be there." In that brief instance I wanted to reach out and grab David's body and shower him with kisses, but I managed to restrain myself and give myself away with a blush.

Reverend Long was smiling and he mentioned to David about having trust in me. "Son, when you have trust in the person you marry, that means everything. Let me tell you something; trust, faith, prayer, and obedience makes a world of a difference in a marriage." He held up a picture of his wife.

"Sister Long and I have been married for thirty-three years, and I've been a pastor twenty-six years. Sister Long and I started on the rough side of the mountain, our early stages of marriage were troublesome, and we were going to call it quits after four years. It wasn't until I found Christ, that our marriage did a complete 360. Sister and I began to pray more often, and we turned all of our troubles into God's hand, and our marriage has been blessed tremendously." David and I glanced at each other.

"Reverend Long, you forgot to ask Dorothy that question." David grinned and gently tapped my thigh. I looked at David, and forgetting the Reverend was there, I playfully rolled my eyes at him. Reverend

Long waited for me to respond. I told him almost the same things David told him, except I got so emotional at the thought of having David in my life, that I burst into tears. Reverend Long ended the counsel session with a prayer. Then he took my hand and placed it in David's hand. This gesture reminded me of standing at the altar.

"It's all about God's love, and your love and commitment to one another. I can look at you two and see that as long as you both have faith and obedience to each other, you can endure all temptations and believe me, temptations will come and they will try to tear your marriage apart, but you can overcome those temptations through prayer and faith and by communication. Remember what we discussed today, and keep it close to your hearts."

During the ride, David and I sat in silence. I guessed his mind was still on the counseling, but I know my mind altered from the counseling to the wedding arrangements. Mrs. Leonard and Mama argued constantly over what colors would be more appropriate for the wedding. Mrs. Leonard suggested red and white. They fought for hours until I ended the argument when I told them this is my wedding and I decide what colors I want. I suggested my sorority colors. My God, to see the ugly faces when I said that, even David had his screw face working. Mama made another suggestion; turquoise and pink. Mrs. Leonard turned up her nose, definitely not. I finally decided on turquoise and fuchsia. At that moment, I saw an array of sunshine in the room; everyone seemed to like the combination. Mrs. Leonard proudly took credit for it, but Mama wouldn't let it ride. She said, "Elizabeth Leonard, you wouldn't have thought of it if I hadn't suggested we used turquoise in the first place."

Mrs. Leonard smiled in a phony way. "Cleo LaCroix, I have decided that the seven bridesmaids should have their dresses altered. I think they're a little too provocative above the knee. I want them to be longer, say six inches from the floor."

Mama rolled her eyes. “Sugar no! No! No! The girls won’t be able to walk anywhere without tripping. I suggest they alter the dresses to where the hem is nine inches above the floor.”

Mrs. Leonard thought about what Mama said. Whenever Mama came up with a definite solution, Mrs. Leonard would jump into something else.

David and I arrived in the driveway of his parent’s home. This was a temporary spot for the both of us. I was visiting for the holidays and David was there, at least until he completed his residency. I hardly saw him during the day and when I finally saw him he was too tired and aggravated. At first I tried to reason with his frustrations; I’m pretty sure that being a resident at one of the poorest and busiest hospitals in Houston was already taking it’s emotional toll on David. His mother wasn’t making the situation any easier on me. Mrs. Leonard was so paranoid about the wedding, she was driving me crazy. She suggested I set up committees: an invitation committee, a dress committee, an entertainment committee, a food committee, a decorating committee, an usher committee, a security committee and a transportation committee. She even suggested a beauty committee, which was a trio of her best friends: one was a hair stylist, one a manicurist and the third one was a make up artist. Mrs. Leonard drove me to the point where I was near tears, I was burning with frustration and pressure. Every other day I would get on the phone and call Aunt Ruby Jewel.

“What did the woman do now.” I called her so much, she already knew the subject matter.

“Everything, Aunt Ruby Jewel. I just wish I could click my heels three times and vanish to some place, any place other than Houston, Texas.”

She laughed; it was a soft throaty laugh. “Do you still think you’re ready to be a part of the family?”

“Aunt Ruby Jewel everything was so nice at first. I didn’t have any hassles at all with Mrs. Leonard, she was a sweet person.”

"Don't pay any attention to that woman, she's just under a lot of pressure about the wedding."

"But I'm the one getting married here."

"Well darling, don't get yourself upset about it. If she wants to handle it, let her handle it all by her lonesome."

"It looks as though she might have to because no one else will work with her; she's too bossy."

"Well darling, I guess that's the cost you have to pay when you organize a huge wedding. How many people do you have on the list?"

"About 400 people," I guessed.

"Dorothy do you even know 400 people?" she asked.

"Most of the people are family and associates of David."

"What's the main course?"

"David and I wanted roasted duck with steamed vegetables."

"Let me tell you what you should have."

Oh no, everyone was telling me how to run my wedding.

"Dorothy, you should have barbecue, baked beans, potato salad…"

"No Aunt Ruby Jewel, we always have that at family gatherings."

"It's good and it's reasonable."

"No, work with me Aunt Ruby Jewel."

Aunt Ruby Jewel laughed. "Who's making the cake?"

"David's mother is having the dessert designed by Rosseau's. David and I decided to have pineapple-cream cake, it's our favorite."

"That Ole' Mama of his," she said. "She must not be from the South where people cook and bake their own food."

"David's Mama is having everything catered."

"Well I'll say. Well baby, when is this wedding? I didn't hear you mention a date?"

"David wants the wedding to take place on New Year's Eve, so he and I can celebrate the new year as husband and wife."

"How thoughtful. You know everybody's been telling me about him, saying how nice he is, how handsome he is everybody's gotten the opportunity to meet him except me." Aunt Ruby Jewel pretended to sound upset.

"You will Aunt Ruby Jewel."

"And I hear he's a doctor too."

"Yes he is."

"You're a beautiful girl I always knew you would find a wealthy man to take care of you."

"Thank you Aunt Ruby Jewel."

"You know I'm upset with you young lady."

"Oh no, not you too," I whined. "Why are you upset with me Aunt Ruby Jewel?"

"You pass right by Beaumont and won't even come by to see me anymore."

I could hear Uncle Herbie's voice in the background saying something.

"What is Uncle Herbie talking about?"

"He's upset with you too, you and Katherine both."

"Tell him I will drop by on my way home, and I'll bring David with me."

"Baby, she said she will come and bring her fiancé so we can meet him!" He told her something else. "Baby, do you want to talk to her yourself, I'm tired of passing messages back and forth over the phone."

I sat there laughing and listening at those two yell back and forth to each other.

"Darling, he said he can't wait to prance down that aisle with you."

I laughed. "Tell Uncle Herbie I love him and I can't wait to see him prancing down the aisle with me too; I know he'll have everyone in the church laughing."

Aunt Ruby Jewel chuckled. "Honey, you know your uncle."

After I hung up the phone, I thought about the wedding again and fell back against the sofa.

*　　　*　　　*

That night David and I were in the family room talking. He was staring straight ahead at the ceiling. I noticed dark circles around his eyes.

"Dorothy, I don't know about you, but it would be a lot easier if we go to the courthouse and get married."

I laughed. "David, we wouldn't hear the end of it if we did that. You know your mother wouldn't like it if her oldest son got married in a courthouse."

He sighed and rubbed his forehead.

"She's not the one getting married."

"But still, you know your mother." I sat there thinking. "Come to think of it, my mother wouldn't have it said I went to the courthouse and got married either. My sister Katherine had a nice small wedding. So…"

"I just wished it was over; I have too many irons in the fire right now."

"It'll be here before you know it. Years from now we'll look back at it and say it wasn't that bad after all."

"Yeah," he said through a yawn. "We can look back at it, laugh, and say it would've been just as nice if we'd went to the courthouse."

"Shut up, Dr. Leonard." I said as I nibbled on his ear. He closed his eyes and started to smile. "Stop that woman before you start something." I felt his hand creep inside my blouse. "You know, Mama didn't actually come out and say it, but she hinted that you and I need to be in separate places until after the wedding."

I stopped kissing David. "Say what?"

He sighed. "Mama said it was disrespectful towards her and Daddy. She said people in the neighborhood were talking about it and some have confronted her about it." I think my blood pressure rose.

"I'm sorry, maybe I shouldn't have came."

"I told Mama to tell those people to mind their own business. They don't pay the bills over here, and I wouldn't care if they don't speak to me."

I just sat quietly with a blank stare on my face.

"See, that's what I don't understand about Mama. She loves to blow everything out of proportion. She's not being realistic. This is 1965 not the 1930's. Mama needs to loosen up. Now I can see Daddy saying something about it, but he has no problem with it."

"If it's going to be a problem, I can always leave David."

David took my hand into his. "No I can't let you do that."

"I can't stay here."

"We'll work something out don't worry about it, okay?"

I stared into David's sleepy eyes and smiled, "okay."

That morning during breakfast Mrs. Leonard was quiet. She looked like she wanted to say something, but had second thoughts about saying it and kept quiet. I heard David beside me crunch down on a piece of toast. Doc Sr. was at the head of the table sipping coffee and browsing through a section in the newspaper. David's little brother Marcus was home from summer church camp and was buttering his toast and mixing it with grape jam. I sat with my eyes gazing down at my toast and eggs. I wasn't really hungry, but I picked up my knife and began to spread jam over my toast.

"So David, have you and Dorothy decided on your living arrangements?" Mrs. Leonard asked. She was eagerly anticipating an answer from David.

"No, Mama."

"Don't you think it's about time you do?"

David continued to chew his food and pretend he didn't hear.

"Did you hear me son?"

Doc Sr. intervened. "Let's not talk about his in front of the child."

Mrs. Leonard stared at her husband for a second and then at David, before she sipped on her coffee and proceeded to poke at her eggs with her fork. I knew this conversation wasn't over.

Later that day, everyone except Marcus sat in the family room. Doc Sr. sat in his usual blue leather oak chair, across from him was Mrs. Leonard sitting in her blue leather oak chair, on the sofa sat David and I.

"David, as I mentioned before, you and *Bettye* here are engaged to be married, but—"

David help up his hand. "Whoa, slow down Mama, I'm not marrying Bettye."

Mrs. Leonard paused for a second. She realized what she had said and was stunned. "Oh, I'm sorry. Forgive me for calling you by that girl's name."

Thank you. Mrs. Leonard didn't know she was pushing my buttons. If I didn't love David so much, this wedding would've been terminated well in advance.

"But as I was saying, I wish the two of you wouldn't stay together. You know it's awfully distasteful to, to…" Her face was screwed up. "I don't like to mention the slang for it because it's an ugly word."

Doc Sr. interrupted by clearing his throat. "I have no problem with you two staying together, however, I do have a problem with you staying here together."

David leaned forward and clasped his hands together. "All right, Dorothy and I will leave as soon as possible." He glanced at Mrs. Leonard. She sat there with her legs crossed, and batted her eye lashes wildly.

"I still think it's wrong. You shouldn't do it. Dave it's a sin to shh—."

"Shack Mama? Is that the word you're looking for?"

"Eww." She shifted her posture in the chair, squinted her eyes and gritted her teeth. "David I didn't hear that word coming from your mouth. No sir, I didn't!"

David sighed. "I'm sorry Mama."

"That's better. I don't ever want to hear that word mentioned around me again."

David sighed again. I thought I should have a few words to say.

"Excuse me Doctor and Mrs. Leonard but I'm going back to Louisiana first thing in the morning."

I felt David staring at me.

"I'm sorry if I caused any problems." I said.

Mrs. Leonard only batted her eye lashes and glanced at her husband. Doc Sr. crossed his legs. "I hope you and David aren't planning to have a family anytime soon." He said.

"Daddy would you at least let us get through the honeymoon before you give us a family okay?" David said, sounding a little bit annoyed.

"I just want you two to make the right decision that's all."

"Believe me daddy we will."

"Good son."

Doc Sr. stood up and walked out of the room.

Mrs. Leonard wasn't going to let this day pass without mentioning the wedding.

"Now Dorothy, your mother and I talked about the food for the wedding, now she wanted it to be prepared by your relatives, but I remember telling her I wanted it catered by Rosseau's. It'll be a lot easier to handle. All the caterer does is present a menu and all you do is check off the items you want and they'll do the rest. Now isn't that much easier than deciding on who will bring what, and have some people end up bringing the same dish..." As she went on talking about the wedding I rested my head in my hand. I really didn't want to hear about it.

* * *

I was at home in New Orleans lying in bed staring at the ceiling. My wedding was six days away and I was a nervous wreck. David and I talked on the phone everyday. He also made it a habit of sending me roses and gifts. Mrs. Leonard and I too talked on the phone. She managed to calm down after everyone told her how they felt about her bossy attitude. Mrs. Leonard had nerve enough to say that the wedding would otherwise lack taste had it not been for her innovative ideas. I was so lost in my thoughts, that I didn't hear Ophelia come in. She opened the curtains to my room.

"David's here," She said.

I leaped out of bed so fast I hit my big toe on one of the end posts. "Oh Shit!" I screamed and collapsed back into bed. Ophelia was standing by the window laughing.

"That's not funny girl." I glanced at my big toe, it was red and swollen. As I rubbed it, I couldn't help but smell the tantalizing aroma of bacon.

"Is that Mama cooking?"

"No, that's Louis' mother cooking."

"Oh yeah? When did she get here?"

"Around 7:30 this morning, she and Old Man Dix."

"He's here too?"

Ophelia nodded.

The smell only intensified when I opened the door to my room. In the living room Louis and David were sitting near the Christmas tree talking and sipping on coffee.

"Merry Christmas honey," I said in my baby voice.

David's smile was as handsome and bright as the Christmas scenery that surrounded him. When we embraced, I held him in my arms for a long time.

"Hmmm, I'm not familiar with this cologne," I said.

"It's a new one; it's called Lagerfeld."

I heard Mama's voice laughing in the kitchen.

"Merry Christmas baby. Did you just get out of bed?" He asked.

We kissed. "Yes."

He made a face and waved his hand. "Whew did you brush last night?"

I slapped him on the arm. "Now David you know my breath does not stink."

I took his hand and we sat down in front of the Christmas tree. "You know I wasn't going to forget you sweetie." I picked up five presents underneath the tree. David took them. "Oh honey, you shouldn't have, I didn't get anything for you." He pretended to be sad.

"Open them David."

"Right now?"

"Why not?"

"Okay baby I will." He began with the smallest present.

"Baby why don't you open the big present first?"

"Baby have you heard of saving the best for last?" He asked while neatly tearing away at the wrapping paper.

Mama entered the room with Old Man Dix on her arm. "Louis come over here and sit your father down, he's pretty heavy." Louis and Mama both helped him to his chair. He was around 100 years old. He couldn't see very well, but he could hear like a bat. I remember once before he came over, we were all sitting in the living room one night listening to the radio and Old Man Dix made us turn it off. He said he kept hearing animals. I thought maybe he heard a dog or a cat, but he said it was coming from down the hall. Now down the hall was Mama and Louis' bedroom so he couldn't have heard it coming from there, but he argued until he was raving mad and said if those dogs don't stop barking he was going to get his shot gun. So me and Katherine went down the hall and sure enough we heard noises coming from Mama and Louis' bedroom. Unknowingly we opened the door, and they were in bed doing God knows what, and sure enough Louis was barking like a dog.

When Mama and Louis helped Old Man Dix to his seat he sat there staring at Louis. "Good morning Sir!" He talked so loudly it sounded like he was shouting. David stood up and gave Mama a hug. "Merry Christmas, Ms. LaCroix."

"Merry Christmas to you too son. Did you bring Mama something pretty and fancy?"

"As a matter of fact I did," David responded.

It made Mama's day whenever David lavished her with gifts. She was almost as happy as I was.

"You know you'll always be my favorite son-in-law," Mama said before giving him a kiss on the cheek. "What did you get Mama?" She asked anxiously.

David licked his lips. "Oh Mama, you got me I'm the best Christmas present you'll ever have," he said with a smile.

"Don't start with me David." Mama rolled her eyes and picked up Jacqueline who was crying. Louis' mother stuck her head out of the kitchen door. "Breakfast is ready!" She said. She was a short fair-skinned woman with aqua blue eyes.

"Who is she?" David whispered to me.

"That's Louis' mother."

Louis turned to his father. "Pops are you hungry?"

Old Man Dix was chewing on his gums and staring at the ceiling.

"Miss Caroline, this is my son-in-law." Mama introduced David to Mrs. Dix. "He's a doctor in Houston."

"Oh how nice." Her eyes studied David. "You look like Almeda's son, the one that went across seas. Doesn't he to you Louis?"

Louis looked at David. "I knew there was someone he reminded me of, that's it Mama."

David's expression was filled with questions. All eyes were watching him, except for Old Man Dix's. Mama managed to hush Jacqueline. "Well, y'all let's go in the dining room and eat this nice breakfast Miss Caroline went out of her way preparing."

Mrs. Dix's eyes were still on David. "You know you look like Cousin Ned's son too."

David smiled at her, when she turned her back, he frowned at me.

At the table I had a hard time eating; I couldn't stop staring at Old Man Dix. He couldn't help himself, but seeing him spit his food and watching saliva and dough run down the front of his wrinkled chin made me want to gag. I kept nudging David's side, but he pretended the situation didn't exist. He was talking to Mama about his patients at the hospital. Ophelia sat across from me and I noticed she kept hitting my chair with her foot and using eye signals. She took one bite out of her buttermilk biscuit, glanced at Old Man Dix and turned her head the other way. Mama stopped talking to David and noticed Old Man Dix with food stuck to his chin. "Excuse me baby," she told David. "Louis will you go in my room and get me one of Jacqueline's old baby bibs?"

Louis frowned and chewed the rest of his food down, "A baby bib? For Jacqueline?"

"No, for your father over there."

Louis glanced at his father and saw the shape he was in. I excused myself from the table and went to the bathroom.

After breakfast I helped David unwrap the rest of his gifts. He fell in love with the gold cross pen. "Baby you shouldn't have," he kept saying after he opened it. He then opened the brown leather slippers, the blue and red signature robes, and socks.

"Well David, everybody's been in the giving spirit but you." Mama said. She was puffing on a cancer stick. "Where's your present to Dorothy?"

David laughed and pointed to himself. "I am Dorothy's present."

Mama threw one of the sofa pillows at him. "I'm serious, you're playing."

"Seriously, I haven't told anyone this, but I don't believe in the exchange of gifts."

"Honey, stop kidding," I said.

David stood up. "Well, I guess I better leave," he said dragging his feet to the floor. "Nobody wants me around during Christmas."

"I know you're not leaving here without eating." Louis said.

David opened the door. "No, I'll be back. Dorothy could I see you for a second." I followed him outside and we stood on the front porch. He stared out into the busy street. "Oh man." He hid his face. "Oh man, you see that car right there?"

"Yeah, you talking about the mustang convertible parked in front of your car?"

He nervously bit his lip. "That car has been following me since I left Houston."

I felt my heart pounding.

"Hold on you're not serious are you?" My knees began to wobble.

"Yes I am. I thought I lost her when I exited the freeway, but somehow she managed to find me?"

"She?" I asked, "It's a woman?"

His expression was motionless; it was scary.

"I'm going to call the police," I said.

David grabbed my arm before I reached for the door. He held my hand and I saw a smile flash across his face. David was up to something.

"Why are you stopping me?" I asked.

"We can handle this without the cops." David took my hand and we started walking towards the car.

"David what are you doing?" As we got closer, I could see my reflection clearly against the apple red paint. I also noticed a dealership tag stuck in the back window.

"You don't go near people's cars like this!" I shouted.

David ran his hands along the finish and opened the door. I thought I was going to faint as he got in and sat on the passenger's side.

"Dorothy it's real nice." He sniffed the aroma. "Ahhh the smell of new."

"David who's car is this?"

"Come on Dorothy."

I walked away and stood behind the gate. "Are you crazy? Get out of that car. For all you know *she* could have a bomb in it!"

David got out of the car and held a set of car keys. He dangled them from his hands. With a big smile on his face he said. "Merry Christmas Dorothy. If there is a bomb in this baby, that'll be the end of your Christmas present."

"What?" I realized what he said and I was speechless and grinning from ear to ear, I had to laugh real hard at that one, he got me good. I gave David a hug and a kiss. "I ought to get you good for scaring me." My heart was still pounding. He handed me the keys.

"She's all yours, brand new."

"David this is beautiful; I Love it!" I got inside and blew the horn. Moments later Ophelia stepped on the porch, followed by Mama and Louis. They all had wide smiles on their faces. I blew the horn again.

"Well what are you waiting on, let's go for a spin."

I started the ignition. "Oh David, I love this car honey and you say all this is mine?"

"Yes sweetheart."

"Oh baby." I planted him with so many kisses until his face was covered with red lip rouge. "I love you so much."

I couldn't believe I had my own car and a convertible at that, given to me by my man. He laughed. "I wished you could've seen your face Dorothy." He began to mimic my voice, "Don't go near people's cars, she got a bomb! She got a bomb! Aaaah!"

I playfully nudged him in the side.

"You prankster, always full of surprises. You had me believing that lame story."

I pushed the accelerator and the car roared. "Oops, I guess I need to put it in drive first."

"I *guess* you do," David replied. "Easy on it Dorothy." He held my hand. I put this shiny red machine in drive and took off cruising down the street.

"You know you can let the top down if you want to."

"David how much did this car cost you?"

"Don't worry about it *Mrs.* Leonard."

Believe me I wasn't. David turned on the radio switch. He flipped through almost every channel on the radio, and it sounded like each one was playing Christmas Carols. Then the opening music to the Temptations, *My Girl* came on.

"Oh, I love this song Dorothy
I got sunshine on a cloudy day…"

David looked at me and kissed my cheek. I tried to kiss him back and swerved a little to the side.

"Whoa," he said. "You keep your eyes on the road."

I was too excited.

When it's cold outside
I got the month of May
I guess you say
What can make me feel this way
My girl, my girl, my girl,
Talking 'bout my girl. My girl!

I was blushing so hard I was near tears. David was really into the song. He couldn't carry a tune, but he carried me in the palm of his hand. You know, I was loving every single minute of being his girl.

Chapter 6

"Dorothy you need something blue," I heard Joan telling me. I looked at the items in front of me. Already I had something old, something borrowed, and something new. Tiny stood behind me and stared at me in the mirror.

"Oh girl," she cried, "You got something blue all right." And she started crying. I tried to hold back my tears, but I couldn't. I heard everyone sniffing in the room.

"Stop it, all of y'all, stop it before you make me ruin my mascara." I started dabbing at my eyes with a tissue. Everyone in the room started to laugh. The hairstylist grabbed my hair and held it on top of my head, she then took it and twisted it into a ball. I had naturally curly hair, so it wasn't that difficult to deal with.

"Do you like that Dorothy?" she asked.

She had my hair pinned on top of my head with Curly Sues at the nap of my neck.

"Dorothy, don't wear your hair like that, it makes you look old," Tiny said.

"Ummm hmmm." I heard another voice agreeing with her.

The hairstylist took that style down and began to brush through my hair. There was a sharp knock on the door. Everyone ooed and ahhed when Mrs. Leonard entered the room. She was decked in a fuchsia double breast suit with the hat, shoes, and purse to match.

"How's the hair coming Miss Beverly?" she asked gazing at Miss Beverly's reflection in the mirror. Miss Beverly smiled and began to pin the top part of my hair with hair pins. "Dorothy has a lovely head of hair and a lot of it too."

Mrs. Leonard looked at me and smiled. "You look so beautiful honey, let me see your nails." I held up my right hand so she could see them. "You didn't want the French manicure?"

"No ma'am, I wanted to go with the pearl look; it matches my dress just perfect," I said.

"Oh Dorothy, I'm so glad you're marrying my baby."

I wanted to cry when she said that. For a few minutes I stopped thinking about all the bad things I had said behind her back. Mrs. Leonard was all right in my book.

I stared at my grandmother's old brooch, the borrowed costume beads, and the new pair of nylon gloves. "Dorothy, I see you have something old, which is your grandmother's brooch right?"

"Yes."

"Now which one of these are borrowed and new? Don't tell me." She pointed to the costume beads. "These are borrowed and the gloves are new, right?"

"You are absolutely correct," I said.

"Now you're missing something," She said.

"I need something blue," I said.

"That's right."

"Mrs. Leonard you should've seen our faces earlier," Tiny said. "We had something blue all right."

Mrs. Leonard smiled so wide, all of her teeth were showing. "How cute. Anyway, Dorothy I have a blue leather wallet you can use, you know blue is my favorite color."

"Great, then I'll have everything I need," I said staring at my hair, it was turning out to be beautiful.

Joan and Tiny were examining each other's dresses. The dresses were fuchsia, designed with a strapless bodice and v-shaped waistline. Underneath they wore petticoats to give the dresses that Victorian look, which was Mama's idea. Speaking of which, Mama entered the room adorned in her fuchsia and cream colored suit. She had my little sister Jacqueline, my flower girl, with her, and she was so adorable in her little gown.

"Oh Cleo, she's so precious," Mrs. Leonard said to Mama. Jacqueline was pretending to be bashful, which made her even more adorable. Katherine and Ophelia entered the dressing room smiling brightly at me.

"In fifteen more minutes," Katherine said. "My little sister will be taking that long walk and honey I do mean lonnng walk down the aisle. Girl that walk will be so long, you'd swear you were headed for the border."

We laughed and watched as she talked and made silly exaggerations with her face. "Girl be prepared for it; you may need to do away with those pumps for a while and put on some walking shoes."

I laughed. "Katherine, you're so crazy."

Miss Beverly was teasing my hair in the back with her brush.

"That's pretty Dorothy," Mama said.

"Thank you Mama."

I noticed she was fighting back her tears with a smile. "I bet Ole' Vince is upstairs right now smiling down at this very moment."

My heart fluttered as I thought about Papa. I can hear him saying. "Baby girl you've done mighty good for yourself, not a lot of people can find that special someone, but baby you have." I can also hear him say, "Dorothy, marry that man because you love him. Stand by him, honor him. He should be the first person you see when you wake up in the morning and the last person you see when you lie down at night. And another thing Dorothy, never marry just to say you're married, marry because you love who you married."

After Miss Beverly teased my hair she stood back and examined it. "You like?"

I nodded. "Yes." I turned to examine it from the sides. "It's just the way I want it, thank you…"

"Annh, Annh, Annh." She held up her finger. "Never tell a hairstylist thank you after she's finished with your hair."

"Well what do I say?" I asked.

"You just say more hair."

"More hair?" I asked looking at Miss Beverly rather strange.

"Yes." She smiled and picked up her supplies. "You look beautiful girl."

I smiled and touched the back of my hair. Katherine approached me. "Now Dorothy, let's see if you can wiggle your hips into this size five." She went into a closet and retrieved my wedding gown. Ophelia held my veil while Katherine and Tiny helped me into my dress. Once it was on and fastened, Ophelia placed the veil upon my face. Everyone stood around me wide-eyed as if I were a shrine and they came to worship me. I was adorned from head to toe with embroidered rosettes and pearls, even my ten foot long train was trimmed in pearls. To tell you the truth, I imagined myself as a goddess, like Aphrodite, the goddess of beauty and love or Athena, the goddess of art and wisdom.

"Oh Cleo," Mrs. Leonard cried, "My baby's marrying a princess. Oh, I just can't wait to see our beautiful grandchildren."

Everyone including me, gave her the once over. As Katherine placed the veil over my face, I heard Mama and Mrs. Leonard telling the girls to get in their places.

"Where's Whitney and the other one?" Mrs. Leonard asked Joan. Joan was examining Ophelia's dress. "I think Whitney and Alexis went to get fresh gardenias for their hair."

"Well they need to hurry, the wedding's going to start in five minutes." Mrs. Leonard was back to the dragon woman role, just breathing fire everywhere. Mama gave me a hug. I couldn't remember the last time Mama and I hugged each other, but I knew it had been a long time.

"I'm not going to cry," She said blinking her eyes. "I've been through this before with Katherine."

"Mama if you cry, then I'll start crying, and right now I don't need to cry with this mascara on."

We both laughed. Then Mama removed the veil to touch my face. She stared into my eyes for a moment before she mouthed the words, "I love you."

"Oh Mama," I said. I felt my lips tremble and I burst out crying before I knew it. We embraced. She never knew how long I waited to finally hear her say those words to me. It seemed like the wall that separated us all these years was finally torn down. I looked around the room and to my surprise everyone was dabbing at her eyes with tissues and blowing her nose. Katherine took Mama by the hand. "Come on Mama," she said softly. Mama wiped her eyes with her handkerchief and followed Katherine out of the room.

"Dorothy, check your mascara," Tiny said as she started to dab at her own.

"I don't know why we put mascara on," Joan said. "All of us knew this was going to happen." Whitney and Alexis walked in holding their gardenias.

"We were just about to send an APB out for you girls," Mrs. Leonard said. Whitney and Alexis ignored her; they were too busy worrying about their gardenias. An usher stuck her head in the door. "Are you ladies ready to take your places?" she asked. When she saw me in my gown, her eyes widened.

"Isn't she gorgeous? Just look at her in all her splendor."

"Thank you," I said.

"And my, look at that dress, you must've spent a fortune on it."

Mrs. Leonard cleared her throat and looked at the usher. “No, my husband and I spent a fortune on it.”

The usher only stared at Mrs. Leonard and closed the door.

Uncle Herbie and Aunt Ruby Jewel were standing outside in the foyer waiting for me when I walked out.

“Well here she is,” They said in unison.

I embraced them both. “Oh I’m so nervous,” I said, my knees wobbling.

“Don’t be nervous, baby. This is the most important day of your life,” Aunt Ruby Jewel told me. By this time, I was jittering.

“Ruby Jewel, I don’t know if I should walk down the aisle beside this woman.”

I smiled at Uncle Herbie.

“She’s too beautiful and I’m not worthy,” he said underneath that big smile of his. Aunt Ruby Jewel held my hand and looked into my eyes. “You are such a precious jewel,” she said with tears in her eyes. “You deserve only the best.”

“I know Aunt Ruby Jewel and he’s standing at the altar.”

“Yes he is,” She responded. “Yes he is indeed.”

She gave me a kiss on the cheek. “Don’t forget those vows.”

“Don’t tell her that Ruby; you’ll make her all nervous, Sugar.”

Aunt Ruby Jewel blew me a kiss and went inside the church. Although the doors were closed, I heard my Cousin Jacqué singing. I was trembling. Uncle Herbie noticed and he began to rub my arm.

“It’s okay baby girl, just calm down.”

“Uncle Herbie what if I trip coming down the aisle, or…or forget my vows, what if Katherine forgot the ring, what if David forgot his, wh—.”

“Baby, ain’t nothing like that’s gonna happen to you, I’ll make sure of it.”

“Well okay, I’ll try not to think about it so much.”

He turned me to face him. "Now you listen to me young lady, you better straighten up and stop thinking negative like that. You know your Papa wouldn't want you to think like that now would he?"

"No Sir, he wouldn't."

"And I don't either. Now you build up some confidence."

I loved it when Uncle Herbie came to my rescue.

Soon the doors of the church opened and I saw Katherine walk out first, followed by Tiny. I closed my eyes when Uncle Herbie and I were the only two standing in the doorway. Then the organ started up the *wedding march* and I heard the congregation stand to its feet.

"Well baby girl, this is it," Uncle Herbie whispered. "Your last walk as Dorothy LaCroix."

I squeezed his arm and held on to my bouquet. Off we went down the aisle; all eyes were on me. There were so many people that I didn't see their faces, I just saw objects with eyes. Some had tears in their eyes and some had joyful eyes. As I neared the altar, I looked to my left and saw Mama and Louis and the rest of the family, smiling and crying. I looked to the right and saw the Leonards, and their family and friends. Mrs. Leonard was dabbing at her eyes and smiling at David. I looked at the altar and saw David standing there in his black tuxedo. Standing by his side was Jerome. Jerome leaned forward and whispered something to David. David smiled and stepped forward.

I arrived at the altar staring teary eyed at Reverend Long, I was still trembling, my heart was racing wildly and I was perspiring, but I held on to Uncle Herbie's arm. I remembered what he said, and I thought about Papa. I convinced myself to stop worrying, this was a day of rejoicing, it was finally here. I was ready to make a commitment to the one man, whom I intend to be with for the rest of my life. After the music stopped, there was a brief moment of silence, except for the occasional flash of a camera. Reverend Long opened his book and began.

"Dearly beloved we are gathered here today before the sight of God, to unite this man and this woman in holy matrimony..."

As he talked, my mind wondered to David standing on the other side of Uncle Herbie and the flames burning from the candles nearby. My eyes were still teary and it seemed like the flames were a mile long.

"Who gives this bride away?"

Uncle Herbie said, "I do." He released my firm hold and David took his place. David looked straight into my eyes and smiled. It seemed like ages since I last saw that smile, two days to be exact.

Reverend Long began. "If there is one here, who does not see why this man and woman should be joined together, speak now or forever hold your peace."

David turned to face the congregation. He stared around the room with his hand pressed against his ear. "Hark! Do I hear anyone?" I heard the congregation laugh. I glanced at Jerome; he found a little humor in it. Reverend Long waited until the laughter ceased before he continued with the ceremony.

"For this lovely occasion, our bride and groom have written special vows. They will at this time proceed with those vows."

David and I turned to each other; David spoke first.

"Dorothy my love, our day has finally come at last. Here we are, the two of us, standing before God as one. I've had the privilege of knowing you for two-and-a-half years, but it seems like I've known you a lifetime. I am indeed grateful of having shared the last two-and-a-half years with you. You came into my life at a time when I needed you the most. You are the kind of woman a man only dreams about, the perfect picture of how a woman should be: beautiful, obedient, wholesome, patient, understanding, caring, and fine." I heard a few chuckles from the audience. I, on the other hand, blushed when he said that.

"Dorothy you are someone special, and I vow to take good care of you. With God as my witness I'll see to it that this marriage will withstand and conquer all temptations. I love you and I always will."

It was my turn, I was so scared.

"David I've always been told that promises should never be made because they were so difficult to keep, but I am here to say that a promise is something I am giving to you. That promise David is love, unconditional. I promise to serve and stand by you." As I spoke to David I couldn't help but notice Jerome standing behind him staring into my mouth. He stood there with his hands crossed in front of him and his dark ebony eyes dancing back and forth from me to David. As I said my vows, I thought, *how could he stand there and watch his best friend marry his ex* ? You know there are always two sides to everything and I thought, *how could David build up the nerve to ask Jerome to be his best man anyway*? I guess through it all, he and David were Frat brothers and no woman could come between friendship and brotherhood.

"David, I thank God for you coming into my life." I felt a tear in my eye. I kept telling myself to be strong, stop being nervous and sentimental. I heard Katherine behind me whispering, "Take your time sweetheart."

"I am grateful for this opportunity and I vow to never leave you David. I will love you as long as I live and I will honor you and cherish you always."

Reverend Long began, "Do you David Claude Leonard, II take Dorothy LaCroix to be your lawfully wedded wife, to honor and cherish her, for better or worst, through sickness and in health for as long as you both shall live?"

"I do," he replied.

"Do you Dorothy LaCroix take David Claude Leonard, II to be your lawfully wedded husband, to honor and cherish him, for better or worst, through sickness and in health for as long as you both shall live?"

"I do," I replied.

"The rings please."

David slipped a five-carat emerald cut diamond around my finger. I in return slipped a size 11 eighteen-carat gold ban around his.

"By the powers invested upon me by the state of Texas, I now pronounce you husband and wife. You may kiss the bride."

"I may?" David asked jokingly.

Reverend Long closed his book and took off his reading glasses. "Yes you may."

"Really, you're not kidding me are you?" David asked once more.

David had the church laughing again. He lifted my veil. I heard the church stand to its feet applauding when David and I kissed.

"Ladies and Gentlemen, it is my pleasure to introduce to you Dr. and Mrs. David C. Leonard, II."

The organ started up the exit march, and I was bombarded with hugs and kisses. The church was like a microcosm of the Mardi Gras. There were cameras flashing, rice thrown, and people applauding; people whom I've never seen before. The chauffeur opened the door to our limousine.

"Whew!" David shouted once we were inside. I was speechless, I couldn't get over the fact that I was married, it had to sink in for me to finally realize it.

"What's the matter baby, why the dazed look?"

"David pinch me, I mean it, pinch me."

David gave me a perplexed look.

"Pinch me!"

David took my bouquet and placed it on the floor. "I got a better idea." He took me in his arms and kissed me with one of those paralyzing kisses.

"Whew!" I shouted after he released me. "Why didn't you kiss me like that at the altar?"

"I didn't think you and the church could handle it."

I wanted him to kiss me like that again, I thought I heard fireworks explode after the last one.

The photographer snapped at least five shots of David and me with our families. I thought I would never stop smiling. The photographers wanted pictures of the bride's maids and groom's men, more pictures of the family posing for a huge portrait, pictures of David and me cutting our three-tier ten layer pineapple cream cake, pictures of David and me drinking from each other's champagne glasses, pictures of me with Jacqueline, and pictures of David and me dancing for the first time as husband and wife.

Near the center of the room was a small entourage of musicians playing both classical and modern music. I wanted them to play my song, *Unforgettable*, by Nat King Cole. When they did, David and I took center stage. Everyone cleared the ballroom floor for us. David took my hand in his and lead me around to the slow tempo of the music.

"David remember that night in the car when you asked me to be your girl?"

He tried to recall. "Was it that night after we left the coffee shop?"

"Yes, you remember," I replied.

"This song was playing on the radio."

"Yes baby, it was. This is our song, David."

He held me close and we slow danced around the floor. For some strange reason I kept thinking about Cinderella and the handsome prince. I heard David trying to sing, his voice sounded so horrible.

"Unforgettable, that's what you are." He glanced at me. "Stop laughing Dorothy."

"I can't help it," I said. "Do me a favor and stick to your day job."

"Ha, ha, ha; thanks a lot," he said underneath that bright smile of his.

After the dance we sat down to a gourmet feast of roasted duck nestled on top of steamy hot vegetables, seafood etoufée, caviar, fresh cut fruit salad, and a bottle of chilled Chardonnay.

"Dorothy, it's time for the bouquet toss," Mrs. Leonard said. She was starting to get on my nerves again, telling me how to organize the events in the wedding. *Don't start eating until after your uncle has toasted the ceremonies, don't slice the cake until after the main course.* She was flapping so much it was starting to agitate Doc Sr. He turned to her and said, "Liz, will you pleassse, pleassse, pleassse, leave those newlyweds alone. You are driving me nuts. I can only imagine what you're doing to them."

"Honey, I am trying to be of mere help. I don't want our son's wedding to be somber. I want every minute of it to be exciting, and full of vigor!"

"Honey this is a wedding, not the Barnum and Bailey Circus."

Mrs. Leonard excused herself from the table, "Dorothy I will see you in five minutes on the far side of the room."

After Mrs. Leonard left, David whispered in my ear, "You don't have to go over there if you don't want to."

I wiped the corners of my mouth with my napkin. "That's all right," I said calmly. "I'm finished eating anyway; besides, I wanna see the woman who's bold enough to catch my bouquet." David helped me out of my chair. "Honey did you wanna come and see?"

"No Dorothy, there's only one woman I want to see holding my bouquet."

"That's right Sugar." I pecked him across the lips.

Mrs. Leonard had gathered almost every single woman in the ballroom. She was telling them to stand behind some imaginary line and don't step over it until the bouquet is up in the air. She was sounding just like an elementary school teacher.

"Now Dorothy, you turn around and stand here." She took my arm and placed me over some imaginary dot. Although my back was against the ladies, I could still recognize who was telling who not to catch the bouquet.

"Are you guys ready!" I shouted.

"Ready when you are!" They shouted back.

I took the bouquet and tossed it over my head. There were a few screams, a little shuffling, but someone finally caught it. I turned around and discovered that "someone" was a girl whom I didn't recognize. She looked to be about sixteen or seventeen. She was a gorgeous, mahogany-colored girl, who held the bouquet high above her head like a trophy shouting, "I caught it! I caught it!"

I approached this girl. She stopped shouting and timidly held the bouquet in her hands. "I'm sorry; here you can have them back."

"No please, they're yours. What's your name?"

At that moment, Whitney, my soror introduced her. "Dorothy this is Chanel, my sister, unfortunately."

"Chanel?"

"Yes."

Chanel stood there holding the bouquet in her hands, admiring it like it was a prize of money.

"I never thought I'd be the one catching them," she said laughing. "They're so beautiful."

"So who's the lady bold enough to try and take my wife's place?" David asked, I didn't realize he was close behind.

"Miss Chanel here." I said.

David stared at Chanel. "You're not twenty-one are you?" he asked jokingly.

Whitney cleared her throat. "Excuse me but I don't think Dorothy is twenty-one either."

To that remark David replied, "You hear me complaining?"

Whitney playfully rolled her eyes at him. David took my hand. "Excuse us. Honey there's someone I want you to meet." David introduced me to another friend of his from the medical field.

On my way to the powder room, I saw Jerome. He was standing near the balcony sipping on a glass of champagne. He saw me and motioned for me to join him. I pointed to the powder room and told him I'll be back as soon as I can. Inside, Tiny and Joan were powdering their faces.

"You ladies look fine." I said.

Tiny took a tissue and dabbed around her nose. "I just can't stop sweating," she said.

I noticed my lip rouge was wearing off. "You can't stop dancing either?" I replied.

She laughed. "You know me."

Joan was running her hands through her hair. "Dorothy who was that girl that caught your bouquet?"

"Whitney's sister, Chanel." I began to apply lip rouge to my lips. "She looked pretty young."

Tiny began to laugh. "A young one you say?"

"Yes girl about sixteen or seventeen."

"Hmmphf, hmmphf, hmmphf. What business did she have standing in line anyway?"

I rubbed my lips together. "I don't know. Tiny, I wished you could've seen her, she looked so happy when she caught it, she was waving it around."

"Oh yeah?" Tiny replied. She stopped dabbing and put her hand on her hip. "Dot, I don't mean to disrespect your new mother-in-law, but that woman, I could kill her."

"Tiny what happened?"

Tiny was huffing and puffing and gritting her teeth. "She always has something to say to me. Check this out, I was on the dance floor dancing and having a good time with the band you know? Here she comes waltzing her stiff legged-behind out there on the floor; and she says to me, what's going on here? You shouldn't dance that way. I hope you know there are Christians at this reception, and I will not tolerate this display of obscenity."

"Seriously?" I asked.

"Joan is my witness."

I looked at Joan as she nodded her head.

"And Dot, when I cut two slices of the groom's cake she said, 'Christine, I'm ashamed of you. You eat like a hog. You need to stop and lose the weight you already have." Tiny imitated her voice. "I started to tell her, 'Honey you need glasses because I know I'm not fat.' Dorothy that's your mother-in-law and I realize this is a formal setting, but just that moment, girrll, I was getting ready to kick her ass."

"Tiny don't pay any attention to her."

"You know what?" Tiny began to stuff her coin purse with tissues. "She's got one more thing to say to me tonight."

Joan began to chuckle. "Poor Mrs. Leonard. She's in for a serious ass whipping, huh?"

"You damn right," Tiny responded. "Somebody has to set her straight. Forgive me Dorothy. I know you don't like me talking about her."

"It doesn't bother me." I said. At that moment I thought about Jerome. "Tiny, I saw Jerome on my way in here."

"And?"

"He was standing near the balcony alone. He asked me to join him."

"What did you say?" Joan and Tiny both watched me closely.

"I told him I would."

Tiny picked up her purse and flung it over her shoulders. "I knew it. You're not quite over Jerome, are you?"

"Tiny please, I am way over him."

Tiny laughed. "Hmmphf hmmphf, remember those vows and that $5,000 ring."

"Tiny you know better. You know I don't have any feelings for him."

"Denial, hmmphf, hmmphf, hmmphf."

Joan grabbed her purse. "Dorothy if I were you, I wouldn't fall for those lines. You know what I'm talking about. Those I'm-not-the-same-as-I-use-to-be lines," she said. "And the I-still-haven't-gotten-over-you lines."

Tiny replied, "Yeah, and the I'm-lonely-and-can-we-go-somewhere-private-to-talk lines."

"That's what I'm talking about," Joan replied, before she and Tiny left the room.

"You two heffas," I said and followed them out of the restroom. Jerome was still standing by the balcony sipping on his champagne. I ran my hands in front of my gown to smooth the wrinkles as I walked calmly in his direction. It seemed as though I was moving in slow motion.

"Hello Dr. West. Are you enjoying the evening thus far?" I asked.

"Yes I am," he replied. "I've been wanting to tell you that the wedding was beautiful, this reception is lovely, and the view from this balcony is gorgeous."

"Hmmm?"

"I said the view of the city from this balcony is something else."

"Yeah." I replied.

"Where's David? I'm surprised the two of you managed to separate from each other."

"David is somewhere being convivial as usual. He's having the time of his life."

"I would too if I was married to a beautiful woman like you," Jerome said in a low sensuous voice.

I was thinking of a way to end this conversation with another topic other than the wedding.

"Umm Jerome, what time is it?" I asked.

He glanced at his watch. "It's five before midnight."

"Well, you don't say." I noticed his expression was dazed. "Are you going to join the rest of us to toast the new year?" I asked.

He chuckled and shook his head. "No, I'll just stay right here and relax."

I cleared my throat. "Stop being antisocial and join us." I grabbed his hand.

I heard David's voice behind me. "Dorothy, Jerome!"

I turned around and smiled at him. "Sweetheart," I said before giving him a kiss. I looked into David's eyes, but they were still on Jerome.

"Why are you standing over here Jerome?" he asked.

"You know what honey, I was asking him the same thing?" I replied. The expression on David's face revealed that he wasn't at all pleased with me being alone with Jerome.

Jerome chuckled. "David man, the night is mellow. Why not spend it mellowing out with Dorothy over here by the balcony?"

I took David's hand. "Jerome, we're just about to begin the count down. Come on and join the rest of us," I said.

"Don't worry about me," he replied. Jerome titled his champagne glass to David and me. "Here's to a fine marriage and a Happy New Year," he said before taking a drink. David quickly grabbed my hand as I thought we were rushing to get back to the ballroom but instead he pushed me inside the men's restroom. I shrieked when he slammed my body against the cold tile wall.

"In case you've forgotten, this is still our wedding night!"

I looked into his eyes searching for an answer to his outburst. "I don't understand what's going on David, what are you talking about?"

"I'm talking about you and Jerome. What were you doing alone with him?"

"I-I was just talking to him." I smelled David's breath but there were no traces of alcohol.

"About what!"

At that moment my mind froze and my knees became weak. I took a good look at David's eyes; they were like daggers piercing through my body. The pain and humiliation was so unbearable, I thought I was dreaming.

"David please let go of my arm you're hurting me," I pleaded.

David slowly released my arm and backed away from me like I was a total stranger. In the background I heard the sound of our wedding guests counting down the hour. Tears came to my eyes as I thought of how sweet it would have been to bring in the New Year on a happy note. Instead, I brought it in staring into the eyes of a strange acting man who not five hours ago sealed a vow for better or worst with a kiss.

"I'm sorry Dorothy." He came closer and cradled my face in his hands. "I'm so sorry."

I wiped away my tears with my hands. "Why would you accuse me of messing around with Jerome?" I listened as sobs butchered up my sentences.

"Baby I'm sorry, it's just that I saw you standing alone with him and I thought I lost you."

My mouth dropped open in shock, "You thought you lost me! No! I just married you, remember?"

"I know baby." He kissed my lips. "I'm sorry, I won't hurt you again. I promise."

I didn't like the way this was going. Something wasn't right. Somewhere along the way, somebody must have done or said something to David. Then out of nowhere, Bettye's words came back to haunt me. If tonight was a preview of what was to come in this marriage, then I was in for a rude awakening.

Chapter 7

"How was the honeymoon?" Tiny's voice was inquisitive on the other end of the phone.

I rubbed the bluish-red bruise on my right arm and pretended to sound happy. "Tiny, girl that was my first time on an airplane, and I must say it was a catastrophic experience. Tiny, I thought I was going to die. Girl, I hadn't been so religious since the time I prayed for my period after I thought I was pregnant."

"What happened?"

"First of all, it was storming when we boarded the plane. I was apprehensive about that, but the stewardess assured us that the storm wasn't as bad as we thought."

"Wasn't as bad as you thought? Dot, who was this woman kidding?"

"Tiny, we waited for an hour, until the storm gradually ceased. So off we go down the runway and into the air, the turbulence was high of course, and that's scaring the shit out of me, plus right behind us sitting in first class was an old couple. Anyway, the old woman sitting behind us was having a difficult time breathing. So David, being a doctor and a kind and considerate gentleman, offers to help this woman. Tiny, that woman's husband had the nerve to tell David that he didn't want a Nigra Quack helping his wife. David told him that his wife was going to pass out if she didn't have immediate attention, so David tried to give this woman CPR. Meanwhile her husband was shouting and cursing, and it seemed like everyone on the plane was screaming, Tiny. Girl, it was awful."

"Damn Dorothy, what happened to the woman?"

"There was an emergency landing, but it was too late the woman was dead."

"Oh no!"

"Since David was a physician and present when the woman died, he had to accompany the other doctors to the hospital. This delayed our trip for another five hours."

"So when did you and David finally make it to St. Thomas?"

"A day later."

"So were the two of you compensated?"

"Yes, two round trip tickets to Miami."

"After what happened, I'd doubt if I ever want to go there again," Tiny said.

"David was on the news there," I said.

"Really, it's too bad he was publicized under those circumstances."

"David couldn't stop thinking about that old woman, and how her husband's ignorance and bigotry caused her to lose her life."

"Don't tell me David thought about that the whole time you two were on the honeymoon.?

"He thought about it for a day, maybe, until we went to our room that night." I closed my eyes and saw clearly how the night began. David's ego was bruised when the husband of the woman he tried to save snarled at him and called him a "Nigger." I remember David pacing the room ranting and raving about his money, his prestige, and how he wasn't going to be disrespected by anyone, not even me.

Tiny laughed. "Ah girl, did you whip it on him?"

"Yes I did."

"Out of sight, I'm scared of you."

"David was too."

"Go on with your bad self."

"I figure that would be the only way to get his mind off the incident."

"It works all the time."

"Yes it does."

"Enough about the plane ride, tell me about the scenery. Was it anything like you'd imagine?"

"Some parts of it were, David and I lived on the edge of the island in a beach cottage his relatives owned when they lived there."

"David had relatives living in St. Thomas?"

"Yes. David's Great Grandmother and Grandmother were missionaries and they built a school and a church there."

"My goodness, David's regal don't you think?"

"He comes from a wealthy background of doctors, merchants, and educators."

"No shit," Tiny replied. "Go on telling me about the scenery and the food."

"Tiny, each morning we awoke to the smell of fresh brewed coffee and tropical fruits. Tiny the cooks would bring their small grills and cooking utensils and prepared the food right there before our eyes. It was amazing, how fast they prepared the food and the way they prepared it, you know?"

"Yes," she replied.

"Tiny, we tasted nearly everything the island had to offer."

"So tell me about the concert?"

I held my composure as I lied and told her how awesome the Miles Davis concert was and the fabulous party that followed at the hotel, when in actuality they were both disasters. David was obviously jealous of the attention I received when Davis spotted me in the audience and serenaded me on the stage. although I flat out refused, Davis wasn't accepting no for an answer. I stood on stage, halfway embarrassed and halfway astonished as he placed his brass trumpet to his lips and produced a sound so sweet it reminded me of powdered sugar on a beignet. After the set he took my hand, kissed it and lifted my trembling hand in the air as we received a warm and thunderous applause. When I joined David in the audience, he was fuming. He didn't speak to me during the entire concert. During the after party, he kept a tight reign around me, not letting me out of his sight not even for a minute. I finally broke down and told him how I felt that I was tired of feeling like a dog on a leash.

"You didn't seem to mind the attention three hours ago!"

I looked around and noticed a few people staring back at us. "I don't want to talk about this. This is not the time and certainly not the place for you to embarrass me."

"You are right, this is not the place."

With that he grabbed my arm with a grip so tight, I thought the circulation had stopped. I fought back my pain until we were outside and away from the crowd of people. I was glad it was dark so no one could see the tears in my eyes.

"What is wrong with you?" I asked.

"Nothing. I am not the one flirting!"

"I'm not either!"

"Yes you are!"

"David, I am tired of you treating me like dirt, when I haven't done anything!"

"Look, I'm sorry. I got a little carried away, okay?"

He grabbed me and tried to console me. I was so lost in my thoughts that I forgot all about Tiny.

"What happened after the concert?" Tiny asked.

"There was an after party at the hotel, so David and I walked to it. We stayed there for about an hour and walked back to our little cottage by the sea."

"Oooh girl, I don't think I can handle all this romance."

We both laughed. Except Tiny's laugh was sincere.

"I hope you took pictures."

"Yes, we took a lot of pictures," I responded.

"Any nude ones?"

"Perhaps."

"Dorothy Leonard, how could you? See, I knew you had it in you."

"It was David's idea, he's the creative one."

We laughed again.

"So Tiny, when are you and Mike going to tie the knot?" I asked, anxious to change the subject.

"After he grows up and proves to me that he's worthy of a commitment."

"Any clue as to how long it will take?"

"Dorothy, it's questionable at the moment. Mike and I still have to get our acts together. Me personally, I'm not all the way committed to Mike, and I know damn well he's not committed to me."

"Tiny, I never really talked about this with anyone, but do you think David and I kind of rushed into marriage?"

"Dorothy that's a question only you and David can answer."

I sighed, thinking, *Yes, I did rush into it. I should've given it a little more time to develop*. Looking back, David was so much like a gentleman, that I couldn't help but think that maybe the pressures at the hospital were taking its toll on him, and that when his residency is over, things will be back to normal.

"Dot, let me ask you a stupid question?"

"What is it?"

"Do you honestly love David?"

"Yes, I love him." And honestly I do.

"Or do you love the fact that he's a doctor, from a prestigious background of people who have money, and a name for themselves."

"I really love him."

"A lot of times you can convince yourself that it wasn't the money that made you his wife in the first place, it was love, but Dorothy let's be realistic. Love alone does not pay the bills."

I laughed. "No, it doesn't."

"It just gives you a good thrill, I guess, I don't know."

We both laughed. I thought about my big sister, Katherine.

"Have you talked to my sister?" I asked.

"Yes, Katherine and I went to the church revival."

"At who's church? Reverend Massey's church?"

"Yes. I tell you, although he is a man of God, he was raising pure hell last night. Dot you know how he likes to point fingers and throw stones in his sermons? Well last night that man was talking about Jezebel, and girl, he had the nerve to say he see a few Jezebels in the congregation sitting high and mighty like they know they going to heaven."

While I was on the phone, David arrived carrying a load of books.

"I'm gonna let you go. Guess who just walked in?"

"Don't mention it girl."

"Bye."

David took off his coat and hung it by the door. "Who was that?" he asked, sounding like my Papa.

"It was Tiny," I responded and watched as he sat down on the sofa, unbuttoned his cuff links, rolled up his sleeves, and flashed one of those devious smiles.

"Well, aren't you glad to see me? Come here." He motioned with his finger. I moved in closer and received his probing tongue. I oftentimes forgot just how sweet his kisses were, even if he wasn't. I turned my attention away from his stare and picked up one of his books and read the words '*Masters and Johnson: Guide to the Woman's Body*.'

"I must be the luckiest man in the world to come home everyday to a face like yours."

David stared ever so admiringly into my eyes before he opened a notebook of his, mashed the button on the cross pen I gave him last Christmas, and proceeded to write. I picked up a sheet of paper that he had written on. There were so many marks and doodles where he had edited and replaced common words with complex medical terms. I read the first line it said, *'GOD made Adam and gave him the breath of life, seeing that Adam was lonely, GOD gave Adam a wife.'*

"David, what is this?" I asked.

He glanced over it. "Dorothy, that is the intro page to the manual I'm working on."

"Really? Is it a manual about poetry or gynecology?"

He laughed, "The opening sentence must've caught you off guard?"

"Yes, for a moment there, but I see the point you're trying to make."

"Good."

"David honey…" I browsed randomly through each manuscript and I came across words like IUD and Papanicolaou, medical terms that every woman had come across at some time or another. "Have you considered getting this manual published?"

"Yes."

There must've been over two hundred pages in my hand of where he had written and gone over to edit. "How many pages do you plan to write?"

"Somewhere in the range of fifty to two hundred."

"Are you the only person working on this project?"

"No, do you remember Dr. Corbin from the wedding?"

"Yes, I think."

"He's my co-author."

"You've been working on this for a while."

He pulled out a pair of reading glasses and placed them on his nose. Although David was only twenty-five, those glasses made him look much older.

"Two years now." He continued to read across a manuscript.

"Baby are you hungry?" I asked. He kept reading as though he didn't hear.

"Yooohooo, David."

He looked up. "Oh I'm sorry, what were you asking me?"

"I asked are you hungry?"

"No, Dr. Corbin and I had dinner."

"What did you have to eat?"

"A gigantic catfish platter."

"Hmmm." I licked my lips. "Did you bring me some?"

"Yeah I got you some and the best bottle of Chardonnay."

"Really baby?"

"I sure did, see I was thinking about you." He kissed my lips. "I'm always thinking about you."

"Thank you, you know lately, I've been having these cravings."

"Cravings?" He stopped reading.

"Yes." I paused. "No I'm not pregnant."

He put his notebook aside and began to check my temperature with his hand. "I'm checking just to make sure. You know Mother Nature works in mysterious ways."

"I shouldn't be pregnant; I use birth control."

He lifted my blouse and pressed against my pelvis and my breasts. "Does that hurt?" he asked.

His hands caressed them in a circular motion, and for a moment there I was getting really excited. "No honey, it doesn't hurt." I took my hand and clasped it around his. "However it does feel good." We both laughed. "Nope, you're not pregnant."

"David I really do want a baby."

He sighed. "I know it Dorothy, but right now is not a good time. I'm doing my residency, I'm trying to write this book, you still have a semester left. Just give it some time okay?"

"Okay." I nodded and gazed pitifully at the floor.

"Stop looking like that. We have plenty of time."

I sighed.

"Speaking of school, what happened yesterday?" David asked in a matter-of-fact tone of voice.

"Joan is going to law school."

"Are you serious?"

"Yes, she got accepted into Berkley."

"Congratulations to the little militant; she'll love it at Berkley."

"I'm sure going to miss her, David."

"You can pay her a visit once she settles in."

I poured a cup of hot lemon tea for David and myself. "I don't know what else to do or say." I sipped my tea, the smell from the fresh cut lemon opened my nostrils. I sat David's cup on the end table beside him.

"Give her a dinner or a going away party," David suggested.

"Nahn. It may be a simple dinner party to us, but to Joan St. Julian, it's a political platform, and I am not in the mood for her fire-side chats."

"I know what you mean," David replied.

"I'd rather give her a nice gift instead."

"That'll work."

David and I clicked mugs as a toast to the idea.

*　　*　　*

"My, my, my, I just can't get over I got two babies with degrees from college," Mama said as she stood beaming behind me in the mirror. She glanced at Ophelia, who was brushing Jacqueline's hair. "Ophelia baby, soon it'll be your turn."

Ophelia continued to brush Jacqueline's hair. "Mama I don't want to go to college. I want to be an artist. You know I've been looking at an art school in Chicago that's really good."

"Ophelia there's an art school in Houston," I said as I stepped into my robe and stood there while Mama zipped me up. "Mama can you straighten my collar for me, please ma'am."

"I don't want to go school in the South; I'm tired of the South, I've been living here all my life."

"Ophelia I've been here all my life, do you hear me complaining?" Mama asked. She took my collar and pinned it inside my robe. Ophelia sighed and tied a ribbon around Jacqueline's braid. "Some people can handle the South. Me personally, I can't. I want to see something new and exciting for a change."

"Baby you can see that right here in New Orleans. You know there's always something happening."

"Ophelia, if all possible, I will see to it that you go to the best art school in the country," I said.

Ophelia smiled. "Thank you, big sis."

Mama rolled her eyes. "Will you listen at Miss Money here." Mama lit herself a cigarette. She always reminded me of how grateful I was for marrying David and how grateful she was to David for buying her a new five bedroom house in one of the finest neighborhoods in New Orleans.

"How is my favorite son-in-law's book coming?"

"Mama, he's in the last chapter and check this out, his agent told him that the contract for the book is worth, now check this out, $50,000."

Mama's eyes got so big, I thought I saw dollar signs in them. "You got to be kidding me Dorothy."

"Yes Mama, it's true. My man is bringing home big dough!"

"Dorothy, just think of the things you can buy with that kind of money: a beautiful home with a swimming pool and tennis court, a big fancy car with a phone in it..."

"You'll never have to work again," Ophelia said.

"Hmmphf, some of God's children have it so easy. By the way Dorothy, is that mother-in-law of yours coming?" Mama paused and waited for me to answer.

"No, I don't think so. She and Doc Sr. are in Georgia this weekend at a Martin Luther King rally."

"Good," Mama replied. "I can't stand that woman. I feel so sorry for her husband."

I opened the door to my closet; there were dozens of shoes with various designs on them, but I stepped into a pair of sky blue two inch pumps instead. Mama sat down on the bed. "Dorothy if you don't hurry up, we won't be able to find a parking place and you know I hate walking with these bad feet of mine."

"Yes I know, Mama."

Mama glanced at her diamond encrusted watch which was another gift from David. "Your sister told me she won't be able to make the graduation. She said the swelling in her feet has gotten worst."

"Mama when did she tell you this?"

"She called late yesterday afternoon to tell me." Mama thumped her ashes in a nearby porcelain flower pot. "I can't believe she's having a baby, can you picture me, a Grandma?"

Ophelia and I glanced at Mama then at each other. We both said yes. Mama rolled her eyes."Both of y'all can just kiss my ass."

Jacqueline held her hands over her mouth, sniggling.

"Mama stop cursing like that in front of Jacqueline. You know she picks up curse words real easy, just the other day she called David a s-o-n-o-f-a-b-i-t-c-h." I had to spell it, so Jacqueline wouldn't comprehend. Mama thought it was very funny. "Don't you agree?" she asked me. "Frankly I couldn't have said it better myself."

David walked in startling everyone. "Dorothy." He glanced at his watch. "Are you aware of the time? We need to be on the road now if we plan to be in Baton Rouge by 11:00."

I grabbed a pair of earrings from atop the chest-of-drawers. "Honey I know what time it is."

"Well act like it and put some pep in your step."

David got to the point now, where he liked to boss me around in front of Mama and everybody else. I didn't like it, but I kept my mouth shut.

"David you look handsome as usual," Mama said.

David turned around, sucked in his shoulders, and stood in a profile stance. "And everyone said I should become a doctor." I grabbed my sorority banner to wrap it around myself. "How do I look?" I asked.

"Look like you're ready to get that degree to me? Doesn't she to you David?" Mama asked.

David smiled and nodded.

I stood near the platform and listened as the dean announced the girl's name ahead of me. She jumped up and down and ran across the stage like a thoroughbred, "I did it!" She shouted once she got her degree. She had everyone laughing, even the president wiped a tear from his eye. Then the dean announced my name. I glanced out and saw a sea of faces staring at me. I heard the dean call out my major, and I felt him shake my hand. In my other hand he gave me a small blue notebook with the words Southern University and the Jaguar mascot engraved in gold. I felt relieved that my undergraduate years were over and a new life awaited me. I felt too, like jumping and running across the stage, but I held myself and took this new found relief in stride. What a blessing.

"Surprise!" I finally opened my eyes to see a house filled with relatives and friends. I was so overwhelmed with exultation that I peed on myself. I had tears in my eyes when I saw the words, '*Congratulations Dorothy we are so proud of you.*' I felt myself grinning from ear to ear.

"Speech! Speech!" the voices echoed throughout the room.

"Shhh! Shhh! Let my baby talk!" Mama shouted. I was still overwhelmed with joy, but I managed to say a few words. "Thank you very much I'm speechless and I think I have to go to the bathroom."

I heard everyone laugh as I ran upstairs. Meanwhile in the bathroom I pulled off my panties, which were soaked in urine and sat on the toilet. A few minutes later there was a knock on the door. "Hey. Are you okay in there?" It was David's voice.

"Yes honey."

"You left out of the room in a hurry."

"I know David. Hey David, can you tell Ophelia to come here?"

"Is there something wrong?"

"I need her to do a favor for me."

He opened the door halfway and peeked inside. "I can do it for you, what is it?"

"Honey go get Ophelia for me."

He opened the door all the way. "What happened did you pee in your panties?"

I was red with embarrassment. "Yes honey, I peed in my panties. The surprise was a bit too much for me to handle."

He titled his head back with laughter and closed the door. I threw my wet panties. Lucky enough for David the door was closing. I still heard him laughing as he walked down the hall. I grabbed a wash cloth nearby to wet it, grabbed a bar of ivory soap, worked a good lather, and commenced to wiping and digging.

Moments later Ophelia opened the door with a pair of panties and some Wind Song perfume powder. "David told me." She was giggling.

"I don't see what's funny."

"Dorothy, I wished you could've seen your face."

I opened up my panties and sprinkled some Wind Song in them. "Ophelia, who's idea was it to throw me a surprise party?"

"It was a joint effort," she said, while she examined her hair in the mirror. I examined my own before I went downstairs to a hand clapping, feet tapping, backbone breaking family room.

"Dot!" I heard Mama's voice calling me. She stood near the den puffing on a cancer stick, holding a small drinking glass. "Dot baby, would you come over here for a minute?" I danced my way to her. "You called me Mama?"

"Girl, what took you so long, I thought you went upstairs and died."

"No, Mama." I noticed there were more older people conversing in the quiet room than in the family room. "I just had to freshen up."

Mama leaned forward and whispered, "David told me you pissed on yourself."

I flashed Mama, an I'm-tired-of-the-piss-situation look. She puffed on her cigarette and smiled. "You gon' do more than piss after you find out what David got you for graduation."

My eyes widened. "What did he get me Mama?"

"I'm not gonna tell," She said smiling.

"Is it a car?"

"I'm not gonna tell," She said still smiling.

"What is it then, keys to a house, a trip to Europe?"

Mama shook her head and started smiling. "Dot, you'll have to wait and see."

"Where is David, do you know?"

She shrugged her shoulders and puffed on her cigarette.

"See what you did Mama? You got my blood pressure worked up and now I'm anxious."

She blew out a cloud of white smoke. "They say that exercise is good for high blood pressure, so do what the other kids in here are doing and

Wang Dang Doodle." Mama started dancing and popping her fingers. "See won't that calm you down."

"Ah Mama." I waved my hand at her and searched for David. Mama didn't have to tell me David had a bigger surprise waiting on me, now she had me jumpy.

"Jacqué, have you seen David?"

Jacqué frowned and searched around the room with her eyes. "No," she said in her whining voice. "Not since the party began."

I sat down beside her. "Mama said he had a surprise for me. You wouldn't happen to know anything about it?"

Jacqué shook her head. She had an under-bite out of this world, but the girl could sing like a bird. I spotted David coming out of the kitchen. "I'll be back." I stood up and dashed through the room like Superman.

"There you are," he said. "Are you feeling better?"

"Not quite, I hear you have a big surprise for me."

"Huh?"

"Don't pretend you don't know what I'm talking about."

David was perplexed. "Dorothy what are you talking about?"

"Mama said you had a graduation gift for me, but she failed to say what it was."

He licked his lips; I noticed he always did that when he held back something.

"See David, unnh hunh, you are hiding something from me."

David fought back the laughter. "Dorothy I-I."

Tiny passed by singing *Wang Dang Doodle (All Night Long)* .

"Tiny." David grabbed her hand as though he were happy she came by. "Tiny, I am glad to see you. Talk to your cousin, she thinks I have a surprise for her."

A questionable look fell across Tiny's face. "A surprise? I don't know anything about a surprise."

"From what Mama was saying, it sounded as though David might've had a car or something big of that nature."

They both shrugged their shoulders and mumbled. "Tiny, I don't know what Mama could've meant."

"I don't either," Tiny replied. I sucked my teeth. Hmmphf, someone was hiding something.

I went out back where Louis and some other guys were playing dominoes. Aunt Ruby Jewel and Mama's older brother, Uncle JB, were standing over the barbecue pit and pressure cooker. Uncle JB was flipping the huge golden brown ribs like pancakes, while Aunt Ruby Jewel added more cayenne pepper to the crawfish.

"Hmmm, it sure smells good out here."

"Hey Graduation girl!" Uncle JB said as he turned around to give me a hug. He was a brawny man with a loud husky voice. "What you know good?" he asked.

"I know this barbecue smells good, what's your secret?"

"Shhh." He put his finger over his mouth and leaned towards my ear. "If I tell, then it won't be a secret."

"Come on, Uncle JB."

He bellowed out; it was a loud cackling laugh. He held the handle to a pot smoking with the aroma of brown sugar, lemon, wine sauce, and beer. He then dipped a brush into the base and slapped it over each brown, succulent, piece of beef.

Aunt Bridgette came outside with another tray of ribs, seasoned with black and lemon peppers, red peppers, and white seasoning salt. Although the ribs were raw, they already had a rich hickory-smoked aroma.

"That raw meat sure smells good Aunt Bridgette."

"It does doesn't it," she said laughing. Aunt Bridgette always stuck her tongue between her teeth when she laughed.

"Fifteen!" I heard Louis shout. "Now take that to the bank and buy you a new set of teeth!" Louis had everyone sitting at the round table laughing.

"He must be referring to Otis over there, that man has teeth that look like picket fences," Aunt Bridgette said.

Uncle JB shouted, "Lou Dix you can talk dirt all you want to, just wait 'til I come back over there and we'll see who do the walking and talking to the bank!"

"JB you bring your jolly fat ass on over here then!"

I glanced at the table full of so-called pro domino players, everyone over there was over fifty and talked much trash. I stood there thinking, *old men sure do talk a lot of noise when they're playing dominoes.* Louis had a two gallon jug of gin sitting in the middle of the table. No wonder everyone was so loud, they were all drunk as hell.

"That sure was nice of your husband to buy your mother this beautiful house," Aunt Bridgette said while eyeing the two and a half-story, 2500 square foot Victorian-style structure. "She ought to be grateful to God to have him as a son-in-law."

I must have heard that comment a thousand times today.

Meanwhile inside, the 'jerk' and the 'penguin' were in full swing. Tiny was in the center, of course with everyone around her cheering her on and laughing. I passed by David chatting with Uncle Herbie near the door.

"Uncle Herbie, don't talk to this man. He's keeping secrets from me."

David covered my mouth with his hand. "Uncle Herbie, Mama Cleo was telling Dorothy that I had a huge graduation gift just waiting for her."

"I declare. Well have you son?" Uncle Herbie was inquisitive.

David shrugged his shoulders. "This party is it Uncle Herbie, this is as big as it gets."

"But David, from the tone of Mama's voice she had me thinking it was something else."

"Where is Mama Cleo?" He asked.

"I don't know, but she talked as though she knew something that I didn't."

David stared at me, his eyes had that devious air to them, like he was holding back something from me. I noticed Tiny and even Uncle Herbie had the same look.

"We'll have to discuss this after dinner won't we honey."

"Why not discuss it during dinner?"

David chuckled.

After dinner, in which I stuffed myself with a combination of smoked barbecue ribs, three pounds of flaming hot crawfish, roast duck, and helpings of Aunt Bridgette's strawberry shortcake. I managed to find a sofa in the far corner of the den and plopped down. I was burping, sucking and picking my teeth like no one's business. My older relatives were shaking their heads. Ms. Queenie, my paternal great aunt said, "Miss Dorothy at the rate you was going, I thought you was going to eat the furniture baby."

I was too full to respond, too full to even laugh at the remark, although it was so true. Lately, I had been eating like a hog.

"Dorothy!" I heard Tiny's voice. She shook her head and laughed, "Girl what am I going to do with you."

I was too weak to move, I gave Tiny my hand. "Tiny help me up!" Tiny took my hand and pulled me to my feet, it felt like I hadn't stood on them for ages.

"You need to stop eating so much. If you keep on," she whispered in my ear. "You are going to end up like Sister Birtha back there. You know that woman got on the scale to weigh herself and it said 'to be continued.'"

I was too full to laugh at that. I had to take a deep breath, cover my belch and move on.

"There she is." everyone said when I entered. The living room looked like a huge family portrait with all eyes and smiling lips on me.

"Sit here." Mama said. She sat me down on the sofa next to Aunt Ruby Jewel. "This is presentation time where we pay tribute to the graduate. We say good things about her, make her cry, give her gifts, just anything to let her know that we are proud of her for going through college, and getting what some Negroes can only hope for. A good husband and a college degree."

"AMEN!" Uncle JB shouted. He sounded like the cheering deacon section of the church. Everyone in the room gathered around in a circle, Ophelia stood in the middle and next to her stood a tripod stand with a white cloth draped over it. She smiled at everyone. "I need everyone to be quiet, and all eyes on me."

"This here ain't no school house!" Uncle JB shouted.

"Shhh, let the girl start JB."

"Thank you Mama. I'm not a person who thrives on poetry, nor do I read it, someone told me that it was an art form, and since I'm an artist, I feel I'd like to share a poem. I wrote one especially for my sister. I simply entitled it 'Sister.'" She glanced at me and smiled when everyone oohed and ahhed. "It doesn't have a perfect rhyme, but who cares. It's the thought that counts right? So I wrote the first thing that came to mind."

Ophelia cleared her throat and began,

A sister is someone who you can talk to
When there's no one else,
She's everybody's friend,
She's someone no one can keep to themselves.

I heard someone blowing his noise, and a few sniffles, and someone mumble, "How sweet."

Anyone who is someone can clearly see
That my sister means everything to me.

There was a scattered applause. Everyone anticipated more but Ophelia was finished. She glanced around the room and waited until the applause ceased. Then she unveiled a portrait of me dressed in a golden Cinderella gown. I was adorned in jewels, and above my head was a crown. It was unbelievably gorgeous. I heard everyone in the living room gasp; it was breathtaking.

"Ophelia, I love it. Girl that's beautiful." I stood up and gave her a hug. "Thank you." I had to remove it from the tripod and hold it in my hands and touch it. "Ophelia, what was going through your mind when you painted this?"

She shrugged. "I don't know. David treats you like a queen, so I decided I would portray you in that manner."

"Thank you." I gave her another hug, and held up the portrait. "This'll go great in our living room, honey."

Jacqué stood up. "I want to dedicate a song to you Dorothy for overcoming the odds, working diligently and patiently. You proved that you could do anything, so I'm gonna sing, *Climb Every Mountain,* for you." She cleared her throat and crossed her hands in front of her like an opera singer and opened her mouth.

"Meee! Meee! Meee!" She belted out in a loud, clear soprano voice, before she burst out laughing, which caused everyone in the room to laugh. Jacqué cleared her throat once more and proceeded to sing. She had a voice out of this world; the notes just flowed from her mouth like a bird soaring in the air. She added a little soul to the *Sound of Music* song, and of course her gracious heart. I was near tears. I looked at my arms and saw the hairs were standing straight up. After she finished I gave her a hug, then David stood up.

"First of all I'd like to say thank you Dorothy for a wonderful first year of marriage; it was blissful, perfect, and need I say more."

I tried not to think about the night of my wedding and the nights during our honeymoon and concentrated on the present.

"No baby, don't say nothing else, just get to the nitty gritty!" Mama shouted.

Everyone laughed. David waited until everyone stopped. "I know my woman has a big heart, and she deserves big things."

Oh big heart, big things, enough of the beating around the bush.

"Now about two years ago I purchased my wife a Mustang, but now she has to move on to better things. So one night I was thinking, hmmm." David folded his arms. "My wife isn't a mustang, she's a Southern University *Jaguar*. As a matter of fact my baby is a Jaguar, all the way down to the car she drives."

I noticed Mama was patting her hands and smiling big. David pulled out a set of car keys from his pocket. I grabbed my heart, Oh God another car! "Dorothy Leonard, in my hand I hold keys to a two door, 1967 Jaguar convertible."

"Honey, no!"

"Yes, baby. You said you've always wanted one."

I held my hand over my heart. "Honey you didn't get me a Jaguar!" David escorted me to the door. I stood on the porch and waited until he pulled the sparkling crystal, blue baby in front of the house. He honked the horn, BEEP! BEEP!

"Go ahead Dorothy!" everyone shouted. With my hand locked on my chest, I just basked in the glow of the occasion.

Chapter 8

"Dot, where do you want me to hang this portrait?" I searched the family room over with my eyes. "Over there next to the fireplace."

Ophelia took the portrait she painted of me and hung it next to the large framed photograph of the family at the wedding. My new family room contained every piece of photograph of almost everything and almost everyone. I even had a baby picture of me lying on my stomach. I was naked and I had this horrible look on my face. I couldn't have been more than a couple of months old. There were old pictures of Papa, even old pictures of great-grand relatives that had faded over the years.

David and I found a home in Houston's upscale MacGregor section. It was a four bedroom, three-and-a-half bath, split-level home with sun roofs and a small swimming pool out back. I loved plants, so of course, I had a small greenhouse built to nurse them.

"Dorothy look."

Ophelia held up an old black and white photo of Mama and Papa, which was taken on the day of their wedding.

"I forgot all about that picture. Let me see it."

"You know there was a lot of love in this picture."

"Tell me about it." Mama wore a straight A-line dress over her small frame, with a smile that reminded me of Katherine's. She had her arms wrapped around Papa's shoulders with her face next to his. Papa, on the other hand, had a mellowed-out relaxed look, which gave me the impression that as long as he had Cleo Montague-LaCroix by his side, everything was all right.

"I think this will look perfect next to my wedding picture," I said, admiring the warmth and affection that was displayed between Mama and Papa. I placed it next to my wedding picture and Katherine's wedding picture.

"I won't unpack too much, there's just no telling when you and David'll move again."

"You got that right," I said.

I heard a knock at the door. "Ophelia will you get that for me dear?"

I stood up to inspect the room; I couldn't get over the number of boxes I had yet to unpack.

"Hello Dorothy!" It was Mrs. Leonard, wearing a loud yellow polka dot two piece set.

"Hello, Mrs. Leonard. You're looking just lovely as always. Where are you going?"

"To do my usual shopping. I stopped by to ask you along, but I see you have your hands full here." She looked around the room and looked at the ceiling. "Exquisite indeed. I just love a home with a sun roof."

"There's also one in the washroom and one in our bedroom as well."

"How lovely. I hope you and David are satisfied with this house. It's eccentric, not bad for a colored neighborhood? As a matter of fact Dorothy, I told Sylvia, your next door neighbor, that you and David were coming and she's preparing a wholesome dinner party just for the occasion."

"How thoughtful."

"Yes, Solomon, and Dave's friendship goes back to medical school, so they're like a part of the family to us."

Mrs. Leonard opened the glass sliding door to the patio and surveyed the backyard with her eyes. "Just fabulous. Though, you have to be careful with my grandchildren around this pool."

I glanced at Ophelia who was perched against the fireplace sipping on a bottle of coke. We both shook our heads. "Dorothy I think it's about time for you and David to start a family, don't you think?"

Mrs. Leonard always found a way to pinch my nerves. "David and I talked about it."

"And?"

"Mrs. Leonard believe me, I want a child, but David just doesn't see it happening right now."

She waved her hand. "David isn't getting any younger. In three years he'll be thirty, I wonder what's the problem?"

"If you get a chance to talk to David, ask him."

She shut the doors. "Believe me, I will." Mrs. Leonard eyed the family room once more. "This room would look a lot better if the walls were cream instead of white. I think cream walls look so much better." She glanced at Ophelia. "Ophelia I was told you had an eye for art. What do you think?"

Ophelia shrugged her shoulders. "It doesn't matter to me. White or cream, they both look good."

Mrs. Leonard opened her purse and pulled out a small carrying case. She held up a pair of brown tint, elliptical-shaped glasses (I called them Cat Mama's) and placed them on her nose. "Well I'm off to do my shopping. Dorothy is there anything you'd like? You Ophelia?"

"No thank you, Mrs. Leonard." I walked her to the car. She turned to me. "Now Dorothy you've known me long enough to address me on a first name basis. Now I'd rather you call me Liz."

"Liz? No, how about Miss Liz?"

"Just call me Liz honey. Oh gracious, this humidity is killing my hair and makeup. Dorothy do you know I spent over $50 in two weeks on my hair alone? Which was silly, now that I look back."

"That's why I keep my hair pulled back and balled up." I said.

I noticed small beads of perspiration forming underneath Mrs. Leonard's nose. "Maybe I should start doing my hair like yours, it would at least keep my neck from sweating." She pulled out a handkerchief and dabbed underneath her nose and neck. I opened the door for her as she got inside the car.

"Bye honey, and don't forget about the dinner party scheduled for Sunday night, and honey go mingle with Sylvia, she's just dying to meet you." She pulled out of the driveway in her vintage Jaguar convertible and sped off. The only bad part about living in MacGregor was she lived five blocks over from our house, which gave her reason enough to visit more often than she should without driving her car.

* * *

David was still at the hospital, and had been since nine last evening. He received a phone call that one of his patients was getting a premature visit from the stork. So he left without finishing the candlelight meal I prepared for him. It was now 3:00 a.m. and I was lying in bed alone with the rain beating against my window. That only frustrated me. I tossed and turned, I even fantasized, though they were crazy fantasies-where David and I run outside naked and make love with the rain beating against our bodies. I opened my eyes and saw the empty place where David's body should've been. Seeing the empty pillow reminded me of the empty feeling I had had that New Year's Eve night. It was our first anniversary. Earlier in the day, David got a call from the maternity ward at Jefferson Davis. I got in my car and followed him because there was no way I was going to spend our first anniversary apart. So I sat in the lobby of the hospital, and waited on my man. I bugged every nurse that passed, and sent countless messages, hoping they would somehow reach him. I read every magazine on the rack and talked with everyone who waited, until he sent me roses through an orderly. There was a card attached, scribbled in someone else's handwriting that said, *Dorothy, I'm in the middle of a rotation, uncertain as to how long it will last. Hey Dorothy I'm sorry we didn't get the chance to celebrate our anniversary as we would have liked, I love you and I'll make it up to you soon. DAVID.* I took the half dozen roses, went into the bathroom and cried quietly to myself. When I got home, I called Aunt Ruby Jewel and Mama just so happened to answer the phone. I told Mama about it and she told me to shut up.

"Shut the hellup! You better be glad David is working. While most folks on New Year's Eve are partying and spending their money, your man is working hard and making his. So shut up crying!"

Since David bought her the house, she's become his biggest cheerleader, even more so than me. Sometimes I wondered if he paid her to cheer like he paid for everything else.

I turned on the lamplight, and got out of bed to slip on my robe. As I walked near the window, a flash of lightning lit the sky so brightly, I saw my reflection against the wall. I opened the door and walked down the hall to Ophelia's room. Her door was open so I peeked in, she was sound asleep. I was amazed at how some people slept through the worst of bad weather. I closed her door and walked into the kitchen to open the refrigerator. The first thing I saw was last night's candlelight dinner staring up at me, I had lost my desire to finish it after David left. I didn't want cold salmon, so I poured a glass of water, closed the refrigerator door, and sat down at the table. It was 3:45 a.m. and the smell of rain made me frustrated.

* * *

David's brother, Marcus, stopped by early the next day to help with the yard. I couldn't get over that at his age, he had grown tall and muscular. When he arrived, Ophelia and I were sitting at the table eating breakfast.

"Good morning Marcus, how is your mother and father?"

Marcus was eyeing Ophelia. "They're okay," he said in a low tenor voice. I noticed a small mustache outlined his top lip. Ophelia continued to eat and carry on as though he weren't there.

"Have a seat," I said.

He shook his head. "No thanks, I'm gonna try and get started."

Ophelia wiped the corners of her mouth and cleared her throat.

"Oh Ophelia, I'm sorry. This is David's brother Marcus. You met Marcus haven't you?"

Ophelia couldn't remember.

"Marcus, weren't you at the wedding?"

"Yes."

"Dorothy, I didn't know David had a brother."

"Ophelia, you're kidding."

Ophelia rolled her eyes. "I'm serious; I thought David was an only child."

The telephone rang. I picked it up only to discover the voice on the other end was David's.

"Dorothy, I'm on my way home; I just decided I'd give you a call to let you know before I left." I could tell David was exhausted. His voice was soft and shallow and I could barely hear it.

"You sure you can make it without falling asleep at the wheel?"

"I'm positive. Hey Dorothy will you have some coffee brewing when I get there?"

"Yes baby, and what else?"

"And a half dozen golden brown pancakes with melted butter, swimming in a lake of maple syrup?" I heard him yawn.

"I will honey. Are you sure you can make it?"

"Yes."

"Are you positive?"

"Yes, now stop worrying and start cooking."

"I love you David."

He sighed, "Yeah me too," And hung up immediately.

"Poor thing. He's been up since seven yesterday morning. I don't see how he does it?" I grabbed a grill and a mixing bowl.

"It's a good thing today is Saturday; just imagine if it was Monday."

"He's done it before."

"That could not be me," Marcus said. "You know a man's got to know his limitations when it comes to work." Marcus cut his eyes at Ophelia. She eyed me. "Did you hear this Dorothy?"

"I sure did."

Ophelia rolled her big brown eyes to the whites, and smiled bashfully. I couldn't believe this fifteen year-old boy had my twenty year-old sister blushing.

"Marcus what do you mean?" Ophelia inquired. Marcus licked his lips, a gesture he acquired from David.

"Excuse me?" Ophelia still wanted to know.

"Ophelia leave the boy alone; he needs to get started on the yard before it gets too hot."

"No, unhh, unhh. I want to know what Marcus is trying to say." She moved away from the table, folded her arms, and flashed her eyes at Marcus. Marcus glanced at his watch. "Oh my, how the time flies; I was suppose to start on the yard about twenty minutes ago."

"We'll have to finish this talk Marcus."

Marcus nodded and stared at her as he walked towards the door; he opened it and not saying a word he laughed and went outside.

"Ophelia, you got that young boy's mind in a whirlwind. I think he likes you."

Ophelia bit into a peeled orange. "You noticed too, huh?"

"I sure did, that among other things."

Ophelia chewed slowly and pondered. "What's his occupation?"

"What occupation? Ophelia the boy is only fifteen."

She spit chunks of orange all over the table.

*　　　*　　　*

David and I were in the family room, laid back against the chaise lounge, listening to Coltrane's *Love Supreme* and feeling his music. Since the incident with the Miles Davis concert, David had trashed all of Davis's albums and now preferred the likes of John Coltrane, Ramsey Lewis, and Thelonious Monk. As I relaxed inside the folds of David's arms, my mind wandered aimlessly. One minute I visualized myself back in St. Thomas on the honeymoon, a minute later, it was on David and the people at the hospital.

"Honey, when do you complete your residency?"

"In six months."

"I know you'll be so happy."

"Most definitely. I'll get the practice off and going."

"If you need a receptionist, I'll be more than happy to answer the phones for you."

"No that's not necessary. I don't want you working outside the house."

"What do you mean?" I raised up to get a better glimpse of David. "What do you mean you don't want me working outside the house?"

"As long as I'm taking care of you, you don't have a thing to worry about."

"You don't have to pay me anything; I'll be more than willing to work for nothing."

"You're not listening to me, Dorothy." David placed his finger over my lips, "Stay here, take care of the house, watch a few soap operas, pay a few bills, but that's it. I don't want you to work. My mother never worked, her mother never worked and my father's mother never worked."

"So you want me to sit at the house all day and watch t.v.?"

"You better be thankful you have a man like me to take care of you. I know a lot of women who would love to trade places with you Dorothy!" David squeezed his eyes shut. "Damn this headache is driving me up the wall," he said before resting his head on the ball of my left shoulder.

"Would you massage my temples?" he asked.

I nodded my head, but inside I was screaming. I got tired of hearing how fortunate I was, if I was so fortunate why did I feel so worthless?

I proceeded to massage his temples, trying hard not to bury my nails into his skull.

David sighed deeply. "It feels great. Can you massage my back and shoulders too?"

The nerve of him, I thought, but I didn't act on it. I wasn't in the confrontational mood tonight, so I played the actress role.

"I'll do anything you want me to honey," I heard myself say out loud. I was beginning to wonder if David wanted a servant instead of a wife.

Later that evening, David lit every candle in the bedroom while I poured a bottle of Merlot into our glasses. I didn't want to spoil the mood by bringing up the conversation, but it ached my mind to think that David really wanted me to be a "housewife." I just didn't see it happening. That June Cleaver Jazz played out in the 1950's. I watched as David unplugged the phone and picked up the glasses. He gave me a glass and proposed a toast.

"To us, to this night, and to many more nights like this," he said before we clicked glasses and sipped carefully and daintily. The response from the Merlot was unbelievable. David put his glass on the nearby night stand. In a sexy and seductive way he removed his robe and stretched out across the bed. My eyes traveled from the crown of his natural, to the tautness of his honey-colored pectorals, down to the ripples of his stomach, and even further down to the veins that held up his erect penis. I opened a bottle of Johnson's baby oil and rubbed my palms until I generated heat. I applied the oil on David's horizontal body, starting first with his shoulders. I had so much I wanted to talk about. I really wasn't feeling sexual, but I played the actress role, you know, anything to keep him happy. My oily hands traveled down to his chest. I was so glad he had a smooth chest. My hands went down a little further to his abdomen. David had a beautiful brown abdomen. I moved my hands in a circular motion. I heard a light moan escape from David's lips. Then in one motion, he grabbed my body and laid me on my back. I found myself staring at the flame from the candlelight in David's sexy brown eyes. David came closer and kissed my lips.

"Dorothy," he whispered against them.

"Yes." I responded.

"Be gentle with me," he said. We both laughed and held each other in a tight embrace.

Later that night I was awakened to the sound of laughter and screaming. I thought I heard it coming from the neighbors next door, but then I realized they lived quite a distance apart from us, so it couldn't have been them. I turned and saw David beside me breathing deeply and sleeping like a baby. I tried not to think about it and tried to go to sleep. Then I heard it again, and it sounded like it was inside. I immediately shook David.

"Honey wake up." I flipped on the lamp switch. The glare from the light blinded him.

"What?" He squinted.

"David listen."

"Listen to what?" He wiped his eyes.

"Shhh."

We listened for it and I heard it again. David glanced at me and without saying a word we both got out of bed, slipped on our robes and went down the hall. David knocked on Ophelia's door.

"Ophelia." There was no answer. He knocked again. "Ophelia."

I opened the door and walked in only to find she wasn't there.

"You sure you heard something?"

There was another crying outburst. "See did you hear it?"

We listened intently and sure enough we both heard it. It sounded like Ophelia's voice and it was coming from the family room.

"What the hell is going on?" I asked.

"There's only one way to find out."

I followed David into the family room, flipped on the lights and lying on the floor were Marcus and Ophelia butt naked.

"Oh my God I don't believe this!"

Ophelia quickly grabbed her night robe and wrapped herself up in it. Marcus grabbed some pillows and placed them over himself.

"Excuse me I'm going to the bathroom."

David stopped Marcus before he passed by. "Hold on there. After you put your clothes on I want to have a few words with you." Marcus disappeared with the pillows shielding himself. "And pronto Marcus. I haven't got all night." David glanced at me, I could tell he wanted to laugh so bad. "What?" he asked.

"You think this is cute, don't you?"

"No, I don't. I think it's time my brother and I had a serious discussion on this matter." He turned and disappeared down the hall. I glanced at Ophelia, unable to grasp a definition of how I felt about her situation. To tell you the truth I was at a loss of words.

"Dorothy, whatever you do, don't tell anyone about this."

"Child please, I'm embarrassed for you. You must've been hard up for some?"

Ophelia held up her hand in mere protest. "Save it Dot; I don't want to hear about it."

I tied my robe and sat on the sofa across from her. Over and over in my head, I kept getting flashbacks of the expression on their faces when I switched on that light.

"Go ahead," she said nodding her head. "Laugh."

"Ophelia, all the men in Houston, and you want to fool around with a fifteen year-old."

"What's age got to do with it?"

"Ophelia that's a boy; you are an adult."

"Marcus is not a boy."

"You are sick," I said imagining what she was thinking.

"So what?" She buried her face in her hands. "I don't want to talk about it, okay?"

I yawned, "Okay I won't talk about it." We sat there in silence for a brief moment.

"Damn. I can't sleep, I'm tossing and turning in bed, I hear you screaming and I immediately assume the worst."

"So? I heard you and David in the room earlier, so don't blame all the noise on us."

"Ophelia this is my house. I will scream as loud as I please. Hell, I feel like screaming right now."

Ophelia waved her hand.

"Anyway, I don't have much else to say." I found myself laughing again. "You old child molester."

Ophelia chuckled. "Dorothy, you can call me what you want, but I can tell you this, I wasn't disappointed."

"You are sick."

Ophelia crossed her legs and twisted her fingers into her hair. "Marcus is blessed at his age; I never thought a fifteen year-old could feel so good."

"Stop it please! Ophelia what else can that boy do for you?"

"Something I bet most twenty year-olds can't."

"And that is?"

"Have me speaking in tongue," she said nonchalantly, "and crawling the goddamn walls." I shook my head and stood up. "I heard enough. Good night, Ophelia."

She sighed and untwisted her fingers from her hair. "Don't tell anyone about this."

"About what?" I pretended I forgot about the situation. "Come on, girl."

She smiled and examined her protruding butt in the mirror. "Marcus said I had the kind of ass to ride on."

"Ophelia, good night!"

When David got in bed he was still amused from the incident. "Did you talk to Ophelia?"

"Yes I did, honey, I don't know how I feel about it anymore. Just like you, I'm trying to find some humor in it; it's pretty tough though." David clasped his hands behind his head and stared at the ceiling. "I had a man to man talk with Marcus."

"You tell him about the consequences of being caught in the rain without a rain coat?"

"I sure did."

"I wonder what made her think about—" I hesitated. "She had to have been the one to talk him into it."

"Marcus told me it started when they were outside by the pool. Ophelia kept flirting with him and telling him how good he looked, you know the older, more experienced woman, and the younger, naive boy routine?"

I stared speechless at him. "Well, you wouldn't know, but anyway to make a long story short, Marcus said she asked him to put some lotion on her, she asked him to give her a massage, she asked him to stay over for a movie and some popcorn, bla bla bla. After the movie they start to kiss she asked him how many times had he done it, he told her about ten, and she asked him if she could be number eleven, bla bla bla. They kiss once more, they screw for about five minutes, we catch them and that's pretty much the story."

I sighed, "For some reason I wish I were a fly on the wall of that girl's mind. Just imagine what that would be like."

"Dark, gloomy, perhaps empty, maybe?"

"There's no maybe to it; anyway, finish telling me about you and Marcus?"

"I gave him the lecture and I told him that if he screws up and ends up getting someone pregnant, I'm giving him the abortion. I'm not having Mom and Dad raise his kids while he runs around screwing every piece of poontane in sight."

"You see, that's why these young boy's minds are so corrupt; it's because of women like Ophelia who let their curiosity run out to left field."

"And you know what they say, 'Curiosity killed the cat.'"

"Literally, in Ophelia's case."

David chuckled and pulled my body next to his warm flesh. "Let's not think about that, instead, think about this good loving I'm going to give you." I felt his penis hardening against my leg. "Stop it honey," I said half laughing and half asleep. He pulled the covers over our heads and we wrestled with each other until I went down for the count. I simply gave in.

* * *

I finally met my next door neighbors, the Cartwrights and the Muhammads. Sylvia and Dr. Muhammad dined us all in the tradition of their native Nigerian customs. Their dining area was rich with authentic Nigerian regalia. I was simply amazed. Dr. Muhammad served us red snapper in a spicy red sauce, rice, spinach with jumbo shrimp, and crushed peanuts.

"How do you like?" Sylvia asked.

I wasn't too fond of the food, but I told her it was delicious. She asked everyone in the room if they liked it. I noticed Doc Sr. drank a lot of water; that spinach was a little on the spicy side. Dr. Muhammad dipped his hands into a gold goblet and wiped them on a white towel. "For t'e next dish we make sure t'at t'e hands are clean because we don't use any utensils, we use our fingers."

Sylvia emerged from the kitchen area carrying a huge bowl in her hands. She sat it next to Dr. Muhammad and herself. Dr. Muhammad dipped his fingers into a bowl and held up a thick rice-like substance in his hand so everyone in the room could see it.

"Dr. Muhammad what do you call that?" I asked as I proceeded to wipe the corners of my mouth.

"Fufu," he replied in his heavy accent.

I glanced at Mr. and Mrs. Cartwright. The expression on their faces was perplexed. Sylvia dipped her fingers into the bowl and pulled out a small piece, she passed the bowl to Ophelia. Ophelia dipped her fingers into it before she passed it on to me. I reached into the bowl and fingered it. The dish felt lukewarm and sticky, but I grabbed a piece and passed it on to David.

"Sylvia how long does it take to prepare a dish like this?" inquired Mrs. Leonard before she dipped her dainty little fingers into the bowl. It's some wonder she wasn't complaining about eating with fingers, since she was suppose to be an etiquette fanatic, but she managed to grasp the mush in her hands and study it carefully.

After the dish made a full circle back to Dr. Muhammad, he took the dish and proceeded to eat it. We all did the same. I sat there wishing I had the bowl to me so I could throw this stuff into it. I sniffed it; it didn't remind me of anything. I slowly brushed it against my lips and ate it in a finicky manner.

"Hmmm, this is delicious," I said after tasting it again.

"Here, help yourself to another helping."

"No thank you," I said quickly. "I don't want to make a pig out of myself."

"Oh no go right ahead, eat! It's good for you!"

I hesitated before I took another finger full and stuffed it in my mouth.

"Hmmm," Doc Sr. said. "It's delectable."

Mrs. Leonard frowned and wiped the corner of her husband's mouth with a napkin. "Don't talk with food in your mouth honey," She whispered.

Afterwards, Sylvia showed me almost every room in her elaborate home, which was furnished with some of the most exotic pieces this side of Houston. Each room in her home was decorated with African art and hand-carved furniture. When she showed me her bathroom, I fell in love with the gold-plated faucets, and the marbled tub that contained a mosaic of a Nigerian woman's face. Sylvia's bedroom was also decorated in her native Nigerian, with a mahogany-colored bed and vanity set.

"I'm impressed with your home Sylvia," I said.

"My interior decorator suggest that each room in t'e house have it's own unique quality."

She reached into her mahogany jewelry chess and pulled out a pair of diamond earrings.

"T'ese are for you."

"No thank you Sylvia, I can't take these."

"You can have dem; when I go back, I will bring you more t'ings!"

Mrs. Leonard showed me a diamond ring on her left pinkie. "Sylvia was kind and generous to give me this." I admired the way it lustered in the light.

Mrs. Cartwright was across the room admiring a gold fixture around a small lamp. "Will and I went to Nigeria about nine years ago and I purchased this." She pointed to the small bracelet on her arm. Sylvia admired her bracelet. "Pretty," she remarked in her accent. Mrs. Leonard examined it too. "When was the last time you cleaned it?" she asked.

"I don't know, but I've kept it in great condition."

"Ummm hmmm."

That night, I sat in Sylvia's family room and listened to her, Mrs. Leonard, and Mrs. Cartwright talk about their husbands and their children. I was too young for this. I didn't want to spend day after day sitting at home waiting on my husband. Hell, I wanted to get out and put my college degree to good use. I didn't care what David said, I was getting out.

CHAPTER 9

"Dorothy, stop crying; it's going to be all right," Katherine said as she held my hand. "When I was pregnant with Richard, I admit I was frightened. I didn't know exactly what to expect. But now as I look back, I realize I hadn't anything to be afraid of."

I felt ten pounds heavier than usual and I wasn't even showing.

"When did you find out?"

"Today."

"Does David know?"

I blew my nose. "No, he doesn't."

"He's going to be so happy when he finds out Dorothy. I know when I told Ricky we were going to have a baby, he didn't stop until he told the whole neighborhood."

I blew my nose again and pondered my situation, all I could think about were long needles, numerous examinations, and labor. What if I didn't make it through labor or what if my baby didn't make it through? In the past David and I would talk about preparations for childbirth and the changes which the body undergoes. I'd have nerve racking chills and I'd lock my legs tight when he graphically explained the period during labor like contractions and dilation. He told me it was a miracle for a woman to survive countless hours of excruciating pain. While holding my sweaty hands, David also assured me that he didn't want to discourage me from having children. He marveled all the time and said it was the most beautiful and mystical experience in the world, but the pain is a fact of life and sometimes, well, most of the time it can be unbearable. He said it's like taking a sharp knife and stabbing yourself with quick, piercing, deep, jabs. He told me a story of a woman who was in labor and who wasn't fully dilated. Well she tried to push down in the same manner she would if she were constipated, and ripped her cervix. Oh God, David had some stories, which I thought were very horrible and too candid to hear. Well, here I am six weeks pregnant. I pictured myself with sagging breasts, varicose veins, and ugly stretch marks. When Katherine was pregnant, I remembered she had a lot of fluid in her body which caused her to have a swollen face, swollen feet, swollen arms and a huge nose.

"I would love to stick around and see the look on David's face when you tell him."

"Katherine I think he knows I'm pregnant, he's just not saying anything about it."

"Dot, stop kidding yourself; you're just saying that because you're afraid to tell him."

"No, I'm not," I said abruptly. "A doctor should know the obvious signs, like morning sickness or swelling."

"Maybe he's been too busy to notice."

"I don't know."

Katherine grabbed my hand. "Then tell him, what are you waiting on?"

I rubbed my stomach, I was unable to grasp reality. I still couldn't get over the idea of having another individual growing inside of me.

"I love my Richard so much," Katherine said in her goo-goo-ga-ga-voice, "Dorothy once you have this baby, your whole world will start to revolve around him. Whenever you go out, say shopping for instance, that child will always be in the back of your mind." She grinned to herself. "Dot, just the other day Ricky and I went to town to buy groceries and we passed by this cute little baby shop. Dorothy, I couldn't resist the temptation of going inside and buying my baby something."

"So you ended up buying him some cute outfits."

"I damn near bought the whole store."

I tapped her arm. "Get outta here."

David entered the room with a colorful glow on his handsome face. I sighed and silently thanked God that he was in a good mood.

"Katherine, it's good to see you. How have you been? Where's Ricky and the baby?"

"I've been enjoying these first two months of motherhood. It's a new task for me, but I'm handling it well. Ricky and the baby are upstairs asleep."

"The ride'll do it to you every time."

"Tell me about it."

David kissed me on the forehead. "Hello honey, I have something to tell you."

"That's great because I have something to tell you also."

"Oh yeah?"

"Oh yeah," I said softly.

He sat down in the recliner and gave me his undivided attention, "I'd rather hear your news first."

"No honey, you go ahead," I said glancing at Katherine, who sat there mild-mannered, yet holding back a smile. David eyed us suspiciously. "What's going on; why are you two smiling like that?"

"Honey, go ahead with your news." Katherine said. "It's okay for me to hear too, right?"

"I don't see why not Katherine."

"Well, go on honey."

"Dorothy and Katherine, my publisher called me at the office and informed me that my co-authorized book just sold 250,000 copies; and to that, he offered me another deal worth $75,000 for the upcoming book."

Katherine and I both screamed before we reached out and embraced David.

"Baby the earnings from the last book were insurmountable, and they're growing."

He pranced around the room. "Just think 500,000 more copies and it's a bestseller."

He picked up the phone.

"David, who are you calling?"

He continued to dial. "I'm calling my agent. Hello, Ted?" He disappeared into the kitchen. "This is Dave, how are you?"

Katherine and I had these puzzled looks on our faces. "Katherine he didn't give me a chance to share my news."

She rubbed my knee. "Don't worry he will; he's just so happy and excited."

"I know, Katherine; I am so happy for him. David is doing so well. Just the other day, a writer from *Ebony* called and asked if he could arrange an interview with David."

"Dorothy, that's wonderful."

"Isn't it wonderful?"

"Imagine getting interviewed by *Ebony* magazine. That's all right!"

David entered the room once more, smiling as big as ever.

"All right!" he shouted as he pranced to the bar to grab three glasses and a bottle of champagne. He popped the top and filled each glass. Katherine slapped my hand. "Tell him," she whispered. David did a little dance and gave Katherine her glass. I declined my glass.

"Come on baby, this is a time for celebration. This has got to be the most celebrated day of my life thus far."

Katherine sipped from her glass. "Hmmm this is wonderful."

David sipped his champagne. "1965, here." He poured more into her glass until it bubbled over with foam.

"Thank you, David."

"My pleasure. Drink up, Dorothy."

"I can't right now."

"Why not?"

"It's not good for the baby."

"What baby?"

"Our baby." I paused. "David I'm pregnant."

David paused and stood there for a moment with the bottle in one hand and glass in the other. I noticed he swallowed so hard, he nearly strangled himself.

"You w-what? Baby, you're kidding."

I shook my head, "No David, I'm not kidding."

He put the bottle and glass on top of the table and kneeled in front of me. Taking my hands into his, he smiled. "You sure you're not pulling my leg?"

"I'm positive David; I wouldn't lie about this."

He glanced at Katherine. "I take it you knew about this already?"

"Yes." She took my hand. "And I'm so excited because I'm gonna be an aunty."

"So that explains why the both of you were grinning like the joker. Honey how far along are you?"

"Six weeks. I went to see Dr. Clarke for a check-up and she told me."

He rubbed my stomach with the back of his hand. "How do you feel?"

"I feel great right now."

"Damn. I'm gonna be a daddy. Hotdamn!" he shouted before he gave me a kiss.

"Katherine this is too good to be true."

Katherine smiled approvingly.

"Just think, I'm going to be a father." He gazed starry-eyed at the ceiling. "Hotdamn, I need a cigar to go with this champagne."

He took the glass and drank it until it was at a forty-five degree angle. "Hhhhhhh."

I often found myself watching Katherine and seeing how she nurtured her baby. She held him and talked so softly and gently to him. Ever so often she would hold him high above her head and bounce him up and down until he awarded her with a smile. When Richard cried she held him against her cheek and shushed until he stopped. I held Richard and I imagined myself holding my own baby. A girl, maybe? A boy perhaps? It really didn't matter.

"Dorothy, tell me what's on your mind?" Katherine asked, her dark eyes sparkling. I held Richard in my arms and stared at her reflection in the mirror. "I just can't wait to see how my own baby would look, you know?"

"Yeah I know. When I was pregnant, I often wandered the same thing."

"The joys of motherhood." I held him so close I could smell his soft delicate scent.

"You'll love being a mommy, Dorothy."

"I know I will."

"I can't imagine how some people abandon their children. Children are God's precious little gifts to us." Katherine's voice was filled with compassion. To tell the truth, I think the joys of motherhood overflowed with abundance in Katherine. "I love being a mother those late night feedings, the caring, and the nurturing. Dorothy, I wouldn't trade it for anything in the world."

"I know Katherine."

"That child you're carrying is you. You are the only someone that child depends on."

I kissed Richard's head and gave him back to Katherine. She cooed and kissed him before she nursed him off to sleep. While she nursed Richard, I examined my own breasts, these size 34 c-cups weren't very huge and sore, but that'll change very soon. When Mother Nature kicks in, I hear she's on you constantly up to the very moment of delivery, and sometimes afterward.

Ms. Liz telephoned to inform me about her special dinner party for this evening. She even took it upon herself to spend half her Sunday preparing it.

"Dorothy bring your favorite dish."

"I would, but not everyone likes codfish cakes primavera."

"Codfish cakes primavera? That sounds like a great dish honey. What makes you think no one will like it?"

"It stinks up your house, for Christ's sake."

"Oh that's no excuse; fried chicken stinks up your house! Cabbage stinks!"

"Okay Ms. Liz, I see your point."

"Good, now are you going to church this morning?"

"Yes, of course. You know I can't miss Reverend Long's sweet potato and black-eyed pea sermon."

"Honey, if you see Ms. Cartwright will you please do me a favor and tell her to bring bake chicken instead. The last time I gave a dinner party, she brought a roast and it nearly cracked my jawbone."

I grinned to myself as I got a mental picture of Ms. Liz chewing like a horse and swallowing with the utmost difficulty.

"Is there anything else you'd like me to bring?"

"No thank you, Dave's taking care of everything."

"What happened to Rona, your housekeeper?"

"Rona's under the weather, so I sent her home. She sure picked a good time to get ill."

David walked into the kitchen and wrapped his arms around my waist. "Good morning," he whispered in my ear.

"Good morning honey," I whispered back.

"Who are you talking to Dorothy?" Ms. Liz wanted to know.

"I was talking to your son; he just woke up."

David waved his arms and shook his head, he didn't want to speak to his mother.

"May I speak to my son, please?"

I gave David the phone. "Your mother said, 'please.'"

He grimaced and held it in his hand before he placed it against his ear. "Hello Mama?" He leaned against the island. "Good morning. How are you? How's Dad and Marcus? Mama..."

I could hear her voice jolting away like a high speed tape on the other end. "Mama would you listen for a second?"

Poor David. He couldn't utter a single word. The blunt expression on his face said more than he. I poured myself a glass of apple juice and sat at the table to study his expression.

Then Ricky walked in. "Good morning, Dorothy."

"Good morning Ricky. Are you going to church with us?"

"With who? You and Katherine?" He poured himself a cup of coffee.

"Well, you know David's going too."

We both glanced at David who was gesturing away. "Mama, how many times do I have to tell you. You look fine; stop worrying about what other people say. You know Mama you can definitely benefit from one of those. I hear they're especially good for women over forty-five." David glanced at us and shook his head in disbelief. "I suggest you talk to Dad; get his opinion. Me, I think it's a great idea; it helps you maintain a youthful appearance. Yes Mama. Great, don't catch an ulcer. See you this evening. Love you too. Bye, Mama."

After he hung up, he just stared at the phone and chuckled to himself.

"My God."

"What's wrong? Is Ms. Liz thinking about trying one of those health and spa centers again?" I asked.

David poured a cup of coffee. "Yes. I'm tired of hearing about it."

Ricky chuckled and greeted him, "Good morning."

"Ricky there's nothing worst than hearing someone complain about getting old and wrinkled. It seems I have to hear this every day now."

"It's a stage we all have to go through someday. Me personally, I got about another fifty years or so to think about it," Ricky said.

David looked at me. "Honey, I sure hope you don't act like that when you get fifty-five."

"Don't hold your breath. David, your mother told me it's no fun to scream at the sight of wrinkles."

"She has to face the fact that at her age that's normal. A beautiful face can stop anything but time," David said.

"Amen." Ricky replied.

"Besides, it's her face and her wrinkles."

Katherine appeared in the doorway with Richard in her arms. "What is all this talk I hear about wrinkles, and ugly faces?"

She kissed and greeted us all. I took Richard out of her arms and held him in mine. Richard was wide awake and very alert. In fact, he was so alert, he immediately realized I wasn't his mother and his dark ebony eyes began to wander.

"I just got off the phone with my mother, and she was running off at the mouth, as usual, about her skin and old age. She was telling me that she wanted to go to a health and spa center where they pamper you with mud facials and body massages."

"You know I always wanted to go to those places." Katherine nudge Ricky on the shoulder.

"Honey, why pay a hundred dollars for three hours of pampering when you can get pampered all night for nothing."

"Oh Ricky." She slapped him playfully across the shoulders. "The last time that happened, I ended up with your son here."

Ricky chuckled. "It was worth it."

He and David commenced to chuckling again.

* * *

Ms. Liz opened the door and immediately looked at me strangely.

"What's wrong?" I asked.

She eyed me from head to toe. "Dorothy, you look so-so different."

"Different in what way?" I asked.

David put his arm around me. "Now why would you say that mother?"

She blinked her long eye lashes and opened the door wide enough for us to come in. "I can't seem to put my finger on it, but I've known Dorothy long enough to sense even the slightest change in her."

As we walked to the lavishly decorated dining area, Ms. Liz kept naming reasons for my "change" in appearance.

"Dorothy, I think I know. You've gained weight."

"No, mother. Now will you stop worrying." David winked at me and carried the codfish cakes primavera into the kitchen.

"Ms. Liz, you've outdone yourself this time," I said admiring the set up.

She stared silently at me. "Oh yes, you like?"

"I love it."

"Thank you, I love it too." She proceeded to stare at me.

Doc Sr. appeared, dressed in a smoker's jacket with an ascot necktie.

"Hello," he said in a loud, clear, resonant voice. "Good to see you. Glad you could make it."

"I wouldn't have missed it." I gave him a hug and a kiss.

He stood back and examined me. "There's something different about you," he said.

"You know Dave, I said the exact same thing." I did my runway model turn for them and watched as they tried to figure it out.

"Dave, I say it's the outfit."

He smiled and said softly, "I've been in this field too long. I say you're expecting."

Ms. Liz gasped, and flung her glittering hand of diamonds to her chest. I blushed and nodded my head. "Father knows best."

"Am I right?"

"Yes, Daddy."

"Hotdog!" he shouted.

Ms. Liz couldn't close her mouth, she stood there wide-eyed with her arms open. "Dorothy," she cried and the three of us embraced. I heard David walk in asking what was going on.

"My baby!" Ms. Liz cried. "Come give your mother a hug."

David smiled. "Dorothy told you."

"Yes, son; she told us."

"Dorothy, I can't believe you told Mama that we forgot to tell Ms. Cartwright not to bring her roast."

Ms. Liz dabbed at her eyes with a napkin. "Stop kidding son and give me a congratulatory hug."

While the four of us stood in the dining room embracing, the doorbell rang.

"I'll get that," said Doc Sr.

Ms. Liz's café au lé complexion was bright crimson and I noticed chill bumps were forming on her forearm. She blushed, grabbed my hands, and squeezed them tightly.

"Honey, I can't believe it's happening, me a grandmother." She glanced at David. He knew right there and then she wanted another hug, so he gave her one.

Dr. and Mrs. Muhammad entered with their dish. "Hello and congratulations you two." Mrs. Muhammad squeezed me and ran her hand over my stomach.

"I take it you all received the good news?"

"Yes, we did. Dave told us and t'ats going to be one lucky child," said Dr. Muhammad.

"Not to mention lovely," Sylvia added.

Doc Sr. grabbed Dr. Muhammad and David. "This news calls for a celebration. Would you gentlemen follow me into the family room; we'll leave our three lovely ladies here in the dining area."

"Dave honey, don't forget dinner in fifteen minutes."

Doc Sr. nodded and disappeared into the living room, laughing and celebrating the news.

"You know, when the baby gets here, he's going to be spoiled rotten I can see it happening."

"Don't say spoil. I dislike the sound of the word," Ms. Liz said. "Fortunate would suffice; wouldn't you think Sylvia?"

"Fortunate, yes."

Here we go again with that fortunate business, I thought.

The doorbell rang again.

"I bet that's Missy and Will Cartwright. Excuse me ladies."

"So Mrs. Muhammad, what did you bring delicious for us to eat?" Before I realized it I had opened the top to her dish.

"I made something a little more closer to home."

I smelled butter, ginger, and the tantalizing smell of cinnamon. "Hmmm these yams look and smell so wonderful. You mind if I try one before hand?"

"No, no." She placed the dish on a nearby table. "Help yourself."

"Mrs. Muhammad, you'll have to excuse me," I said between each smack. "Me and the little one haven't eaten a thing since breakfast."

"No, go right ahead."

As I stuffed my face I heard Mrs. Cartwright and Ms. Liz enter.

"Dorothy."

Ms. Liz stood beside me with her hands on her hips. "Dorothy you better put some breaks on your mouth." She playfully slapped my hands. "Stop it right this minute."

"Honey, don't listen to her; you just go right ahead." Mrs. Cartwright embraced me. "Congratulations, baby."

"Thank you, Mrs. Cartwright."

During dinner Doc Sr. proposed a toast. "It has to be the most beautiful thing in the world. I've seen hundreds of them, tiny, precious little babies.

Soon we'll have a precious little baby of our own to kiss, cuddle, and nurture. I'm so happy for our son and our beautiful daughter-in-law, and to that I propose a toast." He held up his glass. "To grandparenthood."

"To grandparenthood," Ms. Liz said underneath her breath, as though she couldn't believe she would finally achieve the status.

"You know there's a lot of territory that comes with grandparenthood," Mrs. Cartwright said.

"We can attest to that. Our grandchild, Nichole has rocket fuel in her blood. She's always full of vigor and energy. When we go to the park, you can rest assured she's going to spend all evening there," Mr. Cartwright said.

"You have to admit it ti's well worth it to romp around t' park all day wit' her," Dr. Muhammad said.

"Oh yes, it gives us quite an adrenaline rush," Mr. Cartwright replied between chuckles.

My mind wandered into a kaleidoscope of imaginations. First I pictured David and myself lying on a pallet in MacGregor Park with our child laughing and tumbling in the grass. I laughed to myself when I pictured Doc Sr. and Ms. Liz romping and playing in the park. Those two wouldn't last a good thirty minutes before they would be panting breathlessly at the first bead of perspiration.

* * *

When David stood in the doorway, he found me sprawled across the bathroom floor in a pool of water.

"Baby, don't tell me your water broke?"

The only thing I could do was nod my head, open my mouth, and pray to God to give me strength to endure several more hours without shitting all over everything.

"Baby just stay calm."

A twinge struck me and at that moment, for the strangest reason, it made me wish I could fly. David grabbed a handful of towels and wrapped them around me. I could see it in his eyes, he was wondering how in the hell was he going to carry me to the car. His eyes were intense though the rest of him remained composed underneath a sea of salty sweat.

"Honey do you think you can move?"

I couldn't talk let along move. My left leg caught a cramp and it began to tighten up. I screamed and grabbed the nearest thing-David's shirt collar.

"Dorothy just breath deeply. Each time you feel a contraction, I want you to breathe deeply from here." He laid his palm upon my chest. I closed my eyes and braced myself, remembering what I learned in Lamaze. I learned deep chest breathing, shallow chest breathing, panting and expulsion. Just the sound of expulsion made me want to explode into a million pieces.

David managed to pick me up and carry me to the car. Once we got going, he held my hand and coached me each step of the way. "Hang in there baby, you're doing good baby, don't stop breathing baby, don't give up, we're almost there!" He sped through stop signs and traffic lights. "Honey, that's the second traffic light you've run. David, I want to get to the hospital, but I would at least like to get there in one piece."

"Shhh don't talk baby, just breathe."

I kept promising inside my head, that if I could get through this pregnancy, I would never have another baby, no matter how much David wanted one. Once we were on the freeway, I felt a contraction that ripped through the walls of my stomach, causing me to stand up.

"Dorothy, stay calm baby."

"I can't dammit!" Before I realized it, I was squeezing the blood out of his thigh. Luckily for David, we were turning up the entrance to St. Joseph's Hospital. From there on out I remained in a horizontal position, gazing "teary-eyed" at the bright fluorescent lights, hearing David's authoritative voice, his reassuring voice, telling the receptionist that his wife was in labor. He grabbed my hand and held it as the doctors rushed me down the corridor. When I looked into his eyes, he kept saying to me, "Hold on baby, you're doing wonderful, just hang in there."

"Dr. Leonard how far apart are her contractions?" I heard Dr. Clarke's voice.

"They're five minutes apart."

Moments later our journey came to a standstill. I opened my eyes and saw David standing just to my right holding my hand. He was wearing surgical gloves and his mouth was covered with a surgical mask. To the left and front of me were Dr. Clarke and another doctor. Another contraction hit. God I wanted to die, it was as if someone were stabbing unmercifully at my stomach and wouldn't be satisfied until my intestines were lying all over the floor.

I heard Dr. Clarke mention that the baby was in a transverse position and that a caesarian delivery would have to take place.

"Oh my God." I cried.

I heard David shushing me and I felt him rub my forehead, "you are going to be okay baby."

Dr. Clarke covered my mouth with an anesthetic cone. Afterwards, I was talking and laughing out of the side of my neck. Then slowly the room began to fade to black.

When I regained conscious, I was in a different room surrounded with flowers and blue balloons that said, *congratulations, it's a boy*. I looked at my stomach and saw that the swelling had gone down, but a sharp, needle-like pain remained.

I heard the latch to the door click and it opened. From a side view I saw a white spot, so I assumed it was the nurse.

"I think she's awake now," she whispered and opened the door wide enough for the other person to enter. My head felt so heavy that turning it meant more pain, so I laid still staring straight ahead. A familiar cologne rushed over my nostrils and I felt the soft, sweet, gentle touch of familiar lips brush against my forehead. David looked into my eyes and held my hand. He had this twinkle in his eyes that made my heart pound.

"How's my queen? You look so beautiful." He pulled up a chair and sat down. "Dorothy it's a boy. His name is Ahmad; he was born at 2:45 this morning; he's 7 pounds 6 ounces, and he's 22 inches long."

I pressed my eyes shut. That was music to my ears, at last my baby was here. I wanted so much to talk and ask David how did the baby look, but the excruciating pain prohibited such.

"Shhh, don't talk. You shouldn't exert any unnecessary pressure on your abdominal area."

I mustered a small grunt.

"Baby you were wonderful; I'm so proud of you." He leaned forward and kissed me again. "I bet you're wondering whose idea was it to name the baby, Ahmad, aren't you?"

I closed my eyes again.

"It was my idea, and before you jump to any crazy conclusions, let me explain to you why I named the baby Ahmad." I braced myself, I knew I was in for quite a long story. "Back in med school," he began, "I had a professor named Dr. Abdul Ahmad. Now he wasn't Arab, and he wasn't black; he was white believe it or not. No one at Morehouse liked him because he was so difficult. Many a man have contemplated homicide against this man because they failed his classes left and right. Yet, in spite of the fact that he was difficult, not to mention arrogant, he regarded me as a prized pupil. I earned the name "Doc Headstrong," during my second year of med school. I will never forget the day Dr. Ahmad was called to the maternity ward at Atlanta's Grady Hospital. Now I was the only student who generally stayed after a lab; I forget what the experiment was. Anyway, I was present during the time he received the call. So Dr. Ahmad asked me to accompany him to the hospital, which I did. When we arrived, he turned to me and said, "Leonard I want you to deliver Ms. X's baby. When he told me that, I stood back and examined him, and I thought, *This man has got to be insane*; I thought he was missing a few screws. Dorothy, I had never in my life delivered a child, and I told him, "Doc I'm just a second year student. I don't know a thing about delivering babies. Do you know how serious this is?" David paused and stared quietly out towards the window. "He said, and I'll never forget it, he said, "Look Leonard I'm serious I want you to perform the procedure; I want you to prove to me that you are worthy of being a good physician." So I went into the delivery room, shaking like gelatin and walking barefoot on pins and needles. After three and a half hours I delivered my first child. The patient was so impressed with my demeanor, that she named her child after me. So after that moment I could've bowed down and kissed Dr. Ahmad's feet. He believed in me and told me that I had the potential of becoming a top-notch physician. He told me I performed the operation like a pro, and if Dr. Ahmad said it, that really meant something to me, because Dr. Ahmad had an impeccable reputation as being one of the best physicians in the country. So I made a promise to him, I told him that if I had a son, I would name him Ahmad, which means, "worthy of praise," in Arabic." David's astounding testimony nearly put me to sleep. Then he studied the identification band on my wrist in silence. "Honey, I wish you could see him now."

I smiled.

"Dorothy, he's a natural born ladies' man with eyes like yours and a healthy physique, like his father of course."

I was afraid to laugh.

"Don't laugh; I know how much you want to."

I couldn't get over how he was an excellent mind reader too.

"Ma and Dad called this morning, they were so excited they telephoned the whole block. Now everyone knows our baby's name and his weight."

David took my hand and placed it next to his cheek. "See what I tell you. Our son isn't in the world a good seven hours and people already know him."

A Catholic nun entered the room quietly smiling at the both of us. "God bless you both." Her smiling eyes looked like sparkling black charcoals. David turned around and shook her hand.

"I'm Sister Rose; I'm here to pray for Sister Leonard. You must be Sister Leonard's husband."

"Yes, I am."

"Would you care to join us in prayer, Mr. Leonard?"

"I guess I have no choice." He laughed and shrugged his shoulders.

Sister Rose bowed her head and proceeded to pray. For five minutes she prayed for my successful recovery and my leaving the hospital with a normal and healthy baby.

"Sister Leonard." She took my hand. "Call whenever you need me. My name is Sister Rose and I'll be in the chapel." She smiled. "God bless you Sister Leonard and thank you both."

* * *

I finally saw my baby. I was standing outside the window, gazing misty-eyed at his diminutive form all bundled up and asleep like the world was at a standstill. I thought, *so you're the little fellow who kept me up all night tossing and turning and craving for food. I gained thirty pounds of fluid, fat, and I kept rashes and yeast infections. You were the same little person who made my nose expand all seven continents, my thighs rub, my feet swell, you also made my mouth so fat that I talked with a lisp. Your little mind can't possibly imagine all those times you had me wishing I hadn't gotten into this predicament in the first place. But now as I look at you, I see it was all worth it, every gut aching pain, every single stitch was worth it. You are so beautiful and to think you came to be on a warm, hot, lustful night about ten months back on a bed filled with passion that expanded the depths of the Nile. In other words, it was deep!*

Every one loved you before you were even born. Grandma and Grandpa Leonard said they were going to "spoil" you, can you believe it, Grandma said "spoil." Grandma Cleo said it too. Believe or not, she's coming all the way from New Orleans to see you. Your Aunt Katherine and Cousin Richard and Cousin Tiny are coming too. You know you are so blessed to have wonderful parents like your father and me who love you so much.

"Dot." I heard Mama's voice whispering rather loudly as she and Louis tip-toed towards me.

"Hello, Mama. Louis." Seeing the both of them look so genuinely happy made me happy.

"Dot, which one is he?" Mama asked.

"There, see right there wrapped up in blue with his thumb in his mouth?"

"Yes. Oh he's a biggun," she said in her Tweety bird baby voice. "Oooh look at how big that boy is, Louis."

"Yeah, I see."

"Mama, I fed him this morning and he had an appetite a mile long."

"I can see it now Dot; that boy is going to eat you out of house and home," Mama said.

Louis chuckled, "How much did you say that boy weighed?"

"Seven pounds, six ounces."

"You know Dot, you weighed eight pounds when you were born, and the terrible part about it, I gave birth to you naturally."

My stomach perished at the thought.

"Well Dot how are you feeling?"

"Better than I was, today is my last day here. The baby and I are leaving first thing tomorrow morning."

"I know you're excited about taking him home."

"Yes Mama, I just can't wait to get him home and show him off."

"Dot, you won't believe it when I tell you that Louis and I went on a shopping spree for the baby."

"Mama, you didn't."

"Yes, we did. I dropped his things off at the house."

"Mama, how did you manage to get everything on the plane?"

"Honey me and Louis said to hell with the plane. We decided to drive this time."

"You two never cease to amaze me."

Mama told Louis to reach into her bag to pull out a camera.

"Now Lou baby, get a couple of snapshots of the baby lying there all sleep looking like a Buddha doll." Mama rambled in her Tweety voice again. "Get him Louis what are you waiting on."

"Cleo, I'm waiting on this stupid thing to wind up."

"It hasn't taken this long before. Louis gimme that thang because you don't know what you're doing."

"Move Cleo. See it stopped." Louis adjusted the various gadgets on the camera. "Now it's ready."

"Well, go on take the picture and take it right."

Louis shook his head. "Dot, have you ever heard of such-a person who doesn't know how to operate a camera yet tells you how to operate it?"

"Just shut up and take the picture," Mama said.

"Louis, I'm afraid if you use the flash against the window, it'll cause a glare."

"I think there's enough light in here for me to do without it."

Louis snapped five shots of my baby.

"Mama did you know Katherine and Tiny are coming too?"

"Katherine called last night and told me."

"It's been a while since I last saw her and Ricky Jr."

"You know Ricky Jr. is spending the summer with us."

"You mean to tell me Katherine is going to let Ricky Jr. spend the summer away from her?"

"Yes, I know; it shocked the hell out of me too. You know how she is about that boy. She cries if he's out of sight a good ten minutes. But she and Big Rick want to spend some time to themselves. To do what? Heaven knows."

I smiled, trying to picture myself telling Mama to keep Ahmad so David and I can spend some time together. Mama nudged me in the back. "Here comes that mother-in-law of yours," she whispered through gritted teeth.

"Mama, be nice to her for a change."

"I'll try, but when it's time for you to leave the hospital, I want to be the first one to keep the baby, you hear?"

I paid Mama no attention, and focused it on Doc Sr. and Ms. Liz who were dressed up in what looked like their church attire. Doc Sr. was whispering something to her and looking perplexed at the stuffed elephant and gray balloons. Ms. Liz, on the other hand was carrying a blue blanket and flashing her ivory piano keys.

"Hello Mr. Dix, Ms. LaCroix," Doc Sr. said as he sat the stuffed elephant aside and shook their hands. "It's good to see you both again, how was the trip?"

"Not bad for a change," Louis said.

"You took a flight?"

"No, no, Cleo and I took the scenic route."

"Cleo, if I may say so, you are looking more youthful than ever." Ms. Liz said as she approached Mama, "I guess between the two of us, the grandparent business doesn't affect the outer appearance much." She winked her long eyelashes and playfully nudged Mama with her elbow. Mama forced herself to laugh. "Thank you Liz, you don't look a day over forty-five yourself." Ms. Liz wasn't sure whether or not the remark was a compliment, but she stepped aside and glanced at me. "How are you princess?"

"Anxious, excited, glad." I replied after I thought about taking my baby home.

"I know you are dear. Look what I've found." She held up the blue blanket proudly.

"Where did you find it?" I retrieved the precious commodity from her and cradled it right under my nose. I was surprised that after twenty-eight years it had a delicate soft odor.

"I found it in the linen closet."

"What is it, Dorothy?" Mama inquired.

"It's David's baby blanket," I said.

"My isn't that something," Mama said. "How long have you had this blanket?"

"Since 1940, almost twenty-eight years ago," Ms. Liz said. "I bundled David in this very blanket."

"That's amazing," Mama said before she sniffed it. "Did you wash it?"

"Of course, I had it cleaned thoroughly."

I turned my attention to Doc Sr. and Louis, who were busy chatting away. "Thanks for the elephant Papa Doc."

"No need to thank me dear; I'm just doing my job." He gave me a hug and kissed me on the forehead. "Do me a favor and don't let those two get out of hand." He whispered loud enough for Mama and Ms. Liz to hear.

"Dave what are you talking about?" Ms. Liz asked as she placed her glittering diamond clad hand on her hip. "I hope you're not talking about Ms. LaCroix and me."

"Yes, I'm talking about the both of you."

"Well you don't have to worry about us ladies, will he Cleo?"

"Good, I'm glad to hear that," He said, then whispered to me again, "Why do I have a hard time believing that?"

"Will you cut it out Dave?"

"All I'm saying is that I'm having a difficult time believing you two."

"Why is that so difficult to believe? Sure Cleo and I have had our spats, but that's all behind us, right Cleo?" Mama only nodded. "Besides, we have a grandson to take care of and what kind of example would we set for him if we kept on behaving like two old biddies?"

Inside the nursery I could hear the baby crying. I looked through the window, and sure enough, he was lying on his back crying so loudly, his little pink mouth was trembling. The nurse rushed to pick him up, to hold him; it wasn't time for him to eat again, so I knew he wasn't hungry.

"I hope she doesn't pick him up every single time he starts crying," Mama said.

When the nurse rocked him in her arms, he immediately stopped. Doc Sr. chuckled. "He reminds me so much of David."

"Yes he does," Ms. Liz replied. Both of their eyes were fixed dreamily on the baby.

"When do you leave Dorothy?"

"Tomorrow morning."

"Is David going to pick you up?"

"Yes, if there isn't a change of plans."

The five of us stood there gazing at Ahmad through the window, anticipating the hours before he came home.

Chapter 10

I didn't recognize my sister Ophelia until she spoke to me. She stood in my doorway, accompanied by a white fellow. The both of them looked like they had joined the cast of Hair. Ophelia had a daisy painted under her left eye, a tattoo of a red rose around her waist, along with one of a Buddhist man on her right arm.

"Hello my dear sister." When she kissed me on the cheek, I stood there frozen solid. Ophelia had really gone off the deep end this time. "What's the matter Dorothy? You look like you've seen a ghost."

"Ophelia, what have you done to yourself?" I bypassed the small talk, came right out and asked her with a nasty attitude, "And who is this?"

"This is my ace boomcoom, my lover, and my friend, Professor Rho." He was a dingy white man with yellow hair that dreaded into long, thick, turd-like braids. He had a mangy beard that was yellow with silver streaks, and he had the nerve to tie a rubber band around it.

"Pleasure meeting you."

I was at a loss of words; I couldn't believe Ophelia was keeping company with someone like him. I wished Mama was here to see this, better yet, Papa. I bet he was turning over in his grave. God, I'd give anything to see the look on his face.

"So Dorothy, aren't you going to let us in? We may look filthy but we're really not." I opened the door wide enough so they could walk in.

"Have a seat." Damn! I said it before I realized it. I didn't want them sitting on my clean white sofas.

"Professor honey, let's sit on the floor."

"Sure no problem." The both of them sat on the floor Indian style with erect backs. *Hallelujah*! They must've read my mind.

"Ophelia would you and your friend like anything to eat or drink."

"I don't want anything. Would you care for anything honey?"

"Yes. Do you boil your water before you drink it?"

I stared at this dingy person a while before I answered, "No."

"No thank you, I'll pass."

Good, I didn't want his mangy, yellow bearded lips on my cups and glasses anyway.

"So Ophelia, tell me about Chicago and how you came about meeting; I'm sorry, what is your name again?"

"Professor Rho to my colleagues, but to you Mrs. Leonard, my name is Sigmund."

"Sigmund? Is that your real name?"

"No, that's my alter ego's name."

"How cute," I responded, not in the least bit amused. "I don't want to sound hostile, but how did you two hook up and what's with the mangy hair and the tattoos and what not?"

They looked at each other and laughed. "Dorothy, haven't you heard of the Nirvanas, the Lotuses, peace and love?"

"No, I haven't." I sat back with my arms folded. "Tell me about it."

"Well, Sigmund and I are Nirvanas. We believe in peace and unity and our main goal is to spread it throughout the nation. I met Sigmund at the Democratic National Convention during the demonstrations and chaos. Sigmund was sitting Indian style in the doorway of the Conrad Hilton meditating to reach the state of Nirvana. He looked so peaceful sitting there so I joined him and we sat there for hours until the fascist pigs loaded us into a patty wagon and took us to jail."

"Who bailed you out?"

"A fellow Nirvana of ours."

"Let me get this straight. Are you a hippie Ophelia?"

"Let me correct you Mrs. Leonard. We dress like hippies but our minds and souls are strictly Nirvana. Nirvana walk different, we eat different, we pray different."

I glanced at my sister. "Are you happy Ophelia?"

"I am groovy; I never been groovier in my life." When she said that she held Professor Rho's hand and stared dreamily into his eyes, sounding as if she rehearsed those lines.

"Are you still living in the dormitory, Ophelia?"

"Yes, I am."

I found that hard to believe. I figured if she was in love, she'd be living with her "Professor Rho."

"Where do you live?" I asked him.

"I live off campus. My father owns a condo near Lake Michigan that he rents out to me."

"Is your father happy with your lifestyle?"

"My father could care less about me or my lifestyle."

"Why is that?"

"My father owns a Napalm plant in South America; he's more concerned with poisoning innocent people and reaping untold profits."

I heard the key latch click and the door open. David arrived, yawning and throwing his coat on the hanger. He looked at Ophelia and her friend sitting on the floor. They stood up to greet him.

"Hello David."

"Ophelia?" David was baffled by her appearance. "What happened to you in Chicago? Don't tell me, you got caught in the riot?" He laughed and gave her a hug.

"No David, actually I became a better person, spiritually."

"Is that so." He glanced at Professor Rho. "Hello Sir, I'm David Leonard."

He and Professor Rho shook hands. "Pleasure to finally meet you Dr. Leonard. I'm Sigmund Rho."

"Sigmund Rho, what do you do?"

"I am a professor of art."

"Wonderful! Ophelia's a wonderful artist. I consider her next in line to Picasso."

"She definitely has what it takes," Rho replied.

"Have a seat; make yourself at home. Do excuse me I've just spent fifteen hours in the delivery room, and I need to freshen up." He kissed me on the cheek. "How are you?" He then beckoned me with his eyes to follow him. "Could you come here for a second?"

I excused myself. Once we entered our bedroom, David closed the door.

"Would you explain to me, what in the hell happened to your sister?"

I shook my head. "I don't know."

"And what on God's green earth possessed her to get involve with a character like that?"

"God only knows."

"No offense, but I've always wondered about Ophelia," David said as he unfastened his tie. "Honey, I'm beginning to think it was a bad idea to send Ophelia to Chicago?"

David sat down on the edge of the bed and rubbed his temples. "I've invested a lot of money into that school."

"I should've listened to Ma." I sat next to David. "She told me not to send Ophelia anywhere because she's not mature enough. You know she's been known to do some outlandish things. You remember the time we caught her messing around with your fifteen year-old brother?"

"Don't remind me."

"And David, did you see the tattoos she had on her? I counted at least three!"

"I saw that. I know a couple of guys with tattoos. Big guys, and they tell me the shit hurts."

"How does it hurt?"

"Well, you know a tattoo artist uses a needle to sketch those drawings on."

I flinched at the sound of a needle. "No!"

"Oh yes. I hear that in order to lessen the pain, a person usually gets drunk or stoned."

"You're kidding."

He took off his shirt and slacks and threw them on the floor. He didn't say anything more, and left it up to me to draw the conclusion.

"I be damned."

"I'm not saying she used alcohol, Dorothy, though she could have." He leaned over and kissed Ahmad who was lying across the bed asleep. "How long has this little fellow been out?"

"About thirty minutes or so. You know he turned seven months today, honey."

David's eyes sparkled. "Our boy is growing up too fast, look at him." David traced the creases in the baby's shirt with his finger. "It seemed like yesterday when we brought him home from the hospital. He was barely a week old."

"I know," I said lost in my world of thoughts. David threw on an old Morehouse Medical T-shirt and some pants.

"Honey, when you go out please tell Ophelia to come here; I want to talk to her alone." David chuckled. "Sounds like you mean business."

"I sure do."

He snickered and closed the door behind him. Minutes later, Ophelia appeared. When she saw the baby she smiled and rushed to his side.

"I haven't seen my nephew until now." She took his fingers and kissed them I noticed her fingernails were painted black, and covering her hand was a tattoo of a butterfly.

"You know I only have one picture of Ahmad, and that was taken when he was three weeks old."

I didn't want to talk about that right now, I had a bunch of questions just bursting from my brain.

"Ophelia, what's really going on?"

She continued to amuse herself with kissing and rubbing the baby. "What's really going on? What do you mean?"

"I'm talking about you, are you on drugs?"

"Hell no," she replied just as quick as I had asked.

"Then tell me why are you involved in this; it doesn't make sense to me. Look at you, you look like a damn fool with all that makeup paste to your face! Have you seen Ma yet?"

Before I realized it, I answered my own question. "I guess it's obvious you haven't, because Ma wouldn't have let you out of the house dressed up like a whore with everything but your privates pierced and tattooed."

"Are you finished?"

"Hell no I'm not finished, I'm upset with you Ophelia. Now I'm having second thoughts about sending you back."

"Dorothy, look, I'm an adult, have you forgotten?"

"Have I forgotten? Look, let's discuss this somewhere else. I don't want to wake up the baby." We stepped into the hallway.

"Ophelia listen."

"No Dorothy you listen. For twenty-one damn years I've been listening to people tell me how to run my life. I'm tired of it. I'm living my life the way I want to, I'm doing things that are going to make me happy."

"I know…"

"Let me finish, Dot. I thought you of all people would understand me and accept me the way I am, no matter what. That's the reason why I came to you first, and now I realize I made a big mistake." She paused and stared at my reaction. "And another thing, Dorothy. I thought you were smart enough to recognize art when you see it."

"So that's what you call it? Art?"

"That's right."

"Just a minute ago, it was a symbol of this new spiritual movement that came about in your life?"

"Dorothy, you still don't understand, do you?"

"Make me understand why you want to waste your time chasing botched up philosophies and a low-life weirdo."

"It's no use." She waved her hands as to say she was throwing in the towel, and whizzed by me like I didn't exist.

"Ophelia!" I shouted as she whizzed out of sight. I thought about what I had said. Maybe I was a bit harsh on her. In my mind I honestly thought I was telling the truth, and if I hurt her feelings it was just too bad. So I made up my mind that I wasn't going to let it bother me and I went into the living room.

Ophelia and her friend were walking towards the door. David looked at me. "Dot what happened?" I heard him but I wasn't actually listening; my attention focused on Ophelia. "Ophellia are you leaving?"

Ophelia opened the door, flashed her eyes at me, and rolled them outside. Her friend stood there.

"Ophelia did you hear your sister?" he asked. In the distance I heard the car door slam. He gave us a perplexed expression. "I don't know, she gets that way, even with me sometimes."

He extended his hand to David. "It was a pleasure meeting you, Dr. Leonard, we must pick up our conversation another time."

"Sure. We'll do that."

"It was a pleasure meeting you too, Mrs. Leonard. Peace." He held up two fingers and had the nerve to smile with his dingy beard.

"Dorothy, what did you say to Ophelia?" David asked as soon as he closed the door.

"I wanted her to tell me what's really going on."

"She was angry when she walked out." He chuckled.

"David, I don't give a damn. I don't like her new lifestyle and I told her."

"You know Dorothy, I was talking to her friend and he told me about the Nirvana group he and Ophelia are involved with. There are chapters in Dallas and Austin, and I hear this group is slowly gaining followers everywhere."

"Sounds like a cult to me, David."

"That thought came to mind too. You know Professor Rho, Sigmund, whatever his name, is a sharp man. He's intelligent and somewhat manipulative."

"Well, he found a sucker in Ophelia."

"It's just a phase; she'll get over it. Hell, she better get over it." I tried my best to entertain that thought.

* * *

David's latest medical book was doing real well. As a matter of fact, I overheard his agent inform him that it was three thousand sales away from achieving bestseller status. David tried not to involve me in his personal affairs, but for one week, well almost one week. Parcel delivery trucks were pulling up left and right bringing certified letters for me to sign. I opened one and it was a check made out to David for $25,000. I broke out into a cold sweat as I held the check in my trembling hands. I felt an adrenaline rush. I knew how David hated for me to read his mail, so I had opened it carefully and neatly. There was enough glue left to make it look as though it went untouched.

One afternoon, David came home from work, told me to pack my overnight bags, take Ahmad to his parents, and get dressed. We were flying to South Padre Island to purchase a beach front home. When we arrived, the realtor, Mr. Handy, met us at the airport. We drove twenty miles out into a crystal-blue paradise with sandy white beaches. We got out of the car and about twenty feet away stood a magnificent 2,000 square foot structure, about two-and-a-half stories, high with double doors and windows so clean they cast a mirror-image reflection when you looked through them. The living room was spacious with high ceilings and a spiral staircase leading almost to the top of it. You could look through the glass sliding doors and see a view of the ocean in the distance. Mr. Handy gave us a tour of the house. It contained three large bedrooms, three baths, a huge kitchen and a dining area, plus a recreational facility with a wet bar and balcony. David had always wanted a beach home, so he couldn't turn down the offer. He purchased it and insisted we find the best damn interior decorator to decorate it in time for the party he was planning to give, celebrating the success of the first and second books, as well as the opening of his practice.

The party came off a hit. The food was fantastic, the music was blasting with the Motown sound, and the atmosphere was perfect. David invited both professional and personnel from his practice to attend. Some of which I had previously met, and some I never knew existed. I met two people in particular who amazed me. Sadaria McCloud, was a receptionist. The Southern Comfort made her a feisty character, but she entertained me and Myranda Corbin just the same talking about her no good ex-husband and no good ex daughter-in-law. Drunk as hell with tears in her eyes she told us her life story. She said she never knew the true meaning of the word hate until she met her ex-husband and ex daughter-in-law. She explained why.

"Honey, I came home one day it was a Friday evening. I had worked eight hours, I was dog tired, and I needed a shot of *penis*cillin, because it had been a long time, you see. And you know how it is when you ain't had none in a long time. Anyway I wanted to surprise my husband and—and I came home a little early to change into something a little more sexy, you see. I be damn if I didn't come home to find that son-of-a-bitch in bed with my daughter-in-law!" I noticed a couple nearby whose ears and eyes perked. Myranda wanted to probe deeper into the discussion, so she asked Sadaria what happened next.

"Honey I didn't say a word," She began. "I went outside, went in my glove compartment, brought out my .38, went back in the house, stood in the doorway, and dared the son-of-a-bitches to move."

I didn't know about Myranda, but I was trying my best not to laugh.

"What happened then?"

"I got tired of standing at the door and left the house my damn self. I said, 'fuck her, fuck you, fuck this damn house, forget you ever knew me, I want my divorce, and I want my half of the shit ready for me when I ask for it.'" She drank more and swallowed hard. "Y'all just don't know how much that hurt poor Sadaria." Her mouth was watering with saliva and she showered us with her spit. When a waiter passed by, she didn't hesitate to stop him and ask for another shot.

Myranda, on the other hand, was less talkative about what went on behind closed doors. She mainly talked about her husband, Dr. Corbin, who also worked out of David's practice and her students at Texas Southern, where she taught history. She also told me about this program she was involved in with the youth called, "Operation Goals." She said it's aim was to teach underprivileged and at-risk youths about Negro history. She told me that most of the children didn't know as far back as slavery. So a few of her sorors got together and taught out of her classroom on the TSU campus. I went off on another tangent and asked her what sorority did she belong to. No wonder we hit it off so well, we belonged to the same sorority.

"You might know my cousin, Christine Jefferson."

A smile lit up her face. "Yes. I remember her, we use to call her Tiny. I was her big sister when she was on line."

"Really, that's wonderful! I'm from the Theta Chi chapter myself." I replied, glad I found a soror out of the bunch.

"This is truly wonderful. You know Faye Farris Kent is here tonight."

"Isn't she secretary of the National chapter?"

"That's her; she and I are from the same chapter and we go way back."

"Well where is she? I can't believe I missed her."

Myranda and I left Sadaria standing near the fireplace.

"This is truly a small world," I said leading Myranda upstairs to the second level where there was yet another crowd of people standing around sipping champagne glasses and acting convivial. I glanced near the champagne bar and spotted David talking to a woman. She was about my height, except she was a little on the stout side, but she was pretty and it looked like she and my husband were involved in a deep conversation. David was holding his champagne glass in one hand and gesturing away with the other. She, on the other hand, stood there absorbing every movement and every word. I wondered what they were talking about, so I didn't hesitate to walk into that direction to find out. I heard Myranda say, "That's Mrs. Kent." I wondered if she was referring to the same lady who was talking to David. I had never before seen Mrs. Kent, I had only seen her signatures on a few documents and periodicals distributed throughout the sorority, here was my chance to ask. Before I opened my mouth Myranda tapped her on the shoulder. David and I glanced at each other he acted surprised to see me. I guess the champagne had him all worked up.

"Myranda Corbin, it's good to see you again," she said in a loud and articulate voice. I watched as the two of them exchange compliments about each other's dress. David slid his arm around my waist. "How are you Mrs. Corbin? Faye, this is my lovely wife, Dorothy; Dorothy, this is Faye Kent."

"It's so nice to finally meet you, Mrs. Kent."

"Same here. Mrs. Leonard you couldn't possibly imagine just how much the Leonard family has affected my life. You know David's father was my, my mother's, my sisters' and my aunts' physician."

I thought she wasn't going to stop calling out her family tree.

"I'm deeply indebted to the Leonard family." She clasped my hand. "Honey, you are fortunate to be part of a wonderful family."

She didn't have to remind me of what everyone else had been telling me since day one. I glanced at David. He had a modest smile glued to his face.

"Myranda where's your husband?"

"Bill's around some place."

"I'm surprised you two managed to separate from each other. Talk about love birds."

Myranda thought that was so funny.

"Dorothy these two meet one month, a month later they're married."

"Wow." I responded.

David explained his story. "See Bill and I were suitemates in college. Because of this woman, Bill was always missing curfew." Myranda blushed at the remark. "If I recall correctly, Mr. Bill was a big time playboy, that's until he met this woman," David chuckled.

Mrs. Kent took a sip of her champagne and glanced at Myranda. "I know I haven't been keeping in touch with you like I should because I practically live on the road now."

"Faye, you know what? Dorothy and I were talking about Operation Goals, and I mentioned our sorority, and Dorothy told me she was a member." Faye's expression lit up like early dawn. "That's wonderful, what is your chapter's name?"

"Theta Chi."

"What alma mater?" she asked quickly.

"Southern University in Baton Rouge."

"Great, as a matter of fact our national conference is scheduled to be held in Louisiana- New Orleans to be exact."

"That's my hometown."

"I love New Orleans, it's a great city. You know each time I go, I end up having to take a lot of medication because the food there is so rich and spicy."

"Excuse me ladies," David said with his eyes fixed across the way. I watched as he strutted his six foot-one inch frame across the terrace and disappeared into the crowd. Faye took another sip from her champagne. "This is something else." She took yet another sip. "Hmmm, I hadn't any champagne this good since I left France."

Myranda and I sipped daintily from our glasses, tasting it like it was bittersweet.

"Dorothy you and David have a wonderful home."

"I love it here." I heard Myranda respond.

"Myranda tell me something, when are you and Bill going to have children?"

"I don't know Faye, maybe when I'm forty."

"Forty?" Faye and I said unison.

"Yes, I want to be able to push my career aside and concentrate on raising my kids. Right now, it's just not in the cards."

"You know I had a cousin who thought like you. She waited until she was forty-two to have her first child." Faye shrugged her shoulders. "At forty-two you don't have the energy like you had when you were twenty-seven or thirty-two. This is my opinion Myranda, you know I like to express my opinion. I want to be able to grow with my children."

"What do you mean?"

"I want to do things I see my children do, like run, turn flips. Sometimes I want to be a friend to my child rather than a parent, do you understand?"

"No," Myranda replied.

"When you turn fifty your child will be ten years-old Myranda. My cousin is fifty-two now, her oldest daughter is ten and the youngest is six. My cousin never had to pop a single pill in her life until she had these kids. You talk about an old witch."

"Faye, soror, best friend." Myranda touched her on the shoulder. "I'm not listening to you dear," she added with a chuckle.

"Watch, I don't like to say *I told you* so, but watch."

I thought about my own mother and how at thirty-seven she gave birth to Jacqueline. Now to me that was pretty old. Before long we were off on another tangent dealing with our husbands. The three of us sat and passed the time talking about our every day lives. I really felt close to Faye and Myranda like I had known them all my life. After the party we exchanged addresses and anticipated seeing each other and getting together to pick up where we left off at the national conference in New Orleans. I could hardly wait.

* * *

David was cleaning the lens on his hand-held camera and checking the focus with stern concentration. He did not want to miss a single moment of Ahmad's first birthday party. My baby was one and it amazed me to see him walking around, trying to put anything and everything into his mouth. You can't imagine how many times I've pulled paper, dirt, pennies, nickels, dimes, cotton, whatever he could get his hands, on out of his mouth. He really scared me out of my wits when he somehow or another unfastened the pin on his diaper and stuck it in his mouth. He poked his little tongue and came wobbling to me with blood trickling down his mouth. What really frightened me was he didn't shed a single tear, just a look of guilt. Since that particular incident, I nicknamed him "Man," because he was one tough cookie. Ahmad could take bumps, bruises and scraps like a hungry person could a free meal and he hardly ever cried.

For the party David and I turned the recreation room into a miniature Disneyland with Mickey Mouse hats, plates, cups, balloons, cake, stuffed Mickies, stuffed Donald Ducks, and Pluto to say the least.

When I walked into the recreation room, David was filming Ahmad through his camera.

"And what does the birthday man have to say today?" David asked as if he were talking to someone older. "I feel grrreat!" I spoke for Ahmad in a high pitch voice and scooped him up in my arms. It tickled him so he couldn't stop drooling.

"Dorothy, I want you to look into the camera and say something mushy."

I bounced Ahmad up and down on my lap and coaxed him to look into the camera to flash his million dollar smile. "Smile baby, look at daddy, look at daddy." When I took his small hands and kissed them, they tasted like Johnson's baby lotion, sweet and clean.

"I want you to say a quick 'Da Da' for me," David said with one eye hidden behind the camera. "Come on, say 'Da Da.'"

"Teach him to say 'Ma Ma.' He sees her more often," I said jokingly.

"Put him down so I can get a shot of him walking."

David ended up following him all around the recreation room and down the hall to the other rooms. I rested my chin on the arm of the sofa and watched the two of them. David was enjoying the last of his three days off. Since day one, most of his time was spent with Ahmad, filming his every move and taking him around to show him off at work. Yesterday, the weather was unusually warm for February and the three of us went to the zoo at Hermann Park. I admit at times I was getting somewhat jealous because Ahmad brought out the kid in him, which lately, had been an obligation I found myself lacking to fulfill.

David put his camera aside and held Ahmad in the palm of his hand. "It's a bird! It's a plane!" David glided him around the room like Superman, taking him up high and down slowly. He played a good five minutes then plopped down, with Ahmad secured in his arms, on the sofa and blew against his tummy with his mouth. It sounded like a loud fart, and it tickled the life out of Ahmad. I found myself beaming at the two of them, and although it sounds corny, I wanted to cry. David had never had this much fun with his son since he was born, because the days and nights he spent at work kept him out of touch with us. As I frequently recall, David missed out on a lot of precious moments in Ahmad's life. I wanted David to be there with the camera to video Ahmad's first step and see the look on his face when Ahmad uttered "Da Da" for the first time. To be honest, it almost hurt my feelings being I was the one who listened to him cry and doctored on his gums when he was teething. I was the one who usually cleaned the shit and piss when he went to the bathroom in his diapers. It was "Ma Ma" not "Da Da" who usually catered to him around the clock when he needed a warm bottle at feeding time.

Ahmad looked at me with those glistening eyes. He was so precious, all dressed up for his birthday party in a Mickey jump suit, wearing the shiny, white high top shoes I bought him yesterday. Just then the telephone rang. "I'll get it," I said reaching to pick it up. "Hello."

On the other end was Mama's voice screaming and hollering, yelling. "She's dead, my baby is dead! Lord have mercy!" My heart rate sped up like a thoroughbred's, and the saliva in my mouth all of a sudden tasted like chalk when I swallowed.

"Mama! Mama! What's wrong Mama! Mama!" Blood rushed to my ears and for a moment I thought my head was going to explode. The look in my eyes told David that something horrible had just happened and he quickly grabbed the phone. I grabbed Ahmad and held him in my arms like a teddy bear.

"Hello, hello, Ms. LaCroix!"

I could still hear Mama's voice screaming, and my whole body trembled. My teeth chattered uncontrollably, and the first thing that came to mind was something horrible had happened to Jacqueline. Ahmad turned and looked at me with a confused look in his sad eyes wondering what in the hell is happening to Ma? Why is she shaking?

David shouted, "Are you sure?" He stared blankly at the floor. "Are you sure Ms. LaCroix?"

"David what's wrong?"

David stood up and paced the room with the phone. "Ms. LaCroix we are on our way, I know. Don't panic, don't panic in front of her, she doesn't need to see you panic Ms. LaCroix!"

My heart was coming out of my chest, something happened to Jacqueline. "David what's wrong with Jacqueline!" I heard myself scream, "I want to talk to Mama!" I reached for the phone before I realized it.

"Dorothy please, I'm trying to calm your mother down!" he shouted.

"Dammit let me see the phone!"

Ahmad burst out crying, I did too.

"Ms. LaCroix, listen to me, do this." I couldn't understand how he could sound so confident and calm at a time like this. "Call Louis, better yet call your next door neighbors and tell them to take you and Jacqueline to the airport immediately. Don't worry about it. I'll take care of the tickets, you hear me Ms. LaCroix? I'll take care of them for you. Bye!"

He hung up the phone and looked at me. "That was your mother."

"What's wrong with Jacqueline?"

He shook his head. "Jacqueline's fine, there's nothing wrong with her."

I grabbed my heart and rested my weight against the arm of the sofa.

"It's Ophelia, Dorothy."

My heart raced up again. "Ophelia! Is she dead?"

"I don't know for sure, I wasn't able to calm your mother down long enough to find out. But as far as I gather from her, Ophelia's either dead or barely hanging on."

I immediately shoved Ahmad into his arms and ran towards the bathroom, unable to retain this gut feeling and threw up in the toilet. I had this guilt-ridden feeling like somehow her accident was my fault. I recalled the time she stepped into my home with that man, and how I came down hard on her about her attitude and the way she looked.

When I close my eyes now, I can't help but see the angered look in her eyes when she stormed out the door for the last time. We never spoke a word to each other since. Not even Happy Thanksgiving, or Merry Christmas. I felt the tension mounting from my stomach and I threw up some more.

I heard David behind me shushing Ahmad, who was wailing. It seemed like everything I had balled up inside me came out in the toilet. My throat was raw afterwards when I crawled to the tub to rest my head there. I thought about Ophelia convincing myself I was to blame for her accident. Moments later I heard Ms. Liz and Doc Sr. behind me talking.

"I got her dad," David said lifting me up from the floor.

"David, I'm sorry." I started wailing like Ahmad. He turned me around and held me in his arms.

"Dorothy, you didn't do anything baby, it's not your fault."

I lost the feeling in my legs and fell to the floor again.

"I can't make it, David."

"Yes you can baby, you have to. Come on."

I shook my head. "No!" I felt saliva dripping from my bottom lip.

"Yes baby, I know you don't want to go, but you have to. Come on let's get you cleaned up."

We caught a 5:30 flight to Chicago. The whole time on the plane, I kept having crazy thoughts and visions of Ophelia's funeral. At the airport I was too weak to walk, so David pushed me around the terminal in a wheelchair. I stopped crying once we got into the cab. But when Sam and Dave sang, *Something Is Wrong With My Baby*, I started boohooing again. When the cab driver looked in his rear view mirror and saw the condition I was in he changed the station. A few minutes later Aretha came on singing, "What you want, baby I got it!"

A nurse met with us in the reception area at Cook County Hospital. I dreaded to hear the news. A physician with the name, Mercy also approached us. "Doctor Leonard, Mrs. Leonard."

"How is she?" David asked.

"She's listed in critical condition."

"What happened?"

"Ms. LaCroix and a companion were headed south bound on I-55. Somehow they lost control of their vehicle and collided with the north bound traffic. It killed the driver. Ms. LaCroix suffered a few broken ribs, and a concussion."

David squeezed my shoulders as a sigh of relief.

"After Ms. LaCroix was taken into the emergency room, we also discovered she was eight months pregnant."

My eyes widened.

"Any word on the condition of the child?" David asked.

"Though premature, the child suffered no major injuries."

I grabbed my chest. "There is a God."

"Ms. LaCroix is right down the hall, would you follow me please?" the nurse said.

"Thank you Doc." David shook his hand.

"I'll keep you informed."

In the other reception area, Mama and Louis were visiting with another nurse. Mama was dabbing at her eyes, while Louis held Jacqueline who was asleep. Mama, David, and I embraced like we'd never seen each other before. "Mama I thought she was gone," I heard myself cry.

"I did too baby."

I sniffed, "Have you seen her?"

"No baby." Mama blew her nose.

"Who was the other person in the car?" David asked.

Mama shrugged her shoulders. "I don't know it must've been one of her friends from school." Mama's nose was crimson.

The remaining part of the day we sat in the reception area, talking and watching the clock, while Ophelia underwent surgery. Ever so often a physician would give us an update on her condition. It went from very serious to serious to stable.

We stayed another day in Chicago to observe her condition. When I finally saw, her my heart dropped to my knees. She was bruised and bandaged with IVs running through her veins. And God, her left eye was swollen so bad it looked unreal. It was purple, about the size of a plum. I walked in to find her half asleep. I whispered softly, "Hi."

Ophelia slowly opened her right eye; it was moist with tears. I was grateful to God she was alive, though it upset me to know she was pregnant all this time and didn't bother to tell anyone.

I tried to make a decent conversation. "I saw the baby; it's a boy." Ophelia closed her right eye and slowly turned her face towards the window. She seemed upset when I mentioned him.

"Ophelia, I'm sorry. I know I was wrong for yelling and fussing at you about your friend. I wasn't trying to hurt you, I just wanted you to know that I was concerned and I didn't want you to do anything to hurt your studies at school." I sighed and looked outside the window. It was snowing. "Ophelia, I still love you, although I don't always approve of what you do, but I love you." I stared at a snowflake that hit the windowpane and melted. "I love you very much, and I want you to get well so you can go back to school." I stood there for a moment, to see if I could get some type of response from her; I got none. Ophelia's eyes were glued to the life outside the window. Poor thing I thought to myself.

* * *

Ophelia totally lost her mind after discovering Professor Rho was dead. At first she lived in complete denial, but when it finally hit her, it got so bad to where we had to send her to a mental hospital under close surveillance. The baby, on the other hand, was healthy and living with

Mama in New Orleans. Mama named him Lucky, because he survived the accident and he was premature.

After a month in the hospital, Ophelia moved in with me and David. I didn't have anything else to do at the time, so I played the nurse role and made sure she took the right amount of her medicine at the right time. Ophelia was subject to do anything and I didn't want her to go overboard and overdose. Each morning at 6:30 we'd swim ten laps in the pool and walk about two miles in the neighborhood. I did anything constructive to keep her body in condition and her mind off the accident. But sometimes late at night, I'd subconsciously hear her crying, and I have to awake out of my sleep to give her a sedative to calm her down. Her doctor said it was normal for her to have long periods of grief. The question is, just how long?

Ms. Liz and I were sitting on her patio gazing out into the backyard. It was a peaceful morning and the only noise came from the chirping of the birds.

"I know it's none of my business," Ms. Liz began over a cup of hot lemon tea, "but maybe you ought to send her back to the hospital. She's not ready to function on her own yet."

I stared into my cup at the bleak expression on my face. Tapping it, I amused myself at the ripples I created. Then Ms. Liz added as an afterthought, "Have you thought about Ahmad? She could possibly be a threat to him."

"That's nonsense Ms. Liz. Ophelia wouldn't hurt anyone." I took a sip like the tea wasn't still hot. "Except for herself maybe." My tongue was scorched.

*　　　　*　　　　*

Myranda Corbin sent me a letter. She didn't have very much to say, only that the "Operation Goals" kids went on a field trip to Chicago to the Johnson Publishing Company and they were going to be featured in a *JET* magazine article. She also wrote there was an opening for a History professor at Texas Southern. Amazingly, a brilliant thought came to mind. Graduate school! A master's degree, and while I'm at it get a certificate to teach. Myranda, my soror, gave me an idea. So the next day I went and talked to the Dean of Graduate Admissions at Texas Southern. After our meeting he gave me an application and a couple of brochures to fill out and return. I was excited when I got home, I filled out the application, and when David arrived I shared my information with him.

"Why do you want to go back to school?" he asked, obviously annoyed while he flipped through the pages of the application.

"I was sitting down one day attending to a twenty-two year-old and a one year-old and something told me, 'Dorothy it's time out for babysitting and playing a bored housewife.' So I went and had a talk with the Dean."

"You did what?" he asked, inching closer to me. I sucked in my breath and explained to him what I did and I told him that I was going back to school. Before I could say anything else, he hauled off and slapped me across the face.

"What did I tell you, Dorothy?" he asked.

I touched my stinging face with my hand and looked him in the eye. "Why? Why do you always keep me locked up in this house! Why won't you allow me to better myself!"

He stood up and towered over me like a giant. "You don't get it, do you? I am the breadwinner, the head Negro in charge. I told you that you didn't have to work, that you need to be at home raising our son. Why are you so anxious to get out of this house, huh, are you seeing someone else? Tell me?"

"No."

"Then why do you want to leave, what's out there for you? Nothing! Stay your ass at home! I got enough troubles to deal with at the hospital and now I come home expecting to get some peace and quiet from my wife and she throws her goddamn graduate school application in my face!" He took the lamp fixture from the end table and threw it to the floor, shattering it into a million pieces. "If you want something to do, clean this shit up!" He shouted before he charged out of the room, slamming the door against the wall. If I had the strength, I would've charged right after him, but I didn't. My pride and my self worth were at an all time low. Maybe it just wasn't meant for me to be anything but a bourgeoisie housewife. Everyone kept singing to me like a broken record of how "fortunate" I was to be in my situation, little did they know that right now I would trade places with a poor woman in a heartbeat, if she was rich with independence, and a peace of mind.

I heard a knock at the door.

"It's open." I mumbled.

Ophelia opened the door and glanced at the shattered lamp. "Uh excuse me, Dorothy. Could you come here?"

I felt aggravated not with her, but at myself. "What do you want Ophelia?" I asked.

She hesitated. "Nothing, I guess I can get it myself."

"Shit," I cursed at myself before getting out of bed.

Meanwhile, Ophelia was standing in the bathroom, holding a glass of water and inspecting the glass for what she called microorganisms.

"You didn't take those pills, did you?"

"No, remember you have them locked in the medicine cabinet." I grabbed my keys and unlocked the medicine cabinet to retrieve a bottle of Prozac. I swear watching her was like watching Ahmad, and God knows I didn't need another child on my hands. Not right now. Ophelia stared at my face and the expression in her eyes wanted to know what was going on with me and David.

"I talked to Mama," she said, not delving into the subject, before popping each pill into her mouth, "She said Lucky was doing fine, and..."

Ophelia burst out crying and stopped. "I miss him so much Dorothy, but half of me wants to see him and half of me says you don't need to see him. You know he's all I got to remind me of Rho." Tears went dripping off the tip of her keen nose. I grabbed some tissues. "Here wipe the snot off your top lip."

She blew her nose and wiped it.

"Ophelia, I'm going to Mama's this weekend, do you want to go?"

She continued to dig deeper into her nose. "Yeah I guess." She pulled out the tissue to inspect it,

"When did you talk to Mama?" I asked.

"This afternoon when you were out?"

"What else did she talk about?"

"Lucky mainly. She said she bought him this cute outfit to take a picture in, she said she was going to send it to me." Her bottom lip trembled again.

"Dorothy this afternoon when I was talking to Mama, I heard him crying in the background." She erupted again. "I felt so helpless Dorothy."

"I know, come on." I grabbed her arm and escorted her to her room. It was cluttered with drawings of men: blue men, green men, red men, and all of them had vague and colorful eyes. I sat on her bed and looked on the floor to discover she had the plate from yesterday's dinner with crumbs of dried food stuck to it.

"Dorothy could you take my plate to the kitchen for me. I forgot where it was." I pulled back the covers so she could get underneath them.

"How could you forget where the kitchen is?"

She settled underneath the covers like a two year-old and blurted out, "Dorothy, it sure is good to be alive." I smiled, I couldn't agree with her more. Though I wish I were somewhere else instead of here. I glanced at another sketch of a man that she was currently working on. He had a beard and sorrowful blue eyes. I didn't bother to ask her who the person was.

"You know Dorothy, I use to be skeptic, but I am living proof that there's life after death."

"Really, tell me about it?"

"It's really hard to explain, but this feeling came to me when I was riding in the car. At the moment I felt the impact, I saw this magnificent glow. Dorothy it was so bright that I couldn't look directly into it. But I felt my way to it; it was like something was pushing me, so when I got past the light, I ended up in front of a tall golden gate, and standing at the gate was a man with a long golden beard."

"Who was it?"

"Hell if I know, he scared the shit out of me because he appeared out of nowhere. He took one look at me and asked in a loud deep voice, "Are you lost?"

I laughed. "You sure this wasn't a dream?"

"I'm sure, I'm not playing I actually saw a place that looked like heaven and I saw a man who I believe was God."

I yawned and continued to listen. "So you think you saw God?"

"I be damned. You don't believe me do you?"

I didn't want to argue with her so I told her I believed her and to make her think I was interested I asked more questions.

"Dorothy, I swear everything was white and gold and it smelled like honey Dorothy, like they say in the bible."

I nodded with my lips. "Go on."

"He asked me." Ophelia tried to imitate his loud, deep, voice. 'What is your name child?' I told him Ophelia LaCroix. He had these reading glasses and put them on the tip of his nose and out of nowhere came a huge scroll; he scanned the scroll for about twenty minutes searching for my name. He called out LaBarren, LaBassett, LaCraig, LaCannes, he called out Aunt Vivian's name, Cousin Til's name, and someone else's name that ended with LaCroix, then he went to LaRue. I said, 'hold up. What happened to my name? You called damn near everybody with a

La something on that list and didn't call my name.' He said, and Ophelia began in his voice, 'I'm sorry child but your name isn't on the scroll.' I said, 'Could you give me a pen and let me sign it?' He laughed in sort of a jolly, wicked ole' way and said, 'Sorry my child, we don't allow fornicators, idolaters, and sinners through these gates.' I said, 'Hold up, hold up, wait one goddamn minute…' and before I could say anything else he went Presto! And I found myself in another place. There was fire everywhere and it seemed like everywhere I stepped there was a snake."

My blood crept through my flesh. I hated snakes. Ophelia continued with the story.

"From what I gathered, this place was like hell. There were people standing everywhere cursing and screaming and calling me names I almost got into a fight but the man at the gate stopped me. He was an ugly man, with a black widow's peak and a chin longer than eighty cents in pennies."

"Ophelia, are you sure this wasn't a dream?"

She raised her right hand. "I swear to God on Professor Rho's grave this wasn't a dream."

"Go ahead."

She stared at me for a moment. "This wasn't even a damn nightmare, I swear to God this was real Dorothy."

I chuckled. "Okay."

"The man at the gate didn't ask for my name, he just asked me was I Negro or white?"

"Why did he ask you that?"

"He said if he let another Negro enter through his gate he was going to have to relocate because the Negroes he had were down in the furnace trying to put the fire out!"

I laughed so, tears came to my eyes. "Ophelia what am I going to do with you?"

Ophelia kept a straight face the whole time, which made it even more funny. I laughed until my stomach was in knots. I stopped when I realized she had that look in her eyes which wanted to know what was going on with me and David. She reached out and touched my hand. "If you don't want me to say anything about it, I won't."

"What are you talking about?" I asked, pretending not to know what she was talking about.

"I'm talking about you and David. If you don't want me to say anything about it, then I won't."

"Won't what?"

"Tell anybody."

I began to taste the salt from my tears as they fell quickly to my lips. "There's nothing to tell, David and I had a simple argument, everybody does."

"Dorothy, I may be crazy and under a lot of medication, but I know what's going on, so you don't have to pretend with me."

"Things'll get better Ophelia."

"They won't if you don't start fighting back."

"Ophelia, promise me, you won't say anything, okay?"

She didn't, and when I looked into her chestnut-colored eyes I knew my secret was safe with her.

* * *

I spotted Tiny time I stepped into the terminal. She was sitting in the food court area, sipping on a pop, waving at me.

"Hi." Tiny extended her arms out to embrace me. "You look so pretty, Dorothy. You don't look like a woman who just had a kid."

I checked out Tiny; I noticed she'd lost weight. She use to be short and plump, but now she was short and petite, and the teal green outfit she had on accented all the right areas.

"Tiny you look good; I can tell you lost some weight!"

Tiny did a runway model turn for me. "And you are really wearing that dress. Just look at you."

I glanced at her narrow hips and slim waist line as she sat down.

"You know Dot, there's a saying, 'When ya' got it, ya' flaunt it."

"Well you better keep it, is all I'm saying."

"Got to honey, I have my reasons now."

"Reason number one, Mike."

Tiny gave me an ugly stare. "Give me a break. Mike is old news, child."

"What happened?"

"Dorothy, I thought I knew the man. Here it is seven years deep into the relationship and I don't know if I'm sleeping with a thoroughbred, or a jackass." Tiny's expression was tense and agitated. "I'm tired of games Dorothy, you know? Some people just go too damn far."

"So how long will it take before you're back in his arms again?"

She rested her hand on her chin and rolled her eyes. "For as long as heaven is happy and hell is hot."

"That's a long time," I replied, staring at her expression. Tiny couldn't fool me.

"So how is David and the baby?"

"They're fine; David's slowly coming back down to earth, you know his books have been selling like crazy now."

"Yeah, my girlfriend from law school just had a baby and she told me about the books. She said she had never known a physician to know so much about a woman's body, and emotions; you'd swear a woman wrote the book. She had a lot of good things to say about it."

I laughed to myself knowing deep down inside I knew the truth. "So she really liked it."

"Yes, she's even recommending it to her friends."

"That's great. You should see the letters he receives."

"It's too much for him to handle, huh? Where's my book? I'm entitled to a free copy aren't I?"

"Speaking of which, I have one in my briefcase you can have."

"I'm gonna have to level with you Dorothy. Since your baby shower, all I think about now is having a kid."

"You know it takes two to tango," I said thinking about Mike.

"Hell no, that's out of the question. I'm not having Mike's baby."

"Then who?"

"That's the part I'm working on. See I met this guy while I was in law school and we have been hitting the sheets pretty regularly now." She paused. "He's a high powered attorney from Florida."

"Is he married?" I asked.

She nodded up and down. "Yes, but it hasn't stopped me."

"Does his wife know about you?"

"What kind of question is that? Of course not, and I intend to keep it that way."

"So you're going to have this man's baby and raise it by yourself?"

Tiny rolled her eyes. "Enough about me, what's going on with Ophelia? Katherine told me she was fine, her ass just takes advantage of you and David."

"She tries to, but I gave her an ultimatum. Either she start chipping in on the mortgage or get the hell out."

"Your sister is trifling, how old is Ophelia?"

"Twenty-one or twenty-two."

"That doesn't make any sense, she would definitely have to leave, I'm sorry." She chuckled and sucked on her straw. "But that's your business, your problems." Her eyes wandered into the crowd of passerbys. Someone or something caught her eye.

"Oh my goodness, will you check out sister girl, Dorothy. I know she's not trying to switch."

I giggled and searched for the guilty party. I gave up because there were thousands of people roaming around the terminal.

"Well cuz, what's on your agenda for today?" Tiny asked.

"I don't know about you, but I'm going shopping, and I'm grabbing a bite to eat at Dookie's."

Tiny turned up her nose. "Is that a restaurant?"

"You haven't heard about Dookie's?"

She shook her head.

"Dookie has the best alligator this side of the Mississippi."

"No thank you."

"Yes, girl you don't know what you're missing, Dookie'll fix an alligator up just right."

"Dorothy, I figure with a name like Dookie, he can't fix me shit." We giggled. "The name itself will make you gag on a maggot."

"Shut up, Tiny."

Tiny and I met up with Myranda at Rosseau's on the Riverwalk for drinks. We had a hallelujah time, well at least Tiny. Myranda and I acted like two old biddies and stayed in our corners, while Tiny flirted with every pair of pants that waltzed by her. It mattered not what color they were, whether or not they were single. Once she got on the tipsy side, there was no point in stopping her.

"I don't give a damn if I ever hear from Mike again." Tiny wrapped her ruby red lips around a champagne glass and titled her head back to finish it. She thought about what she said and stared at the flickering flame burning from the candle. "He could come through that door right now, carrying a six pack of good stiffs, fourteen bars of pure gold, a red '69 Corvette convertible, singing 'Please, Please, Please like JB and I still wouldn't go with him."

A tall dark gentleman passed by our table and caught Tiny's attention.

"Say tall, dark and handsome, what are you doing tonight?" Tiny asked. He wiggled his tongue in a sexy suggestive way and continued to walk right out of the room.

"Oh no, he didn't."

Myranda took her napkin and began to fan the air around her. I started to sip from my champagne glass.

"He's too dark and besides I don't want nothing that black but a Cadillac, and it gots to have some white-walled tires."

"Amen," Myranda replied, which was one of the few things she had said all night.

"I feel like having a toast," Tiny began. She stood up holding her glass. Myranda and I stood and did the same.

"First of all, I'd like to propose a toast to the sorority for bringing us here together." Tiny rubbed her temples. "A toast to our chapters, our families, our friends, our men, that's if you claim one." Tiny looked at me. "No it's not Mike, thank you."

"Now did I say anything about Mike?"

"In case you were entertaining the thought."

"Tiny, go on with the toast."

"I want to toast to everything and everybody that made this occasion possible, I love you girls, you're my sisters, beautiful black sisters."

"Somebody bring out the violin," Myranda added.

We giggled and drank up before we walked down Canal Street to the hotel where we spent half the night talking and laughing about the good old days. Not once did I think about David.

* * *

Ms. Johnson was happy to see me, when I arrived one afternoon with Ahmad in tow. Ms. Johnson was one of David's nurses, and she was by far the sweetest person who ever walked God's green earth. I met her at the beach house and since then we've clicked like birds of a feather.

"There she is Miss America." Ms. Johnson's face was glowing when I entered the place. I noticed quite a number of patients from all ethnic backgrounds waiting in the lobby. They all looked at me wondering who I was strutting in wearing my charcoal gray Yves St. Laurent suit with the pumps to match.

"Is my husband here?" I smiled giving Ms. Johnson a peck on her cotton-soft cheek.

"He's here, but I don't think he'll be going anywhere anytime soon. Did you see the lobby?"

I sighed, "Yes, I couldn't help but notice."

She laughed and played with Ahmad before she motioned for us to follow her down the corridor to another waiting area where a couple of patients sat.

"Now you'll have to wait right here, I think he has someone in his office."

"Okay." I said before helping Ahmad into the seat next to me. "Ms. Johnson, if he has fifteen minutes to spare, that'll be just fine."

"Okay sweetie." She winked before she disappeared down the hall.

I glanced at the other two ladies sitting across from me who both appeared to be around my age, in their mid-twenties. They both had huge sandy brown naturals, or "afros" crowning their heads. I checked out at their dress attire; they looked like they were going to a club than to the doctor's office. The light-skinned sister was dressed in a paisley tank tube mini dress with black, patent leather platform boots, while the dark chocolate sister was blazing from head to toe in a brick red jumpsuit with brick red platform boots to match. The light-skinned sister leaned forward and waved her hand at me. "Excuse me, which doctor are you waiting to see?"

I took my time before I answered. "Dr. Leonard."

"Honey, you'll be waiting all day to see that man; he's always packing the house."

This conversation was becoming interesting so I asked her to elaborate. The dark-skinned sister added, "All the ladies come here just to see him."

"Why?" I asked while offering Ahmad a piece of a butter-flavored cookie.

"Because he's easy on the eyes and I just love the way he examines me, don't you?"

It was obvious that she nor the light-skinned sister could read the shock on my face for they went on telling me how they would achieve orgasms just from the touch of his large hands when he examined their breasts.

"If that nurse wasn't in the office, I think I would give him some wouldn't you?" The dark-skinned sister asked as she slapped high five with the light-skinned sister. By now I was steaming underneath my suit. It was on the tip of my tongue to curse them out but I wanted their stupid asses to keep on talking; I wanted to hear the truth before I set the record straight.

"So you get orgasms?" I asked.

"Right on, and honey it's good enough to smoke a cigarette afterwards." The light-skinned and the dark-skinned sister laughed and slapped high fives again.

"Excuse me sister, what is your name?" I asked the dark-skinned sister.

"Lisa?"

"And what is your name?" I asked the light-skinned sister.

"Monique."

"Well I'm Mrs. Dorothy Leonard, Dr. Leonard's wife."

To see the looks on their faces when I said that. They both looked like deer caught in headlights.

"Well," the light-skinned sister responded before she glanced at the reaction of the sister sitting beside her.

"Thank you ladies for shedding some insight on what really goes on at the doctor's office."

"I apologize Mrs. Leonard." The light-skinned sister's cocoa-buttered complexion was now crimson. "I had no intention of disrespecting you."

I felt some gratification from seeing the disappointment in their eyes, it taught them a lesson to be careful who you gossip to because you may never know the status of the other person.

"What is it like being the wife of a gynecologist?" Lisa asked.

I thought about the life I lived with David. Material-wise it was great; I loved my lifestyle, but from an emotional stand point, it was beginning to take its toll on me.

"I love it; I'm not worried about what goes on up here, because I know at the end of the day he's coming home to be with me and his son, whom he absolutely adores." I kissed Ahmad on top of his curly ringlets and gave them an eye-full of my diamond wedding ring when I crossed my legs. When Ms. Johnson reappeared in the doorway she told me to follow her. I gathered Ahmad and flashed a phony smile at the two ladies.

"It's been charming," I said before following Ms. Johnson into David's office. He was sitting behind his massive mahogany desk with his eyes buried in a stack of papers.

"Doctor Leonard, I have someone here to see you."

He looked up from the top rim of his reading glasses. "What a pleasant surprise."

Ahmad was too excited that he abandoned my grip and jumped into David's lap. I watched as David bounced him up and down on his knee.

"I came by to see if you wanted to join us for lunch," I asked.

David's eyes traveled from mine to Ms. Johnson's. "Ms. Johnson would you close the door on your way out, please."

"Sure." She smiled and gave me a pat on the shoulder.

Once the door closed, David's smile vanished. "Dorothy, as much as I want to I can't; you saw the waiting area outside."

"Yes I know, but Ahmad cried all morning after you left."

David looked into his son's eyes. "Ahmad did you do that?"

To his surprise, Ahmad nodded.

"Okay son, for you, I'll take a thirty minute break."

He took Ahmad off of his knee and placed him on the floor. Ahmad, at one year-old, could sense that he had his father wrapped around his little finger. He was chipper and for a little bit; I was too, until I thought about the two girls sitting in the waiting area. When we got inside the car, I couldn't hold my tongue. "David, are you having sex with your patients?"

"What in the hell..." He stopped, realizing that Ahmad was sitting in the back seat he lowered his voice. "What would make you say a stupid thing like that?"

"I just had a talk with two of your patients, and they told me how they would achieve orgasms from your examinations, care to explain that?"

"Dorothy that's my fuc- that is my job. I examine women's bodies. I am not responsible if they have orgasms and I don't intentionally try to arouse anybody. My nurse is present, my gloves are on, I do my job and that is that!"

"Why do they dress like that, you and Bill ought to enforce a dress code. Some of those women dress like they're going to bed, David."

"Dorothy, I can't tell my patients how to dress."

"Yes you can. You are supposed to be operating a respectable practice, but from the looks of your patients, it seems to me like you're running a whorehouse."

"You know, I would expect you to say something like that."

"You damn right, I don't appreciate it David."

"So what do you want me to do, give up my job?"

I didn't respond and instead, glanced out the window at the objects that zoomed by. I didn't concentrate on anything one thing in particular. "Sometimes I wonder."

"Wonder about what Dorothy?"

"Nothing."

"What?"

"Nothing."

David stopped the car and turned to face me. "Speak your mind Dorothy; sometimes you wonder."

"If the reason why you don't want me working at the office is because it interferes with you trying to score with one of your patients."

"Dorothy let me get this straight and you can take this two ways, either you get it, or you just plain stupid. Why would I risk my career and my marriage, on a piece of p-u-s-s-y?" he spelled it out. David tried so hard to convince me that he was indeed faithful, but my heart was saying what Bettye had told me, "Dorothy, beware."

Chapter 11

Four years had come and gone. Four reunions had come and gone, and my marriage to David was not without its highs and lows and for a young girl of twenty-eight, I found myself just plum exhausted. I became a nervous wreck, walking on pins and needles, trying to make everything appear happy from the outside, when it really wasn't, but I left it up to my acting skills. I think the only joy I got was getting Ahmad prepared for private school. I spent my days on the sofa reading to my baby and when I wasn't doing that I was making out a list of things to buy him for school. David, on the other hand, ran across the country. If he wasn't at the hospital, he was at the office. And if he wasn't at the office, he was checking out the site of our new home. It was almost finished, and the only things needing to make the 8,500 square foot structure complete was the furniture. David started plans for the house back in 1972. He wanted the locale in a retreat-type atmosphere so he found 30 acres of land in Southwest Houston. I was excited. David talked all the time about building the ultimate dream home, and it seemed his dream was just days away. He told me it had six bedrooms, five baths, a five car garage, a game room, a library, a jacuzzi room, a tennis court, which I thought was extra, considering the fact I didn't play tennis, an Olympic size pool, a music studio; which was another luxury item he just had to have, and a huge kitchen, I mean huge with a sun roof stationed right above the island, with an industrial refrigerator and stove, just like I wanted. I think David counted sixteen rooms.

I was pondering really hard on what I needed to get Ahmad when the telephone rang. I picked it up. "Hello."

I heard absolute silence on the other end.

"Hello."

Still silence, so I hung up. That's the second time today it's happened; the first time happened this morning, right after David left for work. I guess someone felt the need to call and hold the phone to his face like an idiot. I pulled out a writing pad and pen and started listing the things Ahmad needed: shoes, pants, shirts, socks, drawers, undershirts, sweaters. Ten minutes passed and RING. I let it ring three times before I picked it up and held it.

"Hello."

Silence.

"Hello."

Silence.

"Hey, get a fucking life and stop calling here!" I didn't want to say that, but I did. I slammed the phone down and unplugged it. Ophelia walked in and stared at me rather strangely.

"What was that all about?"

"Just someone with nothing else better to do."

She sat on the sofa across from me and twiddled her thumbs around her knees. At twenty-six years-old, she was still lacking a year of art credits at the Art Institute of Chicago, still jobless, and still depressed about stuff that happened five years ago. Lately she's been in and out of rehabs trying to get the jones off her back. What started three years ago as a minor accident turned into a freaking head on collision. Ophelia started experimenting with drugs. I blamed myself partially; I shouldn't have let her come with me and David to the Ali and Frazier fight. David threw a wild after party, and though I never saw it with my own eyes, I suspected there were drugs involved. Initially she tried marijuana, and when that high didn't satisfy her, she turned to heroin. I discovered this ugly side of her when I came home and heard the stereo blasting Jimi Hendrix, and you know how an electrical guitar with the volume to the max sounds in a house. I thought it was World War III in her bedroom. I rushed in and there she was sitting on the floor looking like a zombie. I went hysterical.

When the drugs started, the stealing started. Money came up missing from my purse; some of my fine antiques came up missing. She went so far as to stealing the painting she painted of me. That's when I drew the line. I told Ophelia to get out, if she didn't give a damn about herself, I sure as hell didn't either. Ophelia wasn't gone a week before I got a call from HPD. They found Ophelia wondering around town, barefoot and crying, with a purse full of stolen credit cards, all in my name. They asked if I wanted to press charges. My mind said yes, go ahead, but I heard myself tell the officer, "No." When I picked her up, I took her straight to rehab; not a word exchanged between us. All I remember is how I wanted to strangle her, dismantle her, do anything to put her out of misery. I was running from rehab to rehab spending unnecessary money. Hell, I even sat in on some sessions and offered to counsel her myself. I managed to do all this, while at the same time, deal with my problems with David. If you ask me, there were times when I thought I needed psychiatric help. I swear the stuff I tolerate is enough to drive me to an early grave.

"Dot, I think I'm ready," Ophelia blurted out.

"Ready for what?" I was anxious to know.

"I think I'm ready to go back to school."

"And I think I'm ready to have the big one. Ophelia, who in the hell do you think I am? You think every time you do something, I'm suppose to jump?"

"I must've been sick in the head thinking I'd get your support."

"Yes, you are sick in the head, because I'm not spending another dime on you."

She nodded and bit her bottom lip, acting as if I made her feel two feet tall.

"That's a cold thing to say to your sister, your own flesh and blood."

"Ophelia, get out of my face."

"If I can't get help from my own family, who can I turn to?" Ophelia said aloud to herself, "Everybody wants to dwell on what I did in the past. I admit it, yeah I fucked up, but that's behind me. I don't have no use for drugs no more, I seen what they can do to you, they destroy your mind, they destroy your soul; Dot, they destroy the people you love, they destroy everything."

I blocked Ophelia from my mind and continued to write the list I had been trying to write for thirty minutes. I heard her get up and run down the hall. A few minutes later I heard the door slam.

* * *

I must've spent hours deciding on food, alcohol, and fourth-of-July decorations. Tonight I was hosting a house warming party and I had just the right foods, just the right decorations, and just the right music to spice it up right.

The first three guests arrived around 9:30. They were my cousins Mary and Claire and Helen, their childhood friend, who had flown in from California. When Mary made her grand entrance she looked around the room and shouted, " Hey, there are no men at this party! Where they at?"

"Give them a few minutes, they'll show up," I said and ushered them to a seat.

"Dorothy, I just envy you; you seem to have everything," Mary began. "You have a man bringing home a six figure salary, a gorgeous home, a beautiful child; cousin what more can you ask for?"

I sat down in my hot pink Oscar de la Renta outfit David had purchased. "A bigger set of boobs perhaps."

"Here you can have mine," Claire added. I noticed for a woman who couldn't have weighed more than 120 pounds, she had a voluptuous bust-line, just like the actress, Pam Grier, who she bore a striking resemblance to.

"Stand up girl, show us what you have on? I'm scared to look at it, it's so bright."

I stood up and modeled for the ladies. I admit it was a bit on the bright side.

"I like that skirt, does it unfasten? And check out that split, uh oh."

"Where did you get it? Hell, I want one myself."

"David was in Miami about a week ago and he got it for me. He told me the moment he saw it, he knew he had to get it."

"Now that's what I like," Helen, began, "a man with taste; why can't I find a man with taste?"

"Why can't you find a man period?" Mary added.

I laughed; I missed my cousins who both went on to college and had thriving careers. Mary, the oldest, worked with public relations at Capitol Records, Claire; on the other hand, worked as a photographer with *Life* magazine's Los Angeles bureau. She brought her portfolio and I was pretty impressed with her spread, especially the one she did on Billy Dee Williams.

"What was it like working with him?" I asked.

"I tried so hard not to get star struck, but honey, with Billy Dee it was hard not to." Claire began to fan the air around her. "But he's a perfect gentleman, down to earth, really a neat person. It's just too bad he's married."

"And?" Helen began.

"And that's not my style; see some of us still have class Helen," Claire responded while shaking her index finger at Helen. I noticed a pear-shaped diamond solitaire ring.

Helen, who sported an ebony styled afro, rolled her long black eye lashes at Claire. "I would've taken advantage of his attention," she mumbled.

"See, that's why you can't find a man," Mary added. "You act too desperate."

I heard myself laughing.

Helen glanced at me. "Okay, we'll see who's laughing when I leave here with a doc-tor."

"Oooooh," Mary and Claire said in unison.

"I know you're not talking about my man." I said jokingly.

"Your man and nine other men just like him, okay?"

"I'd like to see you try and get through that door with ten men dangling from that big afro of yours."

Mary and Claire laughed. Helen shook her finger at me and laughed. "That's a good one, real good."

"You ladies can get up and look around if you feel like it, the band should be here in a minute."

"Dorothy, if you could just kindly direct me to the champagne I'll be just fine," Helen said while opening up a purse that contained her cigarettes.

"Go outside through those double doors, dear."

"Thank you sugar, and while you're at it, could you kindly direct me to your man?"

"Helen, could you kindly direct your 'fro through those double doors like I told you?"

She waved her hand and strutted her skin tight blue denim bell bottom jumpsuit in that direction.

More guests arrived. Some were from David's practice, some I didn't recognize but who knew David, and one person in particular whom I hadn't seen since the night of my wedding. He was dressed in white and smelling like Irish Spring and expensive cologne.

"Jerome."

"Little Dorothy."

"Jerome."

Jerome embraced me and when it seemed that wasn't enough he kissed me on the lips. Not a peck, but a real kiss. It caught me off guard, and it took a while for me to gain back my composure. I kept looking around for David, for fear he might make a scene like he did the night of our wedding.

"Look at you." Jerome stood back and admired my outfit. "You haven't changed one bit, you still look the same as you did ten years ago, Dorothy."

"Thank you Jerome, come in and have a seat."

He walked in, or should I say glided into my living room. I closed the door behind me and checked out his appearance. He changed a lot, especially in the hair part. Jerome was bald like Isaac Hayes, and he was a little on the stout side too. But he was still handsome and suave as ever.

"So were the directions hard to follow?" I asked, ushering him to a seat.

"No, not at all. I stopped by my parent's house and talked with them for about an hour, I left there and caught up with a friend of mine from med school. So I would've been here a lot sooner, but hey, I'm here." He smiled and gave me a light pinch on the jaw.

"Where's my frat at?"

"He's upstairs."

"Upstairs! What is he doing upstairs? The party is down here."

"Good question, Jerome."

"Well, tell him to come down. His long lost Frat has finally arrived."

"I sure will."

"Where's the restroom, Dorothy?"

"It's right down the hall, first door on the right."

I walked upstairs and entered the bedroom. It was empty, so I glanced around the room and noticed the light from the bathroom was on, so I walked inside. I was overwhelmed with shock at what I saw. David was sitting with his face buried on the marble bathroom counter.

"David!" I said it so fast.

He raised up quickly and wiped his nose.

"What?" he answered, sounding aggravated.

I shook my head in disbelief. "David, tell me that's not what I think it is."

David said to me with a smile emerging from his lips, "It's not what you think it is." His voice was deep and breathy.

"What in the hell are you trying to do!" I was so enraged.

"Dorothy, look."

"David no, I don't want to hear it!"

I turned and walked away. Before I could open the bedroom door, he from out of nowhere, jumped up and slammed it shut. He grabbed me and turned me around.

"Dot, let me explain." When he touched me his hands were cold as ice.

"Explain what, what is there to explain?" I stopped and sighed for a moment. "How long has this been going on?"

"I don't know, since college."

"So that explains it," I said.

David released me and turned away from my stare.

"Were you high on our wedding night?"

"I don't remember?"

"Were you high in St. Thomas?"

David's eyes met mine. "Yeah, I don't remember." His voice was hesitant.

"Where have you been all those times when I was running in and out of rehab behind Ophelia?" The veins in my neck began to tighten up.

"Dot, will you please let me explain!"

"Go ahead."

"Look, when you've gone through as much as I have, and seen as much as I have, the pressure Dorothy…" He stopped. The look on his face was so intense it had me shivering.

"Look Dorothy, I'm tired. I'm losing momentum. Ten years ago I could work all night and go all day without sleep, then show up for work, wide-eyed alert and ready for the next day. Just last week alone, I managed to get only seven hours of sleep."

"Why…"

He held up his hand. "Let me finish. I use to brag about it, take bets on it, but now." He shook his head. "It's wearing on me Dorothy, and all I ask is that you bear with me. I know you feel like I've let you and Ahmad down, but I haven't…"

"So you feel you need something, a crutch to keep you alert."

He took his fingers and squeezed his eyelids. "Dorothy look, I'll make a promise. I won't do it again."

"Shut up, I'm tired of you making empty promises." I tried not to scream for fear the guests would hear us.

"All I needed was one blow, just one to get me through tonight. I realize this party is important for the both of us. But I promise, after tonight no more."

I leaned my head against the wall. This episode was all too familiar. I heard "no more" enough times to send me to the moon and back. "First Ophelia, now you." I laughed. It seemed like the only thing to do to keep from crying. "Oh God, just a minute ago the girls and I were talking about having everything. They said, 'Dorothy, you seem to have everything: a handsome husband, who brings home a six figure check, a beautiful home, a beautiful child-you have everything you want.' I just wish they could see me now." David turned and walked without emotion towards the bathroom. I laughed and opened the door. "You coming down or what?"

"I'll be down in a minute."

"Jerome's here."

"I'll be down in a minute."

I closed the door and stood there holding the knob in my hands. I didn't know how to feel, I didn't know what to say. Something told me to forget about it, shut it off because it'll only get uglier if you think about it. So I walked calmly down the hall and downstairs and laughed louder than I did before I left.

The band was out in the gazebo playing, *Let's Get it On* and anyone who could dance was out on the terrace dancing. It kind of reminded me of Soul Train, the way everybody dressed, the way they moved, and the way their afros swayed. I picked up a bottle of gin and played bartender. If I saw anybody's glass empty, even if they weren't drinking gin, it was getting filled to the rim. I spotted Marcus and his girlfriend, Mercedes, smooching in the corner like high school kids.

"Hey, you guys, give each other some breathing room."

"Hello Sis." Marcus' eyes widened when he saw what I had on. "My brother just had to buy that outfit."

"Of course."

"Dorothy you look sassy and hot," Mercedes began, she was Marcus' main flame, a professional model from Miami with Cuban roots. Mercedes looked sharp and sassy herself, plus she recognized a hot item when she saw one. "Where's David?" She asked.

"Yeah where is he?" Marcus began. "Doesn't he know his wife just started a four alarm fire out here?" I thought about David and faked a laugh. "He'll be down in a minute. He had another long day at the office."

"Tell me something I don't already know." Marcus began.

"So Marcus, are you still hanging in there with Miami next season?"

"Of course, you know Miami's my second home."

"When does training start?"

"In about three weeks."

Marcus had gotten larger, muscle wise. He turned pro about a year ago, and things were going pretty well for him. Since high school, he dreamed of going pro, but you know Doc Sr. and Ms. Liz doted on intellectuals, not jocks, in their family. They wanted Marcus to play football for the sake of recreation, but to Marcus it was more than that. Football was his life; he wanted to tackle the gridiron and follow in the footsteps of Jim Brown and O. J. Simpson. Since his sophomore year in high school, Marcus was determined to get into a top notch university, so he chose the University of Miami. While in college, Marcus was an All-American, setting and breaking school records in football and track. He was a natural born athlete, and if I wasn't mistaken, he played soccer too.

"So Sis why are you holding that bottle?"

"Where is your glass Marcus and yours Mercedes."

"Come on now, you know I don't drink."

"Just one swig."

"No," Marcus protested.

"Marcus, you're a party pooper."

"Here, I'll have some." Mercedes held out her glass.

While I poured, Marcus decided he wanted some.

"No. I thought you didn't drink."

"One swig wouldn't hurt, damn."

I made my way to the band who was playing *I'll Take you There* by the Staple Singers. The bass player in the group was making cute faces as he thumped the strings. So I hung around and entertained him and the rest of the band with my so-called dancing. I heard my cousins and Helen behind me laughing and urging me to do all kinds of dances like the funky chicken, and the watusi. I believed I toned down after that number and went inside. I spotted David laughing and talking with

Myranda and Bill. I didn't want to be anywhere near him, so I went back out and danced until sweat flew everywhere. I stopped long enough to get another shot of gin. When that wasn't enough, I got two more shots, then three shots. I got tipsy and mellowed out by the poolside. After awhile I felt some gentle, masculine hands encircle my body and a penis bulge against my spine. I smelled the old familiar scent of Irish Spring and I knew it wasn't David. "W-www wait a minute," I heard myself stutter.

"Dorothy," Jerome whispered against my ear in a low mellifluous voice. I turned around. "Jerome," I laughed. "I should've known it was you. You better stop."

"I wanted to mention it to you earlier, but then I thought, nanh, bad timing."

"Say what?"

"Are you okay?" He looked into my eyes and saw that I was in a daze.

"I'm fine," I said.

"I wanted to tell you how fabulous you look in that dress."

"Thank you Jerome."

"I talked to my frat, he's a very, very, very, lucky man."

I giggled, "Thank you. I'm a very, very, very, lucky woman."

My mind rewound to what I saw earlier, instantly I didn't want to talk about David anymore.

"Are you hungry, what have you eaten?" I grabbed his hand and led him to the buffet table. "We have honey-glazed chicken, barbecue chicken, smoked turkey, crawfish."

Jerome picked up a turkey drum stick and bit it. "Hmmm. You didn't cook all this yourself?"

"No I had it catered. Here try some of this." I took a small slice of potato pie and allowed him to sample it. He bit it and didn't hesitate to lick each one of my fingers.

"And there's plenty more where that came from." I said.

"I see." Jerome's stare was seductive. He took my hand. "Can we go somewhere and talk?" He asked.

"Jerome, no, look, why are you doing this?"

"I just want to know one thing?"

"What?"

"Are you happy here Dorothy?"

"Is that the reason why you came all the way from California?"

"It's part of the reason, but, nevertheless, it's a very important reason."

"Yes, Jerome, I am very happy, why?"

"If you ever need anything, just give me a call."

I knew I was drunk. But maybe, just maybe, I heard a hint of consideration for my well-being in Jerome's voice.

"I know better than anybody the type of man David can be sometimes."

"Good, but I'm happy, I couldn't have been happier." I responded, trying to sound upbeat.

"Take care Dorothy." He leaned forward to give me a kiss, but I turned my head.

"Jerome, I think you better leave."

He nodded, and without looking back, he strolled through the crowd of people. I stood, with a million-and-one thoughts racing through my mind. I was on the verge of tears when I retreated inside the house. This was suppose to be a happy occasion, but I was so miserable. I picked up another bottle of gin and poured myself a drink. By now my insides were burning and throbbing, like someone was pouring acid inside me. Then suddenly the room started changing colors and I swear it seemed I had infrared vision. I was out of it; I wasn't even aware of the photographer directly in front of me.

"Mrs. Leonard, I'm from the Houston Defender. Would you and Dr. Leonard care to pose for some shots?"

"Sure, where's my husband?" I squinted and looked for David.

"I see him. He's on his way, Mrs. Leonard."

"I'm sorry, I didn't catch your name?"

"I apologize, my name is Carlton Shays." He extended his hand, I shook it. Gosh he had a strong grip, I thought.

"Carlton, excuse me I need to freshen up."

"Oh, go right ahead."

"There's plenty to eat and drink out back; you're more than welcome to something."

My head throbbed and pounded harder as I walked to the restroom. Once inside, I closed the door and looked at myself in the mirror. My hair still looked good, my make-up, except for my lipstick was all in place. Wait, who was I trying to fool. I looked like shit, and I felt like shit too. My head was swimming in thoughts, crazy thoughts; there was absolutely no explanation for the way I was feeling. Needless to say, I felt good some of the time and felt like shit all of the time. Half of me wanted to break down and cry, the other half wanted to forget about all of life's troubles and party like there was no tomorrow. I turned on the faucet, grabbed a towel and wet it just a little enough to dry some of the perspiration on my skin. I turned off the light, walked outside, took the photograph with David, and danced until my legs were sore.

Two hours later…

"Psss Myranda, I want to talk to you." My head was spinning uncontrollably.

"Dorothy, are you okay?"

My mouth was hanging down a mile, and I could barely walk. Myranda caught me before I fell.

"Where's David?" Her voice echoed, just like the other voices around me. Even the music echoed.

"Myranda, help me."

"I will, but you have to help me and take at least one step." My legs were numb.

"I can't walk, Ophelia."

"I'm not Ophelia, okay? Hey, can I get some help!" she shouted.

I closed my eyes and began to sing a song I heard Aretha singing about daydreaming. I didn't care how it sounded, so long as somebody heard it. A few seconds later a familiar voice said, "I got her." A second later I was swept off my feet and carried upstairs. I heard the door open and close and the sound of laughter dying in the distance. I knew I was in my own bed when my body hit the firm mattress. The lamp light came on and blinded me. "I don't need that damn light, turn it off."

Then the smell of Lagerfeld cologne crept into my nostrils; I opened my eyes.

"David?"

David leaned forward and kissed me on the lips. "I'm here baby," he said softly. That was all I needed, a lousy ass kiss from him. I wiped it away because it was cold and wet and tasted like rum.

"Why don't you go on and leave me alone," I said.

"I have been thinking," He began.

"Oh really?" I said. "You still manage to think?"

"I deserve that," he said. "I'm sorry if I disappointed you all these years. I just want you to know that I never really meant to hurt you."

"But you have."

"Shhhh." He put his finger over my lips. "I am willing to put the past with the drugs and my anger behind, if you are willing to start over with me."

I thought about it; he really seemed sincere. "Okay," I said.

"Thank you Dorothy." He put his arms around me and kissed my lips. "I love you so much honey." Pretty soon the rum on his lips began to taste sweet and I closed my eyes.

I awoke to find myself naked and in great pain. *God what on earth*? I thought as I looked around and saw the top of my outfit lying on David's pillow. I tried to get up, but my head felt ten pounds heavier and my neck was sore. I fought the pain and raised up anyway. My stomach and breasts were covered with small red passion marks. I took my bed sheets and wrapped them around me. As I put my feet on the floor, I noticed my panties were lying there along side David's wallet. My body struggled to fight against another bout with pain, before I picked them up. David's wallet came open and out fell a fifty dollar bill and a yellow piece of paper with the initials C. G. and the number 777-7713 underneath it. I wondered what C. G. stood for. Anyway, there was no need in fighting more unnecessary bouts with pain, so I crawled my naked body back into bed.

CHAPTER 12

Dorothy was shaking her head. Dr. Clarke told her some news she didn't want to believe.

"Are you sure, Dr. Clarke?"

"I'm positive, Mrs. Leonard."

"How far along?"

"Twelve weeks."

Dorothy sighed and stared at the ceiling silently praying to God. She was pregnant. Abortion came to mind, but she convinced herself she had a conscience and couldn't continue life with the dark cloud of abortion suspended over her. David didn't want another child; he told her that on numerous occasions. Now she was scared to face him for fear that he would lash out like he often times did. When Dorothy arrived home, she cried and cuddled herself between the pillows atop her king size bed. She blamed the melancholy on hormones, remembering how she went through a bout of it during the first pregnancy. But during that period, it came and went suddenly. This time it lingered with Dorothy.

David came home that evening around nine and slapped on the lights. He paused when he saw his wife balled up like a bug on top of the covers. He slowly took off his brown leather coat and hung it in the closet along with his white medical coat. The flame was almost burning out in the fireplace, so he opened it and turned the charcoal and ash covered logs over. David wasn't satisfied until the fire had rebuilt itself into a row of flames. He then walked into the bathroom and opened the seat on the toilet and laughed quietly to himself, recalling a joke he had heard during lunch. After the toilet splashed and gurgled he washed his hands and wrestled with his conscious. He was dying for another blow, but instead he undressed down to his boxers and slid on top of the bed next to his wife's warm and soft body. Dorothy opened her eyes and turned to face her husband.

"Hello," she said.

Dorothy closed her eyes when David brushed his lips against hers.

"How was your day?" he asked while pecking softly around her neck.

"Okay," She mumbled, feeling her body tighten when David pulled her closer. He couldn't help but notice the dismal look in her eyes. "What's wrong?"

"I went to see Dr. Clarke."

David waited in anticipation for more.

"Honey, we're gonna have another baby." Dorothy said.

"Are you serious?"

"Yes I'm afraid so." Dorothy examined the look in his eyes, she couldn't tell whether or not he was happy, but to her surprise he planted a congratulatory kiss on her lips.

"You're not mad?" she asked.

"Why should I be mad? Ahmad needs a brother or sister."

"I know," Dorothy heard herself agreeing.

"Dorothy we need some more life in this house. Hell, I like hearing the pitter and patter of feet." David turned her face and body away from his.

"I love you, Dorothy," David said as he kissed the nape of her neck and rubbed the long caesarian scar underneath her navel. A minute later he was asleep.

*　　*　　*

"Mama, it's me how are you?"

Ms. LaCroix was ironing Lucky's pants when Dorothy called.

"Hi, dear I'm fine, just ironing Lucky and Jacqueline's school clothes."

Dorothy leafed quickly through a Sears catalogue. "Mama guess what?"

"Don't tell me nothing else about that damn Ophelia, that bitch got more problems than a chicken got feathers."

"Believe me when I tell you, this ain't about Ophelia."

"Good, tell me anything, but don't tell me nothing else about that damn girl, Ole' bitch; she ain't seen Lucky since he been here."

"Now, Mama."

Ms. LaCroix was so steamed she forgot about Lucky's pants and burned a brown ugly hole in them.

"I be goddamn."

"What happened Mama?"

"I burned a hole in this baby's pants."

"Mama, I'm pregnant again."

"Ah shit."

"Mama."

"I didn't' mean you, I'm still pissed off about these pants. I spent too much money on them."

"You can afford another pair."

Ms. LaCroix rolled up Lucky's pants in frustration and threw them on the floor.

"So you and David got another baby coming?"

Dorothy released a tired sigh. "Yes Mama, due in April."

"I thought y'all weren't gonna have any more children."

"That was five years ago; a lot has changed since then."

"Well, look at it like this, you and David aren't getting any younger. Plus you got all that money, you live in a baddass house, you go first class around the world, one more child wouldn't hurt. As a matter of fact, three more wouldn't hurt."

"Speak for yourself Mama, I don't think I can take anymore cuts after this one. That scar from my caesarian operation looks so ugly under my navel."

"Anyway, how's my grandbaby, Ahmad doing?"

"He's doing real good in school; you know my baby reads second grade level books."

"That's good. Lucky just learned how to write his name. Dot, it's so cute. You know I got Lucky enrolled in preschool now."

"Really? How is Jacqueline, Little Miss Fancy Pants."

"That little heffa likes to mess with my make-up and stuff toilet tissue in her blouse. I say keep on, one of these days you gon' have titties so big, you ain't gonna know what to do with them."

"You know little girls go through that stage."

"Yeah, you and your sisters did the same thing."

Dorothy glanced at her chest. "My boobs aren't that big Mama."

"Not yet, but wait until you have this baby. They usually get bigger after the second child."

"Not necessarily, I've known women to have four children and still have small breasts."

"That doesn't stop them from sagging."

Dorothy thought about that. "I guess you have a point."

"I know I do."

Dorothy thought about her oldest sister. "Mama, how is Katherine?"

"I talked to Katherine yesterday and she told me she was getting bored with her secretarial job. I told her to quit that job; it ain't even worth the headache and suffering, so now she's talking about moving back home."

"How are things between her and Ricky?"

"She didn't say, so I assume it's gotten better."

"I know they were on shaky ground for a moment. I remember her telling me, Ricky got laid off and she was the only one bringing home a steady paycheck."

"I don't know what to say about Ricky; I don't understand him. Here is a man with an engineering degree and he claims he can't find a job."

"Well then Mama, it's not so much he can't find a job; I'm sure there are jobs out there. The problem is people aren't giving them to the ones who qualify. They're giving them to their friends."

"That ain't it, that motherfucka' just lazy."

"Mama, stop it." Dorothy got tickled.

"Enough about Katherine's man, let's talk about your man. Did the stuff work for him?"

"I hope it did; I did everything you told me. I prayed over it for ten minutes and sprinkled some under his pillow."

"Did you take his picture and pray over it?"

"Yes I did."

"Did you take his drawers and rub them in olive oil?"

"Yes Mama."

"Sister Devereaux told me if there's anything else you need let her know."

"I hope I won't have to ask for anything like that. Mama I can't help feeling…"

"Feeling like what?"

"Like I deceived him."

"Deceived? Unh huh; if anything you helped him. Tell me what's wrong with putting a little herb under the pillow. Hell, I do whatever it takes to keep my man from doing dope. Now the last thing you need are two dope-heads on your hand. Dot, I keep telling you, it's better to stop him now before he snorts his house, his job, you, and that baby up his nose."

Ms. LaCroix lamented for a second. "Dot, when you first told me about David, that really hurt me. I don't normally let stuff bother me, but that bothered me, and all I wanna know is why would he even think about doing that?"

Dorothy didn't shed insight with her mother that David had been experimenting on an off with cocaine since his undergraduate years in college.

Dorothy released another tired sigh and checked the time on her watch.

"My God, what's next?" Ms. LaCroix asked.

Dorothy remained silent.

"Well Dot, I'll burn a few candles of my own and say a prayer for you."

"Thanks Ma, I could use it."

*　　*　　*

Outside, Dorothy's driveway looked like a luxury car lot. While inside, the aroma of pastries, finger sandwiches, and cream of broccoli soup meandered about the kitchen and den. The den was cluttered with opened packages of baby gifts. Dorothy was well into her third trimester. She knew she was going to have a girl this time, so she told everyone to buy soft feminine colors.

"Thanks you guys," She said after opening a package that contained a baby book with her sorority's colors. Five of her sorors were there along with Tiny, Mrs. Johnson, her mother, Aunt Ruby Jewel, Ms. Liz, Katherine, Mercedes, Myranda, Sadaria and Chanel Gainous.

Ms. Gainous was the newest member of the Leonard practice who started work as a receptionist last summer. After severing ties with her family, and a failed attempt at completing college, she left New Orleans and moved west to Houston. It was during a visit to David's office that she decided she wanted to work. She noticed Sadaria was overwhelmed with paper work and insisted David hire her. David was impressed with her audacity not to mention the creamy white tank tube mini dress that covered her mahogany complexion. He told her to be at the office at eight o'clock sharp. It was 7:59 a.m. when Chanel stepped off the city bus and showed up for her first day wearing a short, black, spandex skirt with a soft pink, low-cut blouse. When she introduced herself to Sadaria and told her that she was working, Sadaria thought it was a joke.

"You call yourself working in that outfit?"

Chanel took one look at herself. "What's wrong with what I have on?"

"Everything. Honey that outfit has "coochie for sale" written all over it." Chanel thought that comment was rather harsh coming from someone who didn't know her, but she learned very quickly that Ms. Sadaria McCloud didn't bite her tongue.

"And another thing Miss Chanel, if you're trying to entice Dr. Leonard or Dr. Corbin, I got news for you; they're both happily married with beautiful wives." Chanel's expression didn't change on the outside, but on the inside her heart fluttered at the thought of David. Chanel moved to Houston with an agenda, and number one on her agenda was finding David. She was obsessed with him from the moment she laid eyes on him almost ten years ago. She still had the bouquet in her possession. Although the flowers had withered a long time ago, she held on to the frozen bouquet as a reminder that her accompanying her half-sister, Whitney to the wedding, and catching the bouquet was no accident; she was destined to be with David. Now she had her foot in the door of opportunity and she wasn't going to let anything, not even his marriage to Dorothy, stop her.

Chanel eventually finagled her way into the Leonard household during a Christmas party and began a friendship with Dorothy. She found they had a lot in common, they were both born under the Taurus sign, they were both crazy about their fathers, and like Dorothy's father, Chanel's father passed away when she was eighteen. Chanel liked to plan parties and Dorothy thought it was awfully nice of her to organize the baby shower. Chanel was very low-key, and quiet. She preferred to stay away from everyone else and busy herself serving punch and cutting slices of cake. Chanel eventually made her acquaintance with everyone and everyone seemed to think it was nice of her to go beyond the call of duty.

"Cuz, who is she?" Tiny asked, biting into a pickle.

"Who?"

Tiny nodded her head in Chanel's direction. "The girl serving the punch."

"That's Whitney's sister, Chanel Gainous."

"Chanel Gainous, the name doesn't ring a bell, make me know her."

"She's Soror Whitney's half-sister."

"Well, I don't consider myself a mind reader, but I'm reading her, and I'm getting some unusual vibes."

"From Chanel? Why?"

"Where did you meet this girl?"

"She works for David."

Tiny paused from chewing on her pickle and gave Dorothy a questionable stare.

"Tiny, I'm confused what are you getting at?"

"Dorothy, watch her. Now I don't know what type of person she is, but whatever it is, I just hope this feeling in my chest is a bad case of indigestion."

"You know Sadaria told me the same thing, I'm not feeling any bad vibes from her, I think she's good people."

"You know Caesar felt that way about Brutus and Jesus felt that way about Judas."

"Tiny, I think you've had too much to drink. You are way out in left field with this Brutus jive and besides, Chanel's got her own thing going, she has a good man."

"Have you met this man?"

"No."

"Hmmphf," Tiny replied.

After the baby shower, Chanel lingered around and helped Dorothy clean up.

"Chanel, you've done enough sweetheart, go home."

Chanel plopped down on the couch. "I would go home, but there's nothing to do there."

"I'm sure your man will keep you company."

"My man is so boring, half the time I end up going out." Chanel looked at Dorothy, "Do you go clubbing?"

"No," Dorothy replied.

"I forgot you don't party."

"It's not that I don't party. I just don't go to night clubs and bars; I normally do dinner parties. David and I use to throw parties all the time," Dorothy said reminiscing about the Ali and Frazier fight. "One time we flew to New York to the Ali-Frazier fight and David along with his colleagues rented a suite at the Mariott and we threw the loudest, rowdiest, baddest after party, and baby we rocked all night long."

Chanel was impressed, at least on the surface. But down underneath, she melted with envy. The stories Dorothy told her was the stuff dreams were made of, somewhat like a fairy tale. Chanel savored the opportunity to tell her friends the same kinds of stories, true stories of how it feels to make passionate love to a married man and go on with life as though nothing happened. To face that person every day and not think about the evening before when he whisked your feet off the floor and into the stirrups of his examination table and ignited passions within you you never knew existed. To face that person and not think about the evenings after five-thirty, when the two of you made his desktop a bed of roses, and made sweaty, hot, passionate love with pictures of his wife and young son nearby staring at you, and you staring back, gloating.

Chanel eyed David closely when he leaned over and gave his wife a tender kiss on the cheek. Chanel smiled quietly to herself, recalling the moments her lips, breasts, and other parts of her body spent being proud recipients of those same lips.

"How are you, Ms. Gainous?"

"I'm fine, Dr. Leonard."

"How was the baby shower?"

"You know honey, I got Ophelia to film it, but halfway through the camera started acting up."

"Acting up. How?"

"Ophelia said it kept getting out of focus."

"You sure it wasn't Ophelia."

"I checked for myself and I noticed too."

"Where's the camera?" David asked.

Dorothy stood up. "In the family room, I'll go get it."

When she left, David and Chanel sat in silence.

"Why are you still here?" David whispered once Dorothy was out of sight.

"I wanted to see you? Is that a problem?"

Before David said anymore, Dorothy entered the room again carrying the camera. "I think you need a new one if you ask me because this baby here is old and worn out."

* * *

David couldn't stop kissing his little girl's cotton soft cheeks.

"She's daddy's little girl," David told the nurse who was there with him in the nursery, "She will always be daddy's little girl." He held Nia's diminutive form in one palm and kissed her good night. Dorothy couldn't let the moment pass without grabbing the camera. "David give her another kiss," Dorothy said as she held the camera over her eye. Through the grainy screen she saw David plant a soft kiss on Nia's forehead.

At three months Nia was already sitting up on her own. It scared the hell out of Dorothy because she started running around screaming. "David quick, go get the camera! This isn't normal!"

David assured her it was a sign of maturity and independence. At ten months she was standing on her own. At her first birthday party, she was singing and miming all the songs to Stevie Wonder's, *Songs In the Key of Life* album, not to mention pulling herself to play Ahmad's piano in the process.

When Nia turned fifteen months, Dorothy was pregnant again. That was the only explanation for her queasy feelings and crying spells. Chanel was pregnant too. When Dorothy asked her if the father was just as happy as she was, she hesitated. "Linus wasn't enthused at all when I told him." Chanel's eyes were filled with tears when she explained to Dorothy that the man, who she called "Linus," insisted she get an abortion.

"Don't do it Chanel," Dorothy told her. "I thought about it once and God forbid me to think about it again."

"Dorothy, I can't support a child; I can barely support myself."

"That's what we're here for. David and I are here to help."

Chanel cried. "Thank you. I don't know what I'd do without you. You and Dr. Leonard are good people." Chanel quickly dried her eyes. She had large, brown, almond-shaped eyes.

"You have my word on that," Dorothy said.

"I really do appreciate this, you know I really do want to have this baby."

"I know you do sweetie,." Dorothy said before giving Chanel a hug and a warm rub across her back. "The less stress you have the better off you and your baby will be."

Chanel nodded and wiped the snot that tickled the tip of her nose with a tissue.

Dorothy picked up a *Cosmopolitan* magazine and flipped randomly through the pages. "You are my soror's sister, and I'll do my best to help you." Dorothy spotted Mercedes splashing felicitously in a fountain, showing off her wide million dollar smile. Mercedes appeared svelte and energetic, a gorgeous woman with a vivacious personality.

"Chanel this Linus guy is meaningless, he's dead weight, the last thing you need is dead weight."

Chanel rubbed her abdomen she wasn't quite showing yet.

"You're right, me and my baby deserve better."

Chanel's thoughts were on David. Her baby's biological father.

* * *

Rona, Doc Sr. and Ms. Liz's housekeeper, ushered Chanel to a Garden of Eden setting. With her eyes covered with Gucci sun glasses, Chanel found a spot at the back, on the edge of the row. Meanwhile David and Dorothy were standing at the altar saying their vows to one another. Dorothy along with Reverend Long and fifty other guests, listened as David stumbled over promises and lines. Chanel took a half bottle of Pepto Bismol just before she came. She knew her stomach wouldn't be able to take the garbage she was about to hear. And to think, Dorothy asked

her to help plan the event. She even asked her to be a bridesmaid, but Chanel told her she didn't know if she was going to be in town.

"I haven't reneged on any promises. Sure our marriage hasn't always been picture perfect." David looked into Dorothy's eyes. "We've had disagreements, but after every rainy day, comes a day filled with sunshine. And I've come to realize when you have a love that's strong as ours, it can withstand the tests of time." They kissed, it was like a scene out of a soap opera. "For ten years you've been the only woman for me." David kissed her again.

Chanel felt her stomach churning into knots. She was on the verge of throwing up, so she stood up and quietly made her exit from the ceremony. She didn't stop walking until she found a bathroom and closed the door.

"A fake son-of-a-bitch, he can't be at all serious," she said aloud. He had Dorothy and everybody else fooled into believing that he was so in love with her. Chanel began to brainstorm the times she and David spent together. For three days last week he stayed all night at her house and each night around eleven he called his wife to tell her he was working overtime. For the last two years Chanel made him forget he had a wife. She made him happy, very happy. She turned that world of his inside out, doing things to him Dorothy couldn't imagine doing. Sure Dorothy was his lady in company, but Chanel was his lady too, not to mention a freak in bed. They went to Las Vegas it seemed every weekend and gambled away hundreds of dollars and enjoyed countless hours of sex. Then slept, got high, and had more sex. David made her feel special, like she was the one wearing his wedding ring. Sometimes Chanel had to catch herself because she forgot he had a wife and two kids to go home to. There was a song that best described Chanel's situation, *If Loving you is Wrong, I Don't want to do Right.* Chanel and David's relationship had spun itself into a web of selfishness. To Chanel it was all about her, she wanted the same first class treatment that Dorothy was often pampered with. To Chanel it was becoming an obligation for David to satisfy her the same way he satisfied his wife, or more so. In her mind she could have David all to herself and make life a living hell for Dorothy.

Chanel realized she was on the verge of crying and stopped herself before she allowed the salty taste of tears to fall down her flushed cheeks.

Outside David picked Dorothy off her feet and carried her laughing and crying down the aisle. The ceremony was almost dejavu of what had happened ten years earlier.

David grabbed Nia, who was dressed in a red suede dress trimmed in white ruffles. Her soft wavy black hair was gathered at the crown of her head with a red and white ribbon tied in a bow. She was adorable in her father's arm. He carried her almost everywhere he went. Ahmad was dressed too, in a little black tuxedo with a red tie and small cummberbund, which he occasionally wore for a bra because it wouldn't stay around his waist.

Dorothy's cousin, Claire, snapped two shots of David and Dorothy along with the children in front of the fireplace. Twelve a.m., after Rona put the children asleep, David and Dorothy had a New Year celebration, Mardi Gras style.

"Happy New Year David!" Dorothy shouted before giving David a kiss. Her mind drifted back ten years ago to the incident in the restroom. For obvious reasons the second time down the aisle seemed much sweeter and Dorothy was thankful that she lasted this long.

Meanwhile, far across the room in a secluded corner, pretending to be elated over the celebration stood Chanel. She glanced at David and Dorothy and shook her head. She grabbed her purse and made an exit into the darkness and loneliness that awaited her.

* * *

Dorothy went into the delivery room, and after six hours, her son was born. This time she named her son, Jamal. David didn't arrive until the following day after Jamal was born. Dorothy was still lying in the hospital drifting in and out of sleep with an extremely high blood pressure, which caused her face to swell twice its normal size. Dorothy told David out of the three pregnancies, this was by far the worst. Dorothy forgot the trouble she went through once she saw Jamal; he was wide awake staring at her smiling.

* * *

Dorothy and Chanel were both walking through the mall pushing their baby strollers and admiring baby clothing in the window display of a baby department store. Chanel had a little girl named Danielle, whom she absolutely adored and couldn't let her out of her sight. David absolutely cherished her too. He even purchased a house for Chanel and Danielle. It was a spacious three bedroom house with a huge backyard and a swimming pool where he and Chanel often swam naked.

Dorothy couldn't pass up the store without going in and purchasing something for the kids. Nia needed a couple of church dresses and Jamal needed an outfit and a pair of patent leather shoes. Dorothy picked out a pink and white dress.

"How adorable," Chanel said. She was eyeing a similar dress for Danielle.

"This is absolutely adorable."

Dorothy and Chanel didn't stop until they bought half the store, so it seemed.

When Chanel arrived home, David was sitting there.

"Hi baby." Chanel rushed up to give him a kiss, but he turned his head.

"You and I need to talk," he said. His voice sounded hard, his stare was cold.

"About what?" Chanel eyed him as she put Danielle down on a pallet.

"About you and my wife," David said. "I want the nonsense to stop."

"What nonsense? What are you talking about?"

"Stay away from my wife!"

"What do you mean stay away? Your wife is my best friend."

David frowned at her in disgust. "Friend? You call yourself a friend?"

"You are not making any sense to me."

"All right, I'm going to put it to you this way. You can have this house, I'll see to it that Danielle has a roof over her head. If she needs anything, you know how to find me."

"So what are you saying?"

"It's over."

Chanel was motionless for a few seconds. "What did you just say? You don't want me? Is that what you said?"

"That's exactly what I said."

Chanel shook her head. "I don't believe this, so you just going to walk out on me and Danielle?"

"I'm not walking away from Danielle."

"What about my needs David, what about my fucking needs?"

"I'm sorry. I have a wife and three children who need me too. I love my wife, and I can no longer go on lying to her."

Chanel's eyes were watering with tears. "You're making a big mistake."

David turned and walked towards the door.

"David if you leave, I swear I will call Dorothy and tell her everything."

He turned around. "You wouldn't."

"You try me!"

Without thinking David grabbed Chanel by her neck and pushed her slender little body up against the wall. Her face was contorted inside the palm of his large hands. "You listen to me and you listen to me good, if you fuck with me or my wife, or my children, I will kill you."

Tears fell like rain drops down her cheeks where they stopped just short of her trembling mouth.

David released her and sighed.

"What's wrong with you David? I thought you loved me!"

"I just don't know anymore. Looking back these past three years, we've had some close calls. I can't risk Dorothy finding out about us."

Chanel put her arm around him. He released himself from her and walked towards the door again. When he opened it, he turned and looked at Chanel. "Give all my love to Danielle, will you?"

Chanel burst out crying when she picked up her shoe and threw it, almost hitting him when he closed the door.

* * *

David arrived home to find his eldest son, Ahmad, entertaining Dorothy and Nia with a story book.

"Hello, honey," Dorothy said smiling ever so lovingly at her man.

"Hello," David replied before he grabbed Nia and sat her in his lap.

"Where's the baby, asleep?" He asked.

"Yes," Dorothy said.

"What's this you're reading son?"

"*The Sounder*."

"Oh yeah," David responded, sounding like a doting father.

"Yes I checked it out at the library," Ahmad said. He had another book, it was much larger. "I checked this book out too."

"This is a thick book Son. You sure you can read all that?"

"Of course, Dad."

David smiled approvingly at his oldest son.

"Ahmad, can you finish reading to Nia? Your mother and I need to talk."

Dorothy didn't like tone of his voice, but without hesitation, she stood up and followed him into the kitchen.

"How was work?" she asked, trying to sound chipper.

"It wasn't bad at all," David replied. He noticed his wife had gained some weight with the last pregnancy. She wasn't the petite size five, she wasn't even a size ten, more like a size eighteen.

"Dorothy, what have you been eating?" he asked.

Dorothy looked at herself. "Honey, that's what happens when you stay at home all day, not to mention having three children."

"Yeah, I guess. Well anyway, I received my American Express billing statement in the mail today. I noticed last month you spent $13,000. You spent $3,500 at Macy's, another $1,500 at Baby World, and $8,000 at Ethan Allen. What in the hell did you buy at Ethan Allen?"

"I bought those Queen Anne chairs in the hallway upstairs."

"Those ugly-ass chairs cost $8,000?"

"They were imported from London."

"I don't give a damn if they came from Timbuktu!"

"Don't yell honey, the kids'll hear you."

David opened his medical jacket and pulled out a Southwestern Bell phone bill.

"Do you have any idea how much the phone bill was last month?"

Dorothy folded her arms and sucked in her breath. "No, David, I don't know."

"$4,500. Who do you know in California?"

"Mary and Claire."

"What do you talk about for three hours Dorothy? What do you think? You think my money grows on trees?"

Dorothy felt a lump of hurt developing in her throat. "What else do you expect me to do all day, you won't let me work."

"From this day forward, number one, I expect you to stay off the fucking phone; number two, I expect you to stop going to the mall; and number three I expect your fat ass to lose some weight!"

"Okay David, what's next? You want me to jump off a bridge?"

"Oh, you want to be nonchalant about all this? Okay, okay, go get your credit cards!"

"What!"

"Did I stutter?"

"David you're not being fair!"

"No shit? Were you being fair when you squandered away my money like you had enough of it to burn?"

Dorothy didn't answer. She just stood with a menacing look in her eyes.

"I'm putting your ass on a two hundred dollar a month allowance. Is that understood?"

Dorothy shook her head.

"Now stop standing there like you got a stick up your ass and get those credit cards!"

Dorothy shook her head. "No!"

"Dorothy stop playing with me!"

"Do I say anything to you when you spend your money on drugs?"

"It's not your place to say anything about what I do with my own money!"

David began to unfasten the belt around his waist. In a rage, Dorothy stormed passed her husband and made her way to the spiral staircase that led upstairs to their bedroom.

"You better be going up there to get those credit cards!" She heard him shouting from below. "I don't want to have to use this belt on your ass!"

Dorothy slammed the door to her bedroom and ran to the closet where she kept the credit cards. In a crying rage she rummaged through her clothes and shoe boxes. She paused when she came across a .22 caliber hand gun. Crazy thoughts began to dance through her mind as she held the shiny black gun in her trembling hands. Dorothy thought about the last twelve years of her life with David. She didn't want to kill him, she loved him too much to do that, but she was so unhappy and she didn't know how to tell him. But oh boy, she could show him with this gun, if only she had the guts to do it. She put the gun inside the box and placed it back in it's proper place. Slowly, she stood up to her feet and retrieved the American Express and Master Cards and walked downstairs like a child who was about to be punished.

* * *

Dorothy tried so desperately to squeeze into the size sixteen gown David purchased for the UNCF gala. Just days earlier she and David were arguing about credit cards and telephone bills. Like clock work, David made up for it by lavishing Dorothy with gifts. This time he purchased

Dorothy a $15,000 diamond necklace to wear with her two-sizes too small Valentino gown.

David walked into the bedroom adjusting his bow tie and saw Dorothy stuffing herself into the dress.

"Baby do you need a little help?"

"No," she snapped just as quickly as he had asked. "I'm in it, see?"

David noticed how her stomach and hips protruded out. Her once coke bottle figure had transformed into a pear. To David, Dorothy wasn't the same, their lovemaking wasn't the same. David could recall the times when her breasts fit snugly into his mouth. Now he had to lift them into his mouth. At times he wandered whether or not Dorothy cared how she looked anymore. He had grown tired of seeing her dragging her feet and dressing so slovenly.

Lately he had been fantasizing about Chanel and how delectable she looked and how wonderful she felt. Although three weeks had passed since he last confronted Chanel, he arranged for her and a friend to attend the UNCF benefit gala tonight.

Once at the gala, he couldn't keep his eyes off her. She wore a red sequined gown with a low neckline that enhanced her large, brown breasts. Her black, wavy hair was in a French twist, her large eyes were sparking and ever so often she would glance seductively in his direction when Dorothy wasn't looking. She even engaged in a little foot action underneath the table, running her toes along his legs.

In David's mind he fantasized about the hours they would spend together after the gala. He arranged a flight to the beach house on South Padre Island to enjoy countless hours of nonstop lovemaking. *My God,* he thought, *I can't wait to get her alone and make sweet, hot, passionate love to her. I just love the way she feels.*

In Chanel's mind, she too was thinking about the hours ahead. She glanced at the diamond watch on her left wrist. It was ten after nine, which meant the flight wasn't scheduled to leave for another three hours. *I knew he couldn't resist this,* she thought. *I knew he was coming back to me. Damn he looks so good, feels good too. I don't know if I can wait any longer, a good quickie is what we both need before we get on the plane.*

Dorothy, on the other hand, was too busy enjoying the swordfish and Chardonnay sitting before her. She didn't realize anything unusual about tonight's festivities. In Dorothy's mind, the only thing that mattered was trying to get the recipe from the chef.

Chanel's date, who was currently doing his residency, was too busy thinking about Monday's operation. Now and then he would strike up a conversation, other times he was daydreaming and staring into space, occasionally thoughts of Chanel's breasts came to mind.

That night Dorothy went to bed alone. David told her he had some paper work to deal with at the hospital, and assured her he would be home as soon as he finished. When Dorothy woke up the next morning, she was in bed alone. She dialed the number to the hospital and asked for David. When no one could locate him. Dorothy concluded he was on his way home.

Chapter 13

"Honey what's on your mind? You haven't uttered a word since we left Houston."

"Dorothy, for the third and final time, there is nothing wrong with me, now stop asking questions."

"You know you need to stop taking that stuff."

"Shhh." David looked over his shoulder. "Those kids are back there."

Dorothy glanced over her shoulders. Nia and Jamal were both sleep while Ahmad amused himself with a book.

"You know it turns you into a madman and it's affecting our marriage."

"Dorothy I don't won't to hear it."

"But it has…"

"Look." David cut her in mid-sentence. "What did I tell you I don't want to talk about it. Period. End of discussion."

Dorothy stared silently at her husband, his cavalier attitude only frustrated her, she literally had to bite her tongue to keep herself quiet. Her eyes gazed at the sign that read, "New Orleans, 66 miles." She forced herself to remain quiet for the remainder of ride.

When Dorothy arrived at her mother's house, her mother could sense right away that something was troubling Dorothy.

"Dorothy, I can't believe you let this child go out with her hair over her head."

"Mama, how are you?" Dorothy pecked her mother on the cheek.

"I'm fine, how are you?"

"Mama, I need to talk with you?"

"You sure do. Look at you, my God, you've gotten fat and slouchy. You don't try to keep yourself up anymore, do you?"

"Mama are you finished?"

"No."

"Yes you are; let's talk."

"Wait a minute, don't rush me off, let me enjoy my grandchildren." She grabbed Jamal and Nia. "Give your Granny some sugar!" Dorothy stood in the doorway of her mother's dining room and watched as David sat in silence in the living room.

David glanced at his watch. "I'm gonna gas up the RV, I'll be back."

Dorothy watched silently as he exited the room. At that moment she felt like the weight of the world was on her shoulders. Dorothy pondered away at her thoughts. She wanted to ride with him and talk to him without the children or her mother around, but when she finally managed up enough nerve to walk out the door, the RV was gone. Dorothy found a spot on the porch swing nestled in the corner of her mother's large veranda. She cursed herself inside, for being so afraid. Afraid of not being able to stand up to David and taking his actions with a grain of salt. Papa prepared her for a lot of things but never for anything like this. Dorothy felt like she was on her own, and to her that was the emptiest feeling in the world. She didn't want to tell her mother just how miserable she was inside, because her mother would accuse her of being soft and say something she didn't want to hear. So she sat rocking on the swing before Ahmad joined her.

"Hey Man." She smiled when he sat next to her. Her little boy was now twelve years-old and three inches taller than her. He had her golden-honey, hazel eyes, fine sandy brown hair and a smile that melted his mother's heart, but today he wasn't smiling and that bothered Dorothy.

"Man? Talk to Mama. What's bothering you?"

"Mom, are you and Dad getting a divorce?"

Ahmad's question left Dorothy speechless for a second.

"Honey no, of course not," she responded.

Ahmad sighed. "I hear you and Dad arguing all the time."

"Your dad and I just have problems, and when you're married as long as we have been, you encounter problems. But the good thing is you talk about your problems and you find solutions."

"Mom, if you decide to get a divorce, I'll stay with you."

Dorothy looked into her son's eyes, he was serious.

"Man honey, I love your father and I love you too, and I'm not going to get a divorce, I promise."

Ahmad's eyes were in wonderment, like somehow his mother's voice and smile offered assurance where there once was doubt.

Dorothy and her mother finally found time to themselves to talk. Dorothy was tired of hearing about Louis' drinking, Jacqueline's boyfriends and Lucky's sissified ways.

"Mama, can you for once today listen to what I have to say?"

"What child?" Ms. LaCroix replied as she thumped her cigarette ash.

"My marriage is falling apart, bit by bit." Dorothy retrieved a cigarette from her mother. "I can't please David, no matter what I do." Dorothy lit her cigarette. "You know Mama," she exhaled a cloud of smoke. "I believe David is having an affair."

"Dorothy that is the most ridiculous thing I heard since, since you asked me for a cigarette just a while ago."

"Mama, I'm serious. Somebody is always calling and hanging up. David stays out all night. I call the hospital and they don't know where he is. I call the office and he's not there, now what does that tell you?"

"Dorothy, it tells me you are over reacting, that man is in love with you."

"No Mama, you don't understand. David doesn't love me; he's jealous, he's abusive, he's controlling, he's a monster, Mama," Dorothy said it before she knew it.

Ms. LaCroix looked at her daughter as she were a total stranger. "You talking about your husband? Your children's daddy?"

"Yes Mama, I'm talking about David."

Ms. LaCroix frowned. "Why are you just now telling me, Dorothy?"

Dorothy hesitated as she tried to think of something to say. "Mama I keep thinking that things are going to get better and one day he'll stop."

"How long has this been going on?"

"A long time, Mama."

"Do your children know what's going on?"

"I try not to let them hear us, and God I try not to let them see us."

"Has he hit you?"

Dorothy closed her eyes. "Just one time," she lied.

"When was this?"

"A long time ago, before Nia and Jamal were born."

Ms. LaCroix shook her head. "I'm angry, Dorothy. I'm angry at you for not telling me this sooner. I could've went to Sis. Devereaux and we could've done something about it."

Dorothy shook her head. "No Mama, I don't need a Voodoo Priestess to get involved in my marriage. I thought she would help out the last time, but her mojo didn't work. David is still on that stuff."

"Maybe you didn't pray hard enough."

Dorothy waved her hand in protest and took a long drag on the cigarette.

"I even came close to killing him Mama." Dorothy's eyes watered with tears. "So he wouldn't hurt me anymore." She burst into a sob.

Ms. LaCroix mashed her cigarette butt in a nearby ashtray and blew out a cloud of smoke. "You know I don't like this, I don't like this one damn bit, Dorothy."

Seeing Dorothy in such a helpless position, angered her. Ms. LaCroix gave her daughters tough love and when they came crying to her, it made her furious.

"Mama, I'm so tired of this, I'm so tired of him." Dorothy slumped over and buried her face in her hands. Ms. LaCroix removed her daughter's trembling hands from her face. "Stop crying, okay?"

Dorothy wiped the tears and snot from her face with the back of her hand.

"Stop crying and listen to me. You got to fight back, because right now, you're trapped in the corner, and as long as you're there, you are going to get beat and kicked around like nobody's business."

Dorothy listened to her mother. She made it sound so easy, but Dorothy didn't have the nerve to stand up.

"Let me tell you one thing, Dorothy," Ms. LaCroix began. "You cannot let this marriage get the best of you. Remember you have three beautiful children who love and adore you."

A smiled rushed over Dorothy as she got a mental picture of her three babies. "Mama, Ahmad asked me if I was leaving David?"

"What did you say?" Ms. LaCroix asked.

"I told him no, that I loved his daddy and I would never leave him."

"Are you serious?"

Dorothy finished off the cigarette.

"Yes I am."

"Don't get yourself hurt Dorothy. If you need me to talk to Sister Devereaux, I'd be more than happy to do so."

"No thanks." Dorothy was firm with her reply. "I don't need that."

Three months later.

Chanel was sparkling like a chandelier in her jade green, silk pant suit when she saw David standing in the doorway in a charcoal gray Armani suit with two long stem roses.

"You look splendid," David said before planting a kiss on her lips.

"You like?" Chanel asked as he held her hand while she did a turn for him.

David's eyes danced up and down her slender frame. "Yes Lord," he replied.

"Daddy! Dadddy!" Danielle screamed as she ran into her father's arms.

"How's my little girl?" David asked as he picked her up and gave her a playful hug and kiss. "Look what I have for you and your mother." David gave his daughter a rose.

"Thank you Daddy! Daddy! I drew a picture of you. Do you want to see it?"

"Sure, can we see it after we come back from the restaurant?"

"Yeah, daddy let's go, hurry up!"

David smiled at his daughter, who was a miniature version of her mother all dressed up in jade green.

"Okay honey, you heard her didn't you?" Chanel asked.

"Oh I see, you two are trying to double team me," David said before giving Chanel another kiss on the lips. Chanel grabbed her purse and locked the door behind her.

During the ride to the restaurant, Chanel smiled to herself as she stared at David. She felt like a million dollars and that made her want to giggle like a school girl. She was finally with the man she loved and celebrating their seven years together with a dinner at their favorite restaurant. After David valet parked his Mercedes, he arrived at the restaurant with his two ladies in arm.

"I made reservations under the name Chanel Gainous," David explained to the maitre d'.

"Follow me this way," the maitre d' responded. He found a seat near the center of the restaurant.

"How is this?" he asked regarding the seating area.

"This is fine, thank you." David pulled out a chair for Chanel and pulled up a high chair for Danielle.

"Here are your menus. There will be a waiter here shortly."

"Thank you." David said before the maitre d' turned and walked away.

Chanel glanced at the menu. "I like this restaurant honey, you know it's one of my favorites."

David glanced at the menu. "Yes I know."

Josephine's was one of the premiere spots in Houston, known for its fine dining, and live entertainment, as well as its host of famous patrons.

Across the room, unbeknownst to David and Chanel, sat Sadaria and Ms. Johnson, the receptionist and nurse from his practice. They spotted David and Chanel the minute they sat down.

"Ms. Johnson will you look." Sadaria titled her glass across the room at David's direction.

Ms. Johnson stopped chewing, glanced over and quickly turned her head. The sight was unbearable.

"You know I always suspected something like that was going on."

Ms. Johnson shook her head. She felt like crying.

"Now I see with my own eyes." Sadaria paused. "Oh my God."

They witnessed David and Chanel engaged in a kiss.

"No, unh unh, I have to go over." Sadaria stood up. Ms. Johnson sat her down.

"No, sit down and mind your own business."

"Who does she think she is Ms. Johnson?"

"I don't know, but we need to mind our own business."

"We need to tell Dorothy, we can't sit back and pretend this is not happening."

"And like I told you Missy, mind your own business."

"Ms. Johnson, Dorothy called me at work yesterday, crying about how distant and cold David was to her and how they fought all day and night. Now you see that bitch over there, she's the reason why their marriage is in the shape it's in. Now I think we should tell her."

The waitress approached their table with the check. Ms. Johnson opened up her wallet and slipped a $50 bill into the check book.

"I don't think it's right, if David wanted her to know he will tell her. It's not our place to do that."

"Dorothy is just like a sister to me Ms. Johnson. I don't want to interfere in her marriage either, but she told me some things that were so unlike David that I couldn't help but wonder."

"I don't want any part of this."

"Come on, ride out to her house with me."

"No."

"If your husband was cheating on you with your best friend wouldn't you want to know about it?"

Ms. Johnson thought about it for a moment. "I'll ride with you, but I'm not getting out of the car."

"Good, first of all we need to get out of here without them noticing us."

"That'll be easy," Ms. Johnson said facetiously.

When Sadaria broke the news to Dorothy, she stood in shock for a moment before she burst out into tears.

"So that's the other woman?"

"Yes, Dorothy," Sadaria said. "Though I tried to convince myself that it could've been a business meeting, but then again, who does business on a Sunday evening and who brings their children to meetings?"

Dorothy buried her hands in a handkerchief and sobbed. Ms. Johnson was sitting across from her, angry, yet hurt for Dorothy.

"God, how could I not see it was her?" Dorothy asked. "You guys, here was a person who I thought was my best friend. I could remember the times she came to me crying about how she was down on her luck and all the problems she was having with this man named Linus. When all along Linus was David." Dorothy let out a loud sob.

Sadaria stood up. "I always suspected something, I knew the minute she stepped into the office, she wasn't any good."

"Sadaria, you didn't see what was going on?"

Sadaria shook her head.

"Thank you Sadaria, I'm glad you finally decided to open my eyes."

Ms. Johnson was trying to wipe away tears from her own eyes.

"I can't believe her, after all I did for her and her baby. She was just like another sister to me, how could she do it?" Tears were streaming down Dorothy's cheeks like rainfall.

Ms. Johnson grabbed Dorothy's hand and held it. Dorothy was so overcome with tears and emotion, that at times it sounded like laughter.

"You guys just don't know how much I'm hurting; you can't imagine." She dabbed at her eyes. "I tried my best to be a good wife to David. Ms. Johnson not once did I ever think about another man."

"I know," Ms. Johnson agreed.

"I gave him fifteen years of my life. Only he and God know just how much I loved him."

Sadaria grabbed Dorothy's other hand.

"What did I do to deserve this?"

"Some men just don't appreciate good women, they rather have a woman, no, a slut, running around just as much as they are."

"Why? I wouldn't run around on David if I wanted to."

"Not every woman has a kind heart like yours, Dorothy."

Sadaria responded. "It doesn't pay to be good nowadays, and that goes for everything."

"You know," Dorothy started. "David use to always say that he would never do anything to hurt me."

"And you believed him," Sadaria responded.

"Yes I did."

"I use to think that about my husband and I told you what happened with him and my daughter-in-law. That hurt me so bad."

"Dorothy why don't you come with us," Ms. Johnson suggested.

"No, I'll stay here, I got a lot on my mind."

Dorothy grabbed the coin purse sitting on the coffee table and opened it. Her Virginia Slims and gold cigarette lighter were inside.

"I know you're not smoking," Sadaria began.

"Yes, I know it's a filthy habit." Dorothy lit her cigarette. "You like Virginia Slims?"

"Yes, I'll take one."

"You smoke Ms. Johnson?"

"No, but give me one anyway."

Dorothy did the honors and lit their cigarettes.

"I'm up to two packs a day now."

"Two packs? Dorothy honey quit, your health is not worth it."

"I can't."

"Are you drinking too?" Sadaria asked.

"Not much, a few shots here and there."

"Dorothy, don't lose your mind behind this man. Leave. That's what I did eventually."

"It was easy for you, your kids were grown when you and your husband split, I still have babies, Sadaria."

Dorothy took one last drag of her cigarette and smashed the butt in a nearby ashtray.

"Oh God," She lamented. "I can't believe she did this to me. I can't believe David did this to me."

Dorothy's eyes welled up with tears again. "She even asked me and David to be Danielle's godparents, and David, that son-of-a-bitch, went along with it, knowing damn well he was screwing her?"

"Dorothy, how old is that little girl?" Sadaria asked.

"I think she's Jamal's age." Dorothy's words trailed off and her expression drew blank. "You're not implying that Danielle is."

Sadaria and Ms. Johnson both folded their arms and shared blank expressions. A long silence filled the room.

When David finally arrived, Dorothy was sitting in the dark, in a lounge chair staring out the window. David unbuttoned his shirt and unzipped his slacks. He turned on the lamplight and saw Dorothy sitting quietly across the room in the chair.

"What are you doing sitting in the dark?" He joined her on the sofa and examined her expression. "What's wrong with you?"

Dorothy didn't respond. David extended his hand to check her forehead. Dorothy quickly moved her head.

"How long have you been having an affair with Chanel?"

"What?" David responded defensively.

"How long David?" She increased the volume of her voice.

David's eyes searched Dorothy's eyes for questions. "It doesn't matter," he said.

"It does too matter!"

David sighed, he couldn't deny it. "I don't know, six or seven years."

Dorothy pressed her eyes shut as the tears started to flow. A soft sob escaped her lips.

"But baby, she doesn't mean anything, she doesn't compare—"

Dorothy cut him off in mid-sentence. "You were with her seven years, evidentially she meant something to you."

"Dorothy honey, I know whatever I say now won't mean a thing to you anymore. You're hurting."

"You damn right I'm hurting, no woman wants to be told that the man she loves and cherishes is fucking someone else. David, I trusted you."

"I know baby."

"I don't think I can ever trust you again."

David shook his head. "Dorothy what will it take to get you to trust me again?"

Dorothy shook her head slowly. "You figure it out Dr. Leonard."

David sighed and lowered his head.

"There's something else I need to know."

"What is it?"

"Is Danielle your baby?"

David braced himself, he anticipated the question to come up sooner or later.

"Yes, she is my daughter."

Dorothy took a deep breath, her heart felt as though it was about to fall out of her mouth.

"Are you serious?"

David nodded. Dorothy picked up a pillow and tossed it at his head before she realized it.

"You son-of-a-bitch! It wasn't enough you had an affair, but you had to get a baby too! I hate you, I hate you, you are a fucking dog!"

"Baby."

"I am not your goddamn baby!" She tossed another pillow and started pounding furiously at David.

"Dorothy, honey." David replied, shielding himself.

"You are a low down son-of-bitch, bringing her to our house, disrespecting me and my children. I hate you!"

"Dorothy I—"

"I don't fucking want to hear it. How could you do this to me and your children?"

David couldn't respond.

"So that's where you were those nights when I called the hospital and left you messages when Nia woke up screaming and crying for you to come home? Huh?"

David's temples started jumping and his silence was too much for Dorothy.

"Is that where all your money goes? Do you have her on a two hundred dollar a month allowance? Fuck you!"

Dorothy dashed across the room and opened the closet door. She got David's suitcase and threw it on the floor.

"If you want to be with your other family, goddammit you, get your shit and get out!"

"Dorothy I'm not going anywhere." He picked it up and put it back in the closet and slammed the door.

"I hate you so goddamn much." Dorothy uttered through gritted teeth.

"No, you don't."

"Don't tell me how I feel; you don't deserve a woman like me David!"

"Yes, I do." He started walking towards her. "Dorothy if you want me to beg you, I'm begging you, let's start over again. Let's do it right this time, I promise I won't hurt you Dorothy, I promise, just give me another chance, I'm begging you baby, please."

"Fuck You!"

David came closer and reached out for her. She slapped his hand away.

"Please."

"Get away from me!"

"Please, give me another chance."

"Are you crazy, fuck you, I don't need you!"

"Don't do this to me, Dorothy."

"Do what? You did this to yourself. Now take your shit and leave!"

"Is this what you really want?"

"You damn right, you hurt me for the last time, David!"

David came closer.

"Get out, David!"

He stood in front of her, his eyes pleading for her to forgive him. Without a word, he walked out of the room. Dorothy stood frozen, her emotions were getting the best of her, she didn't know whether to laugh or cry, all she knew that at that moment she was miserable and the only way she was going to be happy would be getting a divorce.

The next morning Dorothy walked into the kitchen, only to find David sitting there.

"Why are you still here?" she asked.

"This is my house too, and I don't want to leave."

"You just don't understand the seriousness of this do you? You think it's that easy for me to live with you, once I find out you've been screwing somebody else? Not just anybody, but a woman who I thought was my friend, and then you turn around and have a baby, David?"

He couldn't respond.

"I think it's best you leave, right now!"

David was about to respond when he saw Ahmad walk down the stairs.

Dorothy stopped and gained her composure. "Good morning Man."

"Good morning," he mumbled, before opening the refrigerator.

"Honey, do you want eggs and toast?" Dorothy asked, trying to sound upbeat and happy.

Ahmad closed the refrigerator and looked at his parents. Dorothy could see there was something troubling him.

"You know Mom and Dad, I'm not really hungry anymore."

Dorothy and David glanced at each other.

"What's wrong son?" David asked.

"I'm tired of you and Mom arguing and fighting. You two are better off getting a divorce!" He turned and walked out of the room. Dorothy started after him, but David stopped her.

"I'll handle this," he said.

Just then the doorbell rang. Dorothy shook her head and went to open it. Standing before her was none other than Chanel Gainous. She was radiant in her lime green dress and new Gucci sun glasses. Her teeth were sparkling white and her red lip stick was glistening like a flame.

"How dare you," Dorothy greeted her. "You got some nerve showing up at my door, you miserable low-life snake!"

Chanel sensed the tension in Dorothy's voice and switched her approach. "I came to see if David was home. He promised to take his daughter school shopping today. I know it's not a problem." Chanel was brazen with her approach.

"Look," Dorothy began. "If you don't leave my house right now, I swear I will blow you up into so many pieces, they won't be able to identify your teeth."

"I know you not threatening me. I'm not going anywhere until I see David. I will have you know that he takes good care of me and his child and he will continue to take care of us."

"Maybe, you didn't understand what I said," Dorothy began. "I will hurt you Chanel. You don't know who you're fucking with."

"You better tell David to come here and see about his child."

Dorothy slammed the door in her face and ran upstairs to find David.

"David!" She heard herself shout, her bathrobe was swinging carelessly behind her.

She found David in Ahmad's room. "David you better come downstairs quick and tell your friend to leave."

A questionable stare was glued to his face. "Friend?"

"Excuse us dear," Dorothy said to Ahmad as she followed David out of the room and closed the door behind her. "Your bitch Chanel, tell her to leave before I hurt her."

Once downstairs, David opened the door. Chanel was standing with Danielle in hand.

David was furious. "Will you take her and leave!"

"You told us last night you were going to take her school shopping."

Dorothy appeared in the doorway behind David.

"Chanel take Danielle and leave before I call the police!"

"I can't believe you're going back on your word. What did you tell me last night?"

Dorothy shook her head, it was obvious Chanel had a serious problem.

"Chanel don't make this any harder." David tried to appear calm and diplomatic, but a bead of perspiration around his temples and armpits were beginning to tell off on him.

"Will you tell her which one of us you'd rather be with?" Chanel snapped. "Tell her like you told me how you were going to leave her and the kids and marry me?"

Dorothy shook her head in disbelief. "You have a serious problem," she said.

Chanel added a rebuttal. "You are going to have a serious problem if you don't stop fucking with my man." She lunged towards Dorothy but David intercepted her.

"Dorothy go in the house and call the police!" David shouted.

Dorothy turned around and left, she could still hear Danielle screaming and crying, and Chanel cursing at David. She saw Nia and Ahmad coming downstairs, followed by Jamal.

"Ahmad, call the police, and tell them to hurry."

"What's wrong?"

"Just do what I tell you." Dorothy tried talking over Jamal who was screaming. Nia was nearby sniffing and rubbing her teary eyes.

"Mama is daddy going to jail?" Nia asked.

"Your daddy is all right. Shhh."

"I want my daddy!" Jamal cried out.

"Daddy's coming back, shhh."

Jamal broke out in a tantrum. "I want my daddy!" He cried before he fell to the floor and started kicking. Dorothy scooped him up, and shook him without thinking. "Look!" she shouted. "I'm going to spank you if you don't shut up!"

Jamal cut his tantrum down to a low whimper.

When the police arrived, Chanel had calmed down. The police asked if David wanted to press charges. He shook his head.

"Why not?" Dorothy questioned him. "After all the pain and mental anguish she put your children through today, fuck you, I'll press charges on her myself!" David tried to calm his wife down. Chanel, on the other hand, wasn't making the situation easier. She took Danielle by the hand.

"I hope you're happy son-of-a-bitch. You are going to see me in court, oh yeah, I'm making your ass pay me dearly!"

"You can have him!" Dorothy shouted. "He's all yours!" She slammed the door. Dorothy turned and looked at her three children. She didn't want them to see her crying so she ran down the hall to the home office and shut the door behind her and locked it. With tears streaming down her cheeks she rushed to the cherry wood desk where she picked up the phone. She didn't know who she was calling, but she punched in a few numbers and listened to the dial tone. When Tiny answered the phone. Dorothy hesitated.

"Hello." Tiny asked. "Helloooo."

"Tiny," Dorothy sniffed.

"Who is this?" Tiny asked, not quite catching the shivering voice on the other end.

"Tiny, it's me, Dot."

"Dorothy? What's wrong Cuz, you don't sound too good?"

Dorothy broke down. "Tiny I am so tired, I need out."

"What's going on Dorothy?"

"David has gone and lost his mind Tiny."

"What has he done?"

"You were right."

"Right about what, what are you talking about?"

"About that girl that worked with David."

"What happened?" Tiny asked, anticipating Dorothy's response.

"She and David."

"Get outta here!" Tiny screamed before Dorothy could finish.

Dorothy felt a headache coming on, so she closed her eyes and massaged her temples with her fingers.

"How did you find out about it?" Tiny asked.

"Tiny, she had nerve enough to show up at my door."

"Hold up, back up, she did what?" Tiny asked sounding annoyed.

"She came to my house," Dorothy responded.

"And you didn't kick her ass, Dorothy?"

Dorothy could tell her cousin was no longer sitting down.

"Tiny it all happened so fast, I didn't know if I was going or coming."

"Where's David?"

"Gone."

"Where are the children?"

Dorothy thought about her children and started crying. "They're here. God I wish my children didn't have to see this, Tiny."

"I know. Look, why don't you send your kids here to stay with me until you and David can get this situation worked out."

"Tiny, I'm getting a divorce. That's why I called to see if you could find someone to represent me."

"You really serious about this?"

"Tiny, there is a child involved, of course I'm serious."

"She has a child for David?"

"Yes."

"Hush your mouth." Tiny gasped. "Dorothy I am shocked."

"Now you see where I'm coming from?"

"Yes Dorothy, I am shocked."

"Tiny I feel like dying. I swear to God I hate David, I hate him so much."

"Dorothy, how soon can you and the kids come to Atlanta?"

"Tomorrow."

"You work on getting your reservations and I'll work on finding you a good divorce attorney okay?"

Dorothy agreed.

"I love you Cuz and you are going to get through this," Tiny said.

Dorothy hung up the phone and laid her head down upon the desk and immersed herself in tears. Nothing could heal the large wound in her heart. She looked around the room in search for answers. Then suddenly she felt the urge to get down on her knees. She closed her eyes and said a prayer, "Dear God, I know I haven't talked to you like I should. I have a serious problem that I know only you can help me with. Please forget about all those times when trials and tribulations came into my life and instead of going to you, I tried to fight them on my own. God please forgive me for not giving you the glory during the good times. God please, listen to me. I need you, my children need you, and most of all, my husband needs you." Dorothy paused and cried silently to herself. "God please give me the heart to save my marriage, because right now I just don't have it. Oh God, save my marriage for my children's sake. I don't want them to grow up without their father. They love him so much and I want to love him, but God it's so hard." Dorothy wiped the tears from her eyes. "It's so hard. Please give me strength, in Jesus's name I pray. Amen."

The days following the discovery left Dorothy in a emotional roller-coaster. She called Tiny and decided against retaining a divorce attorney. She and David hardly ever spoke to each other, and when they did, it was small talk, like strangers. There were days when Dorothy hated to be around the presence of her husband, so she hid whenever he came home. She hid in the pool-house, she hid in Nia's room, she even spent a night outside in the RV.

Chanel didn't stop calling, nor did she stop coming to the house and to the practice. She caused so much commotion and confusion that David fired her from the job, then went to court and put a restraining order against her. David had to pay her a special visit to settle things with her once and for all.

"You son-of-a-bitch as long as you live, you are going to regret the day you fucked with me!" Chanel shouted.

"Look Chanel, how much money do you need? If I give you fifty grand, will you promise to stay away from me and my family?"

"Your money don't mean nothing to me."

"You didn't say that last week."

"Me and Danielle need you."

"Chanel cut out the bullshit, okay. I'm sorry. Maybe in the past I had my priorities a bit screwed up, but I look at my home, my business and my children and I see how far I've come. I can't risk losing it."

"You have a good thing with me and Danielle."

"You don't get it do you, before you there was Dorothy, Ahmad, Nia and Jamal. I love them more than you can ever imagine. I love Danielle too; she is my child. And although I told you, when you first realized you were pregnant, to terminate the pregnancy, I can't imagine life without her. But I've got to place my priorities on the lady who's wearing my wedding band, and that's Dorothy LaCroix Leonard, not Chanel Gainous."

Tears spewed out of her eyes, and before David saw it coming, she up and slapped him. "We don't need you anyway! Leave if you want to, go back to your little happily ever after!"

David just sat. Any other time he would've went off, but he tasted the blood in his mouth, and sat, engulfed in his thoughts.

"I don't need you!" Chanel shouted with tears rolling down her cheeks. "I hate you, God I hate the day I met you! Get out! Get out!" She pointed towards the door.

David quietly stood up and made his way to the door. He opened it and turned to look at Chanel. "Give Danielle a kiss for me," he said before leaving Chanel and a life with her behind him. This time for good.

CHAPTER 14

Dorothy opened her door to see a UPS guy with a notepad standing in front of her.

"Special delivery for Mrs. Dorothy Leonard. Will you please sign here?"

With a questionable look glued to her face and without explanation, she signed the pad. The man presented her with a large rectangular box with a Gucci emblem. She didn't have to ask from where the gift came. She knew it was from David. She unwrapped the box to find a white sequined gown inside accompanied with a small white card that read: *I have a surprise for you* written in David's hand writing. She took the box with the gown inside upstairs to her room. For some reason Dorothy couldn't resist smiling, but this time she wasn't giving in. Her feelings could not be bought. She threw the box on the bed.

"Why don't you try it on."

Dorothy jumped when she heard David's voice behind her.

"Why do you always think you can buy me out of my misery?" She asked.

"To show you how sorry I am for being a jerk."

"A sincere apology would suffice."

"Sometimes that's just not good enough."

"That's good enough for me David."

David stood in silence for a moment. "Why don't you try it on for me Dorothy."

Dorothy removed the top from the box and looked inside at the beautiful white gown.

"You like it?" he asked.

Dorothy nodded.

"I'm going to step outside for a moment, I'll see you downstairs, in your dress, in about an hour."

"It's going to take me more than an hour to get dressed."

"Okay, an hour-and-a-half."

"What's going on David, I'm not in the mood, okay?"

"You get that dress on and I'll show you."

Dorothy walked outside to find David standing beside a egg-shell white Cadillac limo. He was decked out in a black Giorgio Armani suit. His brown skin had a youthful radiance that Dorothy hadn't seen for years.

"Are you ready?" He asked.

"Yes I am." She studied his eyes with hers. When David extended his hand, Dorothy reached out to take it. Once she sat inside and positioned herself in the air-conditioned, leather seats, her heart began to pound wildly. David wasn't too far behind. Once the limo pulled off, David sneaked a peak at his wife.

"You look so beautiful, Dorothy," he said softly. "You care for some champagne?"

Dorothy hesitated before she answered. "Yes, thank you."

He poured her a glass of Dom Perignon.

"Thank you," She said.

"My pleasure." David poured himself a glass and placed the bottle in an ice-filled chiller. They both sipped quietly, hardly saying anything to each other. Then suddenly the opening chords to Teddy Pendergrass's song, *Can't We Try* began to fill the speakers in a lively surround sound. Dorothy's hazel eyes began to glow. She absolutely adored Teddy Pendergrass's music. Though the current tune was rather melancholy. It was as if David was speaking to her through this particular song. She listened to the words and turned her attention to the life going on outside the car. It was funny, how it seemed everyone was going on with their lives. How life continues to go on as usual, even when there's death, a divorce, or two people who are at a standstill, not knowing what direction to go. She was too engulfed in the song and her thoughts that she forgot about David. She felt like she was all alone.

Can't we try, love was never born to say
goodbye, touch me one more time and
make me feel like I'm alive and if we
don't survive, then we can have a moment
here…

"Hey." David gently took her hand. "I'm still here, you can tell me what's on your mind."

"I don't know how I feel about this marriage anymore. I will never forget the hurt you put me through, how you pretended all these years."

"I didn't pretend. Dorothy, I've always loved you first and foremost."

"Don't." She put her hand up. "You didn't love me."

"Yes I did, and I still do."

Dorothy frowned and shook her head. "I find that very hard to believe."

"What's so hard to believe?"

"Who's to say how many more women you screwed besides her."

"I'm not like that, Dorothy."

"I never thought you would do this to me."

He sighed.

"Now I feel so stupid and vulnerable, vulnerable because I allowed myself to place my head and heart into this marriage only to be disappointed and lied to."

David finished off his drink. Dorothy turned her attention outside again. "Where are we going anyway?"

Dorothy found herself sitting on the front row facing an empty stage. David was sitting across from her checking the time on his watch and eyeing the stage. The atmosphere of the club was lively, yet mellowed and relaxed with scented candles burning. An emcee walked on stage to the applause of the crowd. "Ladies and Gentlemen, you are going to have an intimate evening with one of the sexiest, balladeers in the industry. He gave us hits like *If You Don't Know Me By Now*. The audience began to applaud and the applause grew louder as the emcee continued to name hit after hit. Dorothy found herself on the edge of her seat.

"Club Atlantis, you asked for it, up close and personal. Coming to you all the way from Philly, please give a round of applause for Philadelphia International recording star, Mr. Teddy Pendergrass!"

Dorothy stood to her feet with applause when he came on stage dressed in a black tuxedo. He greeted the audience, who greeted him back with a thunderous applause. His band started the chords to his first song, while they played, Teddy improvised. "You look so good Houston, but I need to set the mood right. I hope you don't mind if I…Turn off the lights."

The audience, especially the ladies, stood to their feet, cheering Teddy on as he performed one of his signature tunes.

Dorothy's face was bright, like a thousand watts. David was equally pleased. He was pleased throughout the evening as Dorothy sang along and even danced. After five songs, most of which were upbeat, Teddy slowed the tempo and came downstage. The dim lights in the club went completely out, and the spotlight directed its rays on Teddy.

"I want to dedicate this song to a special couple sitting with us tonight, who is going through some problems. The brother approached me and asked if I could put his feelings into words with one of my songs and sing it to her."

David glanced at his wife, whose expression was submerged in deep concentration.

"He said, 'Teddy, I love her so much, we've been married an X number of years, we have three beautiful children and I just don't want to lose a good thing.' He said, 'Teddy, I did something that I'm really ashamed of and now it seems as if nothing is going right, everything is all wrong.' He said, 'Teddy, we don't even sleep in the same bed anymore."

The audience gasped and broke out into scattered whispers.

"This brother looked at me and said Teddy I love this woman. I love her so much, because she's my latest, my greatest inspiration."

David closed his eyes and smiled, that was his favorite song. Teddy began to sing the words.

I've been so many places, I've seen so
many things, but nothing quite as lovely
as you. More beautiful than a Mona Lisa,
worth more than gold, and my eyes had the
pleasure to behold. You're my latest and my
greatest, my latest, my greatest inspiration.

Dorothy's eyes began to water with tears. She knew who he was talking about. Halfway through the song, she was so overcome with emotion that she got up and walked away. Through the crowd she went, clearing her path until she made her way outside. Dorothy called up the limo and waited staring at the rain, which was pouring so hard, it looked like a thin white sheet. David wasn't too far behind.

"Stop it! It's not going to work out!"

The limo pulled up. "I'm trying to apologize to you the best way I know how, Dorothy." The chauffeur opened the door and closed it immediately after they got in.

"You just had to put Teddy Pendergrass into our business. You think I'm suppose to forget about everything and act like everything is fine and dandy because he sang to me. Yeah, I'm flattered, if you want to know the truth, I'm very flattered, but," Dorothy stopped. "It won't change anything David. I don't think I can deal with this marriage any longer. I want a divorce David, I don't want to continue feeling the way I do. I'm tired of sleeping in separate rooms, I'm tired of you using drugs. I'm sick and tired of you treating me like dirt. I refuse to put up with it any longer."

David sighed. "Okay, okay. I promise I will stop taking the drugs, I will even get counseling Dorothy, but please don't talk about divorce."

"It is very hard for me to live with you knowing you have an outside child." Dorothy paused. "Put yourself in my shoes David, would you forgive me?"

"I know I haven't been a good husband Dorothy, I'm sorry." He cupped her face in his hands. Dorothy could see tears glistening in his eyes. "I screwed up, I admit it, but I'm begging you. Don't give up on me."

"You can do all the begging in the world David, it's not going to change how I feel."

"Dorothy." David's expression was immensely intense. "All I want to hear from you is, 'David I know you're sorry, David I forgive you, David I'm not going to leave you, David I'm willing to give you another chance.'"

Dorothy shook her head in disagreement. The tears in David's eyes were falling down his cheeks.

"Dorothy," his voice cried out in desperation. "I love you, I can't live without you!"

Tears spewed out of her own eyes. "I'm scared David, I refuse to let you hurt me any more."

David got down on his knees. "Dorothy please, please."

Dorothy looked at the helpless man at her feet. Deep in her heart she felt David was sincere. This time he was going to change. Before even she realized it, she took his pitiful face into her hands and began to kiss his lips and respond to his every plea. They became entangled in a web of passion so intense, the windows in the limo became ice white. David unbuttoned his tux and removed his shirt and undressed Dorothy of everything but her shoes. David then positioned himself between her large, tan thighs and made long awaited love to her. They were both so emotionally overwhelmed and charged, the spontaneity of it surprised them. Dorothy couldn't remember the last time she felt like this with David's love making. Nothing could compare to this strange, intensified moment.

* * *

Dorothy opened her hazel eyes to see David staring back at her.

"Hey you," he whispered, before they nuzzled noses.

"Good morning David," She said. Dorothy noticed they were in their bed, together.

"How did you sleep?"

"I slept really good, and you?" Dorothy asked.

"I hadn't slept that good since the first time we made love. You remember that?"

Dorothy began to blush. "Yes, it was years ago. On my twentieth birthday to be exact."

David stared straight ahead at the ceiling. "Dorothy, there are so many things I want to say."

"Like what?"

"Why I act the way I do. The reason why our marriage took a turn the way it did."

"Why do you act the way you do?"

David took a moment to think about it. "I think part of the reason is due to the coke. The other part is due to my upbringing."

"Why would you say that?" Dorothy asked.

"My father was the same way towards my mother."

Dorothy opened her mouth in shock.

"Of course they kept it hush, hush. My father was a successful physician, and an upstanding citizen in the community. If word got out about his reputation at home, his image would have tarnished. So my mother, just like you, kept her mouth shut, and she allowed him to treat her like shit."

Dorothy rested her chin on David's smooth muscular chest and listened as he went on.

"There were times when I resented my mother for it. Hell, she didn't tell me any better, so for the longest, I thought a man was supposed to use fear to keep his woman in line."

"Is that what happened between you and Bettye?"

"Yes, sort of."

"Did you ever hit Bettye?"

David hesitated. "A couple of times I don't remember."

"I remember many years ago, Bettye approached me and she told me to beware, that things aren't always what they seem."

"She said that about me?" David asked.

Dorothy closed her eyes and pictured Bettye as though it were yesterday. "Yes, she had tears in her eyes when she told me."

"Yeah. I have hurt so many people without remorse, Dorothy. That's why I turn to the drugs. They make me forget all about the pain I have caused to so many people."

"I'm so glad we're having this talk, David."

"Yeah. I'm doing whatever I can to make sure I don't mess up a good thing."

They smiled and gazed lovingly into each other's eyes. "I need you Dorothy, like I need air to breathe." They kissed each other's lips.

"Stop. You are going to have me crying in a few minutes," Dorothy said, trying to hold back a tear.

"I tried in every possible way to bring you down, but you persevered. You hung in there with me. I know you didn't always want to and I made life for you miserable, but you showed me that you are the only woman for me."

Dorothy wiped the tear from her eye.

"I love you so much, woman," David said before he lavished Dorothy's naked body with tender kisses.

"I want to show you something." David took Dorothy's hand and led her to their large walk-in closet.

"What are you doing?" Dorothy asked.

"Shhh, don't say anything, just watch."

Dorothy watched as David reached into an old college jacket of his and pulled out a bag of cocaine.

Dorothy gave David a questionable stare. "I promise to never snort another line in my life, so help me God." He led Dorothy from the closet and into their bathroom where he emptied the contents of the bag into the toilet. Dorothy was astonished.

"You don't have another stash anywhere else do you?" She asked.

"No."

"You promise?"

"I promise."

"Thank you baby." Dorothy said as she put her arms around David.

"Let's call around for a counselor, so we can work on getting this marriage back in order. Okay?"

"Okay," Dorothy replied.

EPILOGUE

There was life and laughter in the Leonard household again. Dorothy and David entertained their family and friends often with gatherings, which included barbecues in front of the television or out back by the pool. Everyone could sense that the two were back to themselves again, displaying affection like they did when they first met.

"Dorothy, this Easter gathering is so wonderful," Mrs. Leonard said giving Dorothy a peck on the cheek. "I am so very happy for you and my baby."

Dorothy nodded approvingly. "I'm happy too, Mrs. Leonard."

"Please, for the umfteenth time, call me Liz."

"How about Mom?"

"That's even better." She tapped Dorothy's hand and proceeded on her merry way. Dorothy was amazed at how Mrs. Leonard aged so gracefully. For a woman of sixty-eight, she still wore high heel pumps and fitting A-line skirts.

"How's my angel?" David asked, cradling Dorothy in his arms.

"I'm really enjoying this dinner. You should've seen those kids trying to find the eggs we hid."

"They were excited, huh?"

"Yes. I'm glad you thought of this dinner, David."

"We need to spend more time with the people we care about the most."

"You're right; I couldn't agree with you more."

Dorothy turned around and gave him a quick peck on the cheek. She watched as he turned and walked away. Dorothy's thoughts were interrupted by her daughter's voice.

"Mom! Mom! Lucky and Man are upstairs fighting!"

"What!" Dorothy said. "You go up there and tell your brother I said come here, now!"

Nia turned and disappeared through a crowd of her relatives. At that moment, Tiny entered the kitchen.

"Hi cousin, what's ailing you?" She asked.

"Those horrible children. Tiny, were we that horrible when we were their age?"

"No we were good kids. I was a sweetheart," Tiny commented jokingly. She noticed the sparkle back in Dorothy's eyes. "How are things going with him?"

"Like it was when we first met, Tiny."

"I admire you so much," she said. "You are better than I ever will be in this life or the next."

"So how are you and Mr. So-n-So?"

"Fine," is all Tiny said.

"Is that all?"

"Yes."

"Something tells me there's more, but I won't get into your business."

"I'm trying to understand men, seeing what they want out of life besides sex."

"I can see now the romance is fading."

Tiny poured herself a glass of lemon tea.

"Cheer up Tiny, there are a million fish in the sea."

David's brother, Marcus approached, Dorothy and Tiny.

"Is he available Dorothy?" Tiny asked.

Dorothy turned around and saw Marcus. "Tiny, please."

Marcus gave Dorothy a peck on the cheek. "What's happening?" He asked.

"Marcus, my cousin wants to know if you're available."

"Last time I checked I was." Marcus flashed Tiny a radiant, yet sexy smile.

"What are you doing tonight?" Tiny asked.

"Tiny, stop it. She's not serious Marcus."

"Like hell I'm not. Now move Dorothy I'm trying to score a touchdown and you're blocking me." Tiny moved Dorothy aside. Marcus smiled and licked his lips. Which was something the Leonard men did when they were amused.

Tiny thought it was a sign of approval and she glanced at Dorothy. "He has nice lips; I think I'm going to like him," She whispered.

Marcus gave her his arm and the pair walked arm and arm out of the kitchen.

Dorothy joined her mother who was sitting near the pool puffing on a cigarette, with her legs crossed and sunglasses on.

"Hi Mama. You look calm and cool."

"That's because it's nice and cool out here, have a seat I want to talk to you."

Dorothy placed her cheesecake on the table sitting between them.

Ms. LaCroix took off her sunglasses. "You haven't noticed anything unusual have you?" She asked.

"What are you talking about, Mama?"

"With David."

"No Mama, not lately. Have you noticed something I didn't?"

"No, Mama's just being a mama."

Dorothy proceeded to eat her cheesecake.

"I went to Sister Devereaux."

Dorothy stopped eating.

"Those herbs really helped, that and a little prayer."

"Mama, I don't see why you believe in that stuff."

"Hoodoo is powerful, I seen it work miracles."

Dorothy continued eating.

"I think I need to get some for Lucky. He acts more and more like a sissy every day."

"Have you talked to him Mama?"

"He's denying it, but I know he is. A boy his age ought to have girls calling the house. Hell he have boys and sometimes grown men calling the house."

"That doesn't mean he's a sissy."

"Dorothy have you seen his ears? Both of them are pierced, plus he wears panties. That isn't normal."

"No it isn't. You sure those aren't Jacqueline's panties?"

"No, she took all her panties with her."

"What does Louis have to say about it?"

"Louis acts like he's invisible, and besides he's too drunk to notice."

"What does Ophelia say?"

"Seems to me like she's encouraging him to act like that."

"It doesn't surprise me."

"She's been acting funny too; I think she's back on that shit again, Dorothy."

"Don't say that Mama." Dorothy said with a mouthful of cheesecake.

"I really believe she is."

"What are you guys talking about?" Jacqueline asked, joining them. At seventeen she had grown into a beautiful, graceful and intelligent young lady. She was a dance major at Texas Southern, and had a body that was sculptured by the art form.

Ms. LaCroix looked at her youngest daughter from head to toe. "Where's Lucky?"

"I don't know, why?"

"Tell him to come here."

Jacqueline grunted. "I'm tired Mom, I don't feel like it."

"You can dance for ten and twelve hours a day, but you can't get Lucky for me. I swear, kids these days."

"Okay Mom, geez." Jacqueline rolled her eyes and pranced her size eight inside.

The music was jumping and almost everyone was up trying to dance.

"Go ahead Mrs. Leonard, strut your stuff," Jacqueline said urging her on. Mrs. Leonard waved her hand. "No, I can't."

"Go ahead mother." Marcus stood up and started to dance with her, only then did Mrs. Leonard dance and dip a couple of times to the amusement of the audience.

David grabbed Dorothy's hand and lead her in a dance.

"You remember this?" They cut a few steps that were popular from the sixties.

"Yes," Tiny began. "That's the squirrel."

Dorothy shook her head. "No, Tiny."

She joined Marcus for a dance. "Marcus you remember the Jerk?"

"No, I can't say I do. That was before my time."

Tiny stopped and turned up her nose. "That wasn't funny at all."

Backstroke by the Fat Back Brothers was playing loud and clear over the speakers and the younger generation got a kick out of watching their predecessors laugh and reminisce over dance moves. Even Doc Sr. was enthused and popping his fingers. A few minutes later *Forever Mine* by the O'Jays came on. Everyone stopped dancing, leaving David and Dorothy dancing alone.

"This is the song baby," David whispered.

"I know," Dorothy whispered back. They closed their eyes and slow danced hand in hand. David opened his eyes and looked at his wife. Her hazel eyes were staring back at him. They were more beautiful than ever, and her smile was so refreshing. Dorothy saw a look of love, and affection, in her husband's eyes. Without hesitation they became engaged in a long, passionate kiss. They were oblivious to everything. Even the wooing from everyone around them didn't stop them from kissing. The romance was back.

About the Author

When T. Wendy Williams isn't creating novels, she's flying the friendly skies as a Flight Attendant with Continental Airlines. Ms. Williams is a graduate of Sam Houston State University as well as president and founder of NIA Publishing. Ms. Williams currently resides in Houston where she is at work on her second novel.

9 780595 011155